Praise for **Sweet Tea and Jesus Shoes**—

"Told with humor and honesty from the perspectives of traditional and not-so-typical Southern Belles, the stories piece together a literary quilt of eccentricities in Southern living. **Sweet Tea and Jesus Shoes** is about living and loving and learning, regardless of which time zone you call home."
—*Today's Librarian*

"Those drawn to good storytelling will enjoy this collection of tales. All are by southern women. Most are warm, funny and nostalgic. Some touch on the spiritual aspects of life in the South."—*Baptists Today*

"BelleBooks' first publishing venture, **Sweet Tea and Jesus Shoes** will take readers on a delightful trip through the South and its traditions through charming vignettes from its six southern belle author partners. These fine veteran writers not only treat their fans to wonderful stories but also dish up their favorite recipes like Sweet Tea and Mama's Pecan Pie for readers to savor! Don't miss this simply yummy anthology!"
—*Romantic Times*

"A brilliant compilation of southern women's stories in the tradition of Anne Rivers Siddons."
—*Harriet Klausner*, No.1 Reviewer for *Amazon.com,* as featured in *People Magazine*

"A delightful, bright and sometimes crazy patchwork of Southern life, reflecting a proud and unique heritage."
—Susan Scribner, *The Romance Reader*

MOSSY CREEK
POP. 1700 EST. 1839

1. CHINABERRY
2. LOOKOVER
3. YONDER
4. BIGELOW
5. BAILEY MILL
6. TOWN HALL
7. O'DAYS PUB
8. GOLDILOCK'S SALON
9. DAN Mc. NEIL'S FIXIT
10. MAGNOLIA MANOR
11. THE NAKED BEAN
12. BEECHUM'S BAKERY
13. BLACKSHEAR'S VET.
14. HAMILTON'S DEPT. STORE
15. CANDLE FACTORY
16. HAMILTON HOUSE INN
17. BALL FIELD
18. POLICE STATION
19. HAMILTON FARM

WELCOME TO MOSSY CREEK
"AIN'T GOIN NOWHERE
AND
DON'T WANT TO"

W. MOSSY C

N

SPRUCE ST.

TRAILH

NEW CUT RD.

N. BIGELOW RD.

LAUREL ST.

MOSSY CREEK

MOSSY CREEK

CHURCH ST.

ELM ST.

2.

17.

10.

18. 7. 6.

9. 8.

14.

E. MOSSY CREEK

16.

MOSSY CREEK

S. BIGELOW RD.

HAMILTON ST.

19.

MoSSy Creek

3.

Mossy Creek

A collective novel by Deborah Smith,
Sandra Chastain, Debra Dixon,
Virginia Ellis, Nancy Knight,
and Donna Ball

Authors of *Sweet Tea and Jesus Shoes*

copyright 2001 by *BelleBooks*

ISBN: 0-9673035-1-6

HILLSBORO PUBLIC LIBRARIES
Hillsboro, OR
Member of Washington County
COOPERATIVE LIBRARY SERVICES

Disclaimer:

This is a work of fiction. Names, characters, places and incidents are either the product of the authors' imaginations or are used fictitiously. Any resemblance to actual persons, living or dead, events or locations is entirely coincidental.

BelleBooks
P.O. Box 67
Smyrna, GA 30081

www.BelleBooks.com

Copyright©2001BelleBooks   2722 6900 3/03
First Printing May, 2001

Cover Art by: **Rob Kilgore**
Cover Design by: **Virginia Ellis**
Mossy Creek Map/Mailbox Art by: **Dino Fritz**
Mossy Creek Map Design by: **Deborah Smith**

Acknowledgments:

The authors of the Mossy Creek collection gratefully acknowledge all those whose patience and expertise have played such an integral role in bringing these stories to life:

Laura Austin and Jack Berry—who believed you had to feed a child's imagination as well as her stomach.

Shannon Harper and Libby Hedrick, who know a good story when they hear one.

Pepper Chastain, who would have lived in Mossy Creek in a heartbeat.

Karen, Kim and Lynn, the original softball players who inspired the story of Casey, and Whitney Huffman, who begins a new generation of courageous young athletes.

Greg Hicks, dart-master and Irishman—steady and ever-ready to help.

Hank Smith, who knows his coffee beans, and Dora Brown, who would be happy drinking whiskey and cleaning guns with Miss Ida.

Bob, who cheers me on, and for Mike, Karol, Kristi, and Michael, who believe, and for Mother, who keeps on being the best.

Maureen Hardegree, Bill Dixon, and Rena Brown, who made sure everything made sense.

Stories

The Mossy Creek Gazette
215 Main Street— Mossy Creek, Georgia

FROM THE DESK OF KATIE BELL, BUSINESS MANAGER

Lady Victoria Salter Stanhope
Cornwall, England

Dear Lady Victoria,

Let me introduce myself...I'm Katie Bell, gossip columnist for the Gazette and the unofficial town historian. That would mean that you've come to the right person for stories about the hometown of your recently discovered American ancestor! I'm happy to share what I know and to find out what I can.

Right now I can give you a few sketchy details. Your Great-Great-Great-Great Grand-mother Isabella Salter began the 1859 feud between Mossy Creek and Bigelow, our neighboring town, when she ran away to England with Richard Stanhope. Apparently she jilted a Bigelow in the process.

But like any good gossip columist, I want to check my facts before I say any more about their love affair or exactly who broke promises to whom.

I can definitely tell you that the feud isn't over. In fact, the feud is what's keeping me from getting more details right now. I need to talk to our

Mayor Ida Hamilton Walker, but—as you can see from the story I've sent along—she's been busy this spring. If you knew Ida Walker, you'd know a lot about the kind of woman your ancestor probably was. And about the people in Mossy Creek today.

I look forward to sending you more news when I have it.

Your new friend and very distant relative to you on my mama's side,

Katie Bell

Ida

Ida Shoots The Sign

I was six years old, the year was 1950, and the torch of stubborn Mossy Creek pride was about to pass to me in true Mossy Creek style. I clutched the railing on a rickety wooden scaffold the Hamilton farmhands had hung fifty feet up the side of the whitewashed Hamilton Farm corn silo. My grandmother and namesake, Ida Hamilton, stood precariously on a level of scaffolding above me, wildly waving a small brush dipped in black paint. Big Miss Ida, as people called her, was six feet tall, thick-limbed and as strong as a mountain lumberman. Yet she wore her silver hair in a snazzy French twist and her trademark pearl necklace always showed above the collar of her practical chintz work dress. I was known as Little Miss Ida. I trembled in my overalls and Davy Crockett coonskin cap as I gazed up at Grandma's stocky legs and chintz-covered behind, directly above my head. If Grandma made one wrong move, I'd be known as Little

Miss Squashed Ida.

"Pray like a saint and paint like a heathen!" Grandma sang out, slinging specks of black paint everywhere. Oily dabs speckled my upturned face. I refused to duck. I had to be brave. This had to be crazy. But in Mossy Creek, courage was a given, and *crazy* was a virtue. Helping Grandma re-paint the aged Mossy Creek welcome sign on the big corn silo was as solemn as a prayer in church, only without hard patent-leather shoes. The silo stood in a sanctuary framed by broad cattle pastures, high, wooded ridges, and blue-green Southern mountains. I stared up at Grandma's painting project—the tall, faded words of the town slogan.

WELCOME TO MOSSY CREEK
THE TOWN YOU CAN COUNT ON
AIN'T GOIN' NOWHERE, AND
DON'T WANT TO

Those words had greeted town visitors for generations. The silo faced South Bigelow Road, the country two-lane that led the world to our mountain doorstep with the promise of great charm but also stubborn independence, metropolitan Mossy Creek. You could count on Mossy Creek to stay put, to always be the hometown you remembered, the place you would never forget and never wanted to. We might make only a pinpoint on maps of the world, but that pinpoint was a jewel. And so I, Little Miss Ida The Terrified, vowed to survive and uphold the town motto.

A gust of wind hit the scaffolding. I hung on for dear life. Mossy Creek might not be moving, but me, Grandma, and the scaffolding were headed out on a north wind. "Come on up, Little Miss Ida, the weather's fine!" Grandma bellowed, swashbuckling in her defiance of gravity, Picasso-esqe in her ability to slap abstract dabs of black house paint precisely inside the fading borders of huge words that had been stenciled on the silo's side by a Hamilton ancestor long before either Grandma or I were born.

"Do you think I'll bounce if I fall off?" I asked, eyeing a narrow wooden ladder that led from my level to hers.

"You're a Hamilton! You won't bounce, you won't bend, you won't break! Now clamber on up here. She who hesitates is *last*." The wind puffed Grandma's dress, and I saw straight up her flowered skirt. My grandmother, a pillar of the community, a rich woman who commanded 200 acres of prime cattle farm and owned half the countryside in and around Mossy Creek, wore lacy pink panties. I began to giggle, and the scaffold shook harder.

I pulled my coonskin cap down hard on my auburn Hamilton hair and prayed the way my mother taught me in church, where I was expected to set an example for lesser humans. *Have no fear. Lead and defend.* Hamiltons, like most Mossy Creekites, had a passion for honorable eccentricity and practical self-defense.

Have no fear. Lead and defend.

I climbed the ladder to Grandma's scaffold then held onto her outstretched hand like a squirrel wrapped around a telephone pole. She grinned at me. "See? It's all about shouting down the wild wind!"

Suddenly I felt as tall as the softly molded green mountains around us. I threw back my head. "I hope to shout!"

"Yaaah hooo!"

"Yaaah hooo!"

Grandma placed her small paintbrush in my hands. She gestured at the welcome slogan. "I'm afraid I'll mess it up," I admitted in a whisper.

"Bullfeathers. All it takes is a steady hand and a respect for tradition."

"Ardaleen says the saying's backward and stubborn. She says people down in Bigelow think we're all a bunch of pee-culiar smalltown mountain hicks." Ardaleen was my much-older sister, already sixteen and extremely annoying.

Grandmother snorted. "Your sister's struck with the prissy stick. Firstborns are always a stickler for rules. She liked her diapers too tight from day one. That's why I took a hard look at her in the crib and said, 'Nope, name the next one after me.'"

I beamed at her. "Because you knew I wouldn't be struck with the prissy stick."

"I know I can depend on you to knock sense into your sister's head if she ever sets her sights against her own hometown. And knock sense into anybody *else* who wants to throw out the baby with the bath water, tradition-wise." She nodded at the slogan. "You've got to keep the words up here and their meaning in your heart."

I put one paint-speckled hand over my heart. "I swear I'll knock and keep."

"Good girl. Now, paint." Grandma helped me guide the brush. *Ain't Going Nowhere and Don't Want To.* I put a big dab of black paint on the "I" in AIN'T. "So *I* will always stand out," I said.

Grandma laughed. "See? You've got the knack. You'll be the Big Miss Ida around here some day, and I'll be proud of you in Heaven."

"How will I know you're watching?"

She winked at me and pointed at her behind. "Whenever you see pink clouds in the sky, that'll be me showing off."

I laughed and suddenly understood my place in the world. I, Ida Hamilton The Knocker and Keeper, would shout down the wind, hold onto our best old ways but welcome new ones, and when in doubt look up to heaven for a glimpse of Grandma's pink drawers.

In Mossy Creek, that brand of philosophy makes perfect sense.

❦❦❦

Fifty years passed as quickly as a dream. I woke up on a cool spring morning and lay quietly in my big bed at Hamilton Farm, gently remembering that day with Grandma at the corn silo. I was the Big Miss Ida, now. I put a Best of Fleetwood Mac CD in the sound system of my parlor office, turned up the volume on "Don't Stop Thinking About Tomorrow," drank a swig of scotch straight from the bottle, unlocked my mahogany gun cabinet, and loaded shells into my heirloom twelve-gauge shotgun with the silver-inlaid Hamilton crest.

After my parents disinherited Ardaleen for marrying a Bigelow, I inherited a lion's share of the Hamilton property and buildings, both in town and at Hamilton Farm. Ardaleen lives on a fake English estate down in Bigelow and hasn't spoken to me in twenty years. I'm the mayor, not to mention being the town's biggest property owner and landlord. And, if I do say so myself, I'm a fine-looking woman. I allow a few gray tendrils around the front of my hair now, but I consider them racing stripes.

I dressed in tailored khakis, a silk blouse and a dark blazer. I put my hair up with a tortoiseshell clip and polished my wedding ring. I've been a widow for longer than I care to remember, and though I've had my share of menfriends, I still wear my husband's etched gold wedding band. Over my parlor desk, I have a little bronze plaque he gave me: *Tradition. Courage. Love.* Finally, I latched a single strand of heirloom pearls around my neck. Grandma's pearls.

It was time to knock heads.

The mountains had begun greening like a dime store shillelagh. We were smack in the Ides of March. I walked down the long gravel farm road, through the woods and pastures, carrying the shotgun like a baby. *Caesar will get his due*, I vowed grimly.

Fifty of my fat, tan-and-white Guernsey cows followed me along a pasture fence as if I was the Pied Piper of moo-dom. Beyond the farm's big front pastures, South Bigelow Road still snaked past Hamilton Farm on its way into town, and the old corn silo still stood proudly, bearing the Mossy Creek welcome sign. A big, ugly, neon-yellow state highway truck squatted across from it, on the far side of South Bigelow.

I reached the road, and several workmen looked up from their project. When they saw the shotgun, they backed away, their eyes going wide. They reached into their yellow coveralls, pulled out cell phones, and began calling for backup. I lifted the shotgun. "Just stand back, boys. This is between me and my sister Ardaleen's son."

I looked up at the old silo. Thanks to my fresh coat of paint, its tall black words still stood out against the white sides as if stamped there by a huge hand. *Ain't Going Nowhere, And Don't Want To.* I nodded to that sentiment then faced the road crew's handiwork, an antiseptically modern, green-metallic sign with reflective white lettering:

**Mossy Creek, Georgia
The Town That IS Going Somewhere,
And DOES Want To.
By Order of Hamilton Bigelow,
Governor of Georgia**

I blasted that sign. I shot it again, then reloaded and shot it two more times. By the time I finished, the sign leaned backwards like a drunk in a windstorm. The last blast punched a hole the size of a fist through the metal. There were only a few readable pieces of words left, to my satisfaction.

Ham to Go.

I turned my attention to the blue March sky. A wisp of pink morning clouds showed over the mountains. Grandma's panties.

She was watching, and she was proud. "I hope to shout," I yelled.

And Ham's road crew ran.

Police officer Mutt Bottoms shuffled his feet and bit his lip as if he wished he could drop into a long, dark hole and forget he had a duty to perform. Behind him, in the yard of my big Victorian farmhouse, a Mossy Creek municipal patrol car waited. Mutt was young and he was dedicated, but he looked as if he feared I'd grab him on one ear, the way I had when he was ten years old and I caught him in town hiding stink bombs under the breakfast porch of the Hamilton House Inn. Mutt had already sent five of the inn's guests inside complaining about dead skunks.

All these years later, he put a hand over one ear. "Miss Ida, I feel like you got me again."

"It's all right, Officer Bottoms. I'm not upset."

He cleared his throat so hard his Adam's apple bobbed like a fishing cork. "Okay. Then, uh, Mayor, you're under arrest for shooting the new welcome sign." He sagged a little. "Amos said I had to come get you. It wasn't *my* idea."

"It's all right." I smiled. Mossy Creek Chief of Police Amos Royden did not disappoint me. Amos played fair and square, and mayor or not, I was going to jail. Perfect. I picked up the paisley overnight bag I'd packed with a little make-up, a mirror, my laptop computer, and a press release I'd already written. "See you later, June," I called to my curly-haired Scottish housekeeper.

"Be good, Madam Ida," she chimed back

and stepped out into the hall from the kitchen, waving. June McEvers grinned like a large, blonde, Scottish Shirley Temple. "Or at least *look* good."

I nodded and smiled as I faced poor Mutt, who gulped. "Aren't you going to handcuff me?" I asked.

He backed down my veranda steps as if I'd grown extra heads. "I'd rather be skinned alive."

I sighed. "Let's save your hide, then." I walked past him down the steps, through the front garden, to the patrol car.

He loped to the vehicle and held the door for me, like a chauffeur.

❦❦❦

The news of my assault on Governor Ham Bigelow's sign began to spread. Phones rang in the outlying mountain communities of Bailey Mill, Chinaberry, Look Over, and Yonder. Tongues wagged happily all over Greater Mossy Creek. In Hamilton's Department Store—the grand old three-story stone building that dominated Mossy Creek's town square—my stoic, decent, kind but entirely too serious son, 32-year-old Robert Walker, the store president, received the news in person from his wife, Teresa.

"Chief Royden just arrested your mother for shooting the new welcome sign," Teresa said calmly. "I'm going over to the jail and try to spring her, if she'll let me. You know your mother is always trying to make me feel tougher than I am, and I've been reading up on criminal statutes." She paused, frowning but loyal. Teresa was a tax attorney, not exactly a criminal defense shark. "Maybe I could argue temporary insanity brought on by the start of tax season."

Robert, who had solemnly ordained himself a man at twelve years old when his father died, sat back in the chair of the antique desk where several generations of Hamiltons had commanded a world of clothing, knickknacks, home accessories, and all-purpose practical needs for comfortable living. He didn't even look surprised. "I used to think," he said, "that Mother would run away with the circus someday. Then I realized that the *circus* wants to run away with *Mother*."

True to Hamilton heritage, Robert was a creature of tradition—but not, like his late father and me—a natural-born troublemaker. After graduating from the University of Georgia with a business degree, he'd bought the aging smalltown department store from me with a token down payment he'd saved working part-time as a stockbroker, of all things. I'd never imagined a tall, strong, good-looking son of mine wanting to manage our failing old dinosaur of a department store, staffed by ten longtime employees so slow they chewed cuds. But Robert worked a miracle. He renovated and re-energized the building, he upgraded the merchandise, and he soon had the staff chanting *Smile and Sell* at staff meetings. Recently, he'd put a handsome new sign above the awnings of the main doors.

Hamilton's
Because quality and good service still matter.

There may be cheap, sloppy competition everywhere else on the planet, but in Mossy Creek a smiling clerk at Hamilton's shoe department will still measure a shopper's foot with a metal shoe ruler then bring a choice of potential shoes while the person sits in a comfortable chair, waiting like royalty. At Hamilton's, a little old lady with a measuring tape pinned to her sweater will still help customers shop for a dress. At Hamilton's, an old, freckled doorman will carry a woman's purchases to her car. At Hamilton's, people matter.

Suffice to say, everyone in Mossy Creek adores my son, and so do I.

I just wish he wouldn't expect me to behave.

"Go see if Mother will agree to bail," he told Teresa. "Or bake her a cake with a file in it."

That evening—just in time for the six o'clock news—I stood outside the Mossy Creek jail on Main Street. From the Hamilton House Inn to O'Day's Pub and all the way up to Mama's All You Can Eat Café, citizens, reporters and camera trucks vied for space. The Mossy Creek town square is normally the most peaceful place this side of a Norman Rockwell painting, but on that spring night it became a hotbed of protest. People waved placards out the upstairs windows of the shops, dangled little bean-bag effigies of my nephew from the limbs of the square's towering beech trees among signs that read HAM STRUNG, and had even wrapped the square's looming sculpture of General Augustas Brimberry Hamilton of Jefferson's Third Confederate Division in the official town flag. The flag bore our town seal, a medallion of creek and mountains circled by those glorious words, *Ain't Going Nowhere, And Don't Want To.*

"No New Sign! No New Sign!" the crowd chanted.

Camera lights flooded the whole scene. The entire town council stood behind me, forming a seven-person wall of sorrowful faces and ruffled feathers. I tried very hard to look noble and martyred, as if I hadn't just spent a grueling six hours in a jail cell with window curtains. "Governor Bigelow is ashamed of his mother's hometown," I said into the microphones of all the major Atlanta radio and television stations, which only sent crews to the wilds of north Georgia when winter snowstorms threatened tourists or Hamiltons threatened Bigelows. "He has asked us repeatedly to change our welcome motto to something he considers politically correct. After I told him in no uncertain terms we would never surrender our heritage, he forced a new sign on us."

"Do you want people to think that Mossy Creekers are against progress?" a reporter asked.

"Creekites," I corrected. "Mossy Creekites."

"Uh, sorry, Mossy Creekites."

"We're peculiar, you see. We don't want to be like every other town in the world. We hear the word 'progress' and see bulldozers tearing down the mountains. We hear the word 'growth' and see old farms being turned into subdivisions that all look alike." I paused for effect. "We hear the name 'Bigelow' and see our silver-spoon neighbors in the south end of this county plotting to get rid of us. This is not about us resisting *positive* new ideas and new people. This is about Ham Bigelow wanting to erase his mother's odd little hometown, so we won't embarrass him politically." I leaned forward. *"Because this is about Ham Bigelow planning to run for President of the United States a few years from now."*

Reporters gasped and scribbled feverishly in their notebooks while spewing questions at me. *Will the governor confirm that? Has he said that to you personally? When will he make an announcement?*

"You'll have to ask him when he pulls his head out of the sand."

Albert "Egg" Egbert, a retired Georgia Tech physics professor, second cousin of mine, old and jowly and hangdog, stepped forward with perfect timing, just as I had coached him to do. Professor Egg looked more like a ruined old homesteader than a man who could still dazzle everyone with an explanation of Einstein's theories. He faked a cornpone accent and drawled, "Oh, Cousin Ham, how could you be so durned sneaky? We've been ambushed! No, even worse!" He paused dramatically. "We've been Ham-bushed!"

I just stood there, gazing straight into the cameras, smiling like the cat that ate the ham sandwich. "Ham-bushed," I repeated.

The crowd roared.

❦❦❦

Three hours' drive south of Mossy Creek, Governor Ham Bigelow cursed a blue streak and morosely sank back in his executive chair beneath the gilded dome of the state capitol. He was a tall, broad-shouldered man with shrewd eyes but considerable charm —the perfect, deadly mix of Hamilton charisma and

Bigelow slyness. He only fumbled when confronted by the Mossy Creek magic for absolutely twisting his custom-made boxer shorts into a wad. Now he put a hand over his face and groaned. He could see Ted Koppel turning to the camera on *Nightline*. "Primary voters want to know," Ted would intone. "Is Georgia Governor Hamilton Bigelow a candidate driven by consummate greed and ambition? They remember his own aunt telling the world some years ago that he planned to stake a claim on the White House. So voters want to know—as his own relatives are fond of saying—is Governor Bigelow merely trying to Ham-bush this presidential election?"

Ham lowered his hand. "Mother, what am I gonna do?"

Sitting beside him in a Queen Anne armchair she'd brought up from her million-dollar second home on St. Simon's Island so that she would have her own special throne in her son's gubernatorial office, Ardaleen Hamilton Bigelow glowered at her younger sister on the TV screen. Her green Hamilton eyes narrowed like the gaze of a silver-haired vulture. "I'll teach Ida a lesson," she hissed. She picked up a phone. "I'm calling Judge Blakely."

Ham stared at her. "Mother, you're one mean old lady," he said affectionately.

Ardaleen smiled.

Two weeks after I shot Ham Bigelow's new Mossy Creek welcome sign, I stood beside my nervous daughter-in-law, Teresa, in the packed courtroom of glowering Judge Blakely at the Bigelow County Courthouse. Judge Doom, we called him up in Mossy Creek. He thought civilization in Bigelow County began and ended inside the city of Bigelow. After all, Bigelow was the county seat. Bigelow had a country club and a golf course. Bigelow had a French café and a sushi restaurant. Bigelow had a junior college, and strip shopping centers, and a new ten-screen movie theater with stadium seating and chili nachos. Bigelow had a Super Wal-Mart. What Bigelow did *not* have was pretty, unspoiled Mossy Creek— population 1,700, all nose-thumbing anti-Bigelow rebels. Though our town anchored the county's northern end less than a twenty-minute drive from Bigelow, to Judge Blakely, Mossy Creek was no better than a mud-hut village filled with sign-shooting cannibals.

"Well, Ida, the law finally caught you red-handed," Judge Blakely brayed as he banged his gavel to start court.

"I object," Teresa said.

"This isn't the IRS office, little lady, so unless you got a problem with my tax return, you're *overruled*."

Teresa blushed. I chewed my tongue and gave Judge Blakely a murderous look. "Don't take your gleeful bad mood out on my daughter-in-law—or anyone else."

"You *watch* yourself, Ida Hamilton Walker. I'll hold you in contempt. More'n I already do. Women like you have a responsibility to be ladies and role models. You let society down."

"I think I've lived up to my gender-based public responsibility to society more than *you* have. In the past two weeks, you've handed out hard sentences to every Mossy Creekite who's come to trial here. From what I've heard, those people were all innocent. You're punishing the whole town."

Judge Blakely reared back as if about to explode. Teresa yipped softly. "My client isn't accusing you of abusing your power, Your Honor. She's just upset about some of the new government rulings on tax deductions, and she's taking it out on you—"

Judge Blakely slammed his gavel down, and Teresa jumped. He jabbed a finger at me. "Ida Hamilton Walker, are you questioning my honor?"

"Your honor, Your Honor?"

"You being smart-alecky?"

"About your honor, Your Honor?"

The courtroom erupted in giggles. Judge Blakely rapped his gavel and glowered. Half the courtroom seats were filled by grinning reporters and the other half by dour aides of Ham's, pretending to be ordinary citizens.

Sue Ora Salter, the publisher of the *Mossy Creek Gazette,* chortled from her front-row seat. She was married to a Bigelow husband but hadn't lived with him for years. She knew what was what when it came to co-existing with Bigelowans, as we called them. My son Robert sat near her on the front bench, handsome and formal in a dark gray suit, but frowning at the judge with a jaw-punching threat that made me proud. Robert might one day actually forget himself and act reckless. Sitting beside him, grinning at me and waving when I turned around to look, was Little Ida, my brilliant, eight-year-old, auburn-haired namesake. She was taking notes for her website.

Judge Blakely yelled at me. "You makin' fun of me?"

"No, I'm letting you do it yourself."

"Now I'm gonna *really* hold you in contempt, you uppity—"

"Mayor Ida Hamilton Walker pleads guilty to all charges," Teresa interjected quickly.

The judge froze. He eyed me warily, squinting at me, studying me as if I might be hiding a switchblade or another Your Honor quip inside my sleek blue dress-suit. "Well, well. You gonna holler uncle this quick, Mayor?"

"I've already made my point. I've said what I needed to say. If it will stop you from punishing my townspeople, I'll admit my guilt and take the consequences."

"Well, well." Judge Blakely shuffled some papers. "Mayor Hamilton, you destroyed state property. Therefore, you'll pay for a new sign to replace the one you shot. Plus, I'm giving you six months' jail time—set aside on probation, as long as you behave." He paused, then smiled fiendishly. "But you'll have to complete six weeks of anger management classes at the Bigelow Counseling Center."

Anger management class was the equivalent of being sent to stand in the corner. I wasn't being taken seriously—the whole town of Mossy Creek wasn't being taken seriously. I wanted dramatic punishment—the kind television cameras could film. "I'd rather serve time in the county jail. I will happily wash county police cars or unload garbage at the dump with the rest of the unfairly convicted Mossy Creek citizens singled out in your reign of terror."

"Sssh," Teresa begged. "Your Honor, could I approach the bench and discuss alternative sentencing for my—"

"Nope." He slapped his gavel down. "We'll just see who's funny, now."

To add insult to injury, Judge Blakely ordered the state roads commissioner to put up an identical new welcome sign within a day after my prissy, patronizing sentence hit the news.

I had won the battle but lost the war.

❧❧❧

On a rainy Thursday night when the spring winds carried the first full songs of the frogs, I parked my 1958 silver-gray Corvette outside one of the antiseptically modern, white-brick buildings of a Bigelow office park. I stared balefully at the glow of light coming from the glass doors of the Bigelow Counseling Center. Flinging a soft black cashmere scarf around my black sweater and slacks, I strode inside.

Room 7A was my destination, according to my court-provided instruction sheet. When I rounded a hallway corner, I nearly collided with over six feet of lean, muscular, male body. The owner of that body moved a plastic coffee mug out of the way without spilling a drop. I looked up into a rugged face, deep blue eyes, and short, sandy gray hair.

"Excuse me," I said. "You shouldn't just lurk around corners holding dangerous coffee cups."

He smiled, and I caught my breath.

There are a limited number of hunky men over the age of fifty, and this one could have been a leader in that elite group. I'm never helpless or coy around attractive males, but I gave him and his handsome packaging—loafers, khakis, a sweater and a brown bomber jacket—an unfettered once over, while my right hand rose to my chest and preened at my scarf.

He tilted his head, arched sandy gray brows, and gave me the same head-to-toe scrutiny. "Nice accessories," he said in a deep voice with a crisp Midwestern accent. "I apologize."

My face burned. The rest of me experienced a rebellious jolt of pleasure. I wanted to retort, *You, sir, are no gentleman*, as if I were some middle-aged Scarlett O'Hara, not quite upset but not quite happy, either. "I don't know you, do I?"

"Not yet."

"Are you here for anger management or for a class on picking up women?"

He grinned. "Interested?"

"Do I look interested?"

"Your lips say No, but your smile says Yes."

I clamped my rebellious lips together and sashayed past him into our small, starkly lit classroom. What was the world coming to when a mayor could get hit on by a middle-aged Rhett Butler while attending court-ordered counseling?

Maybe this punishment wouldn't be so bad, after all.

My fellow Mossy Creekites and I–all victims of Judge Blakely's vendetta—sat in hard plastic chairs behind two cold metal tables in a little classroom where the wall posters offered feel-good slogans and finger-wagging lessons. *Think, don't fight. Smile, don't yell.*

Kiss My Behind, I wrote on a notepad.

I nicknamed our group the Mossy Creek Five. I knew two of them—bulldozer operator Wolfman Washington and young Geena Quill, who was the daughter of a friend of mine—but the other two—my rugged Rhett Butler, and a rough-looking young man with kind eyes--were newcomers who must live in the outlying communities of Mossy Creek. I sighed. Look Over, Yonder, Bailey Mill and Chinaberry were just crossroads with country stores to anchor them, but there had been a time when I could name every soul who lived there. I started to introduce myself to Rhett and Rough, as I named them, but the counselor suddenly entered the room.

He was a short, thin, tight-mouthed man who wore a bright yellow badge pinned to his sweater vest. Oscar Seymore, Happy Therapist, it said beneath a smiley face. I distrusted him instantly. Oscar frowned at our little group as he handed out packets of reading material. "I expect y'all to read these papers for class discussion next week," he commanded in a reedy, annoying voice.

Barney Fife, I wrote on my notepad.

Rhett leaned over, boldly invaded my personal space, and read my words. "I'm telling Teacher," he whispered drolly. A mischievous smile lifted one corner of his mouth.

I answered through gritted teeth, "Back off. I'm barely managing my anger."

"My job," Oscar began, "is to provoke this group and make each of you think about appropriate ways to respond to unpleasant circumstances." He stood before us, rapping the palm of one hand with a cigar-sized metal device. "First off, I want you to share your personal background and tell everyone exactly why you were placed in this class."

"Brainwashing 101 was already full," Rough suggested in a carpet-slicing New York accent. Rough was in his early twenties, with dark hair and sharp, amused eyes. He lounged in his desk-chair with dusty, laced-up work boots crossed at the ankles. His shirt was clean but old, and his hands were covered in nicks and calluses. He narrowed his eyes and smiled, but his exhausted posture and the gaunt circles beneath those eyes told me this kid worked hard at some dirty job.

Next to him, Geena fidgeted with the buttons of her demure brown suit and eyed him with shy fascination. She was trying very hard not to cry, and he was trying very hard to look mean. I felt a pang of sympathy for them both.

Oscar's cheeks colored. "Let's get something straight, young man. I put remarks such as yours in my files for Judge Blakely to read. If you don't want to repeat this class—or serve jail time—you'll straighten up. And that includes sitting up straight, too."

Silence. Humiliation crawled through the room. Rough, the poor young guy, looked as if his skin were being sliced off bit by bit. Beside me, Rhett straightened and said quietly, "You must be talking to me, Oscar."

Wolfman, behind us, drawled firmly, "No, must be talkin' to *me*."

I squared my shoulders. "Oh, no. Oscar means me."

Rough's mouth quirked in a smile. "Nah, it's just me." He sat up taller, defiant. Geena darted nervous looks at him and the rest of us. Then she slowly pressed her spine into a proud line and lifted her chin, quivering with brave camaraderie. "No, me," she peeped.

Oscar craned his head and gave us all a look like a worried gopher. "I'll make a note of this sarcasm in the group dynamic." He turned his back, clicked the cigar-shaped device, and pointed it at a poster pad on an easel. A red laser dot speared the first name he'd scrawled on the pad. "Mr. Washington. Stand up and own your shame."

Wolfman, a burly, thirty-something black man with a thick beard, rose from the table like a calm mountain. His beard and mustache were neatly trimmed, and he wore a white shirt and a tie with brown corduroy trousers. The tie had Mickey Mouse on it. His hands were large and hard-worked, his face, friendly. "My name's Wolfman Washington. I been in the earth movin' business since I was old enough for my daddy to set me in the cab of a bulldozer. Got me two big dozers and two bobcats, a backhoe, and a twenty-ton dump truck. Me and my wife got us a nice little farm over in Yonder."

"Get to the point," Oscar snapped.

"Well, yessir. Heavy equipment sure isn't the point." He cleared his throat and launched into a poem. Wolfman was the poet laureate of Greater Mossy Creek, including Yonder and the other outlying communities. "Wife and kids, I'll take no bids, Wouldn't trade 'em, For all the world's riches, I'm just happy, Digging ditches."

"Very nice," I said.

Oscar glared at me, then at Wolfman. "Tell us your crime, Mr. Washington."

"I was doing some work for a developer over in East Bigelow Estates—digging a swimming pool for his backyard—and whilst I was working he set this crew of men to building a gazebo, and one of those men was a Mexican feller, a real hard worker, he has a family, he's a good soul, and, well, I found out that developer wouldn't pay the Mexican as much as the rest of the crew. See, he knew the

Mexican wasn't here legal. So he knew the Mexican couldn't do nothing about being cheated out of pay." Wolfman paused. His chin came up. "I can't watch a person be cheated out of his duly earned money. I can't go home to my boys and tell 'em we live in that kind of country. So I . . . I lost my temper, and I, uh, got in my bulldozer, and I pushed the developer's golf cart into the swimming pool hole." He sighed but kept his chin up. "I did the crime, I'll serve my time, Just don't want the world, To turn on a rich man's dime."

A bad poet, I thought, *but a noble crusader.*

Oscar snorted. "You, next," he said loudly, and pinpointed my name on the pad. I stood, gave my particulars in a firm, loud voice, then started to sit down. "Not so fast," Oscar said. "I believe all of us are familiar with your crime, via television and the newspapers. I'd like some comment from your classmates."

I nodded, and calmly studied the group. Wolfman nodded politely back, Rough shrugged, Geena blushed, but Rhett Butler raised a hand. "What gauge was your shotgun?"

"Twelve," I said.

"Wouldn't a deer rifle have done more damage?"

My heart warmed. "Yes, but the shotgun was a family heirloom. A sentimental choice."

"Next time, try to stand no more than twenty feet from the sign—"

"Enough!" Oscar stepped in front of me. He could have killed Rhett Butler with one waspish look. "You think the mayor's violence and vandalism are a joke?"

"No, I think she betrayed her official oath, and she ought to resign from office. But I was talking technique, not morality—"

"Betrayed my oath?" I echoed. "I'll tell you what would have been a betrayal of my oath: Letting the citizens of my town be trampled by the Bigelow political machine. Letting the governor's arrogance overrule more than one hundred years of devotion to an old-fashioned welcome sign that means something to the people of Mossy Creek. Turning a blind eye when individuals corrupt the system for their own gain."

"You corrupted the system when you did an end run around the law," Rhett countered smoothly. "That makes you no better than your enemies." He paused. "But you're a helluva admirable fighter, I have to tell you."

"Keep your fake compliments."

"Temper, temper."

"This is good," Oscar said, studying my face. "We've hit a nerve. Would you like to describe how you're feeling?"

"Not in language you want to hear," I said flatly and sat down.

Oscar pointed at Rhett. "You." My blue-eyed nemesis stood with a sigh, and began to speak. He had a name as sturdy as his red-blooded attitudes. Delaware Jackson. Newly retired Lieutenant Colonel Delaware Jackson, U.S. Army, to be precise. A civil engineer. Combat veteran of Vietnam and the Gulf War. Fifty-five years old, divorced for more than twenty years from the mother of his son, Campbell, and grandfather of two. He had just bought the old Bransen farm outside Bailey Mill. For now, he was helping out his son, who owned a gym and martial arts studio in Bigelow.

"Mister Jackson," Oscar bawled, emphasizing Del Jackson's lowly new status as a mere citizen. "You conveniently forgot to explain anything about your crime."

"There's a six-year-old boy involved. He's in foster care, and I have to testify on his behalf in a court hearing. I don't think I *should* discuss the details."

Oscar pawed through a sheaf of notes. "Well, I don't care what you think. You tossed the boy's father in a garbage container. You gave him a broken nose and a concussion. Why?"

Del Jackson eyed Oscar as if he were a termite in a woodpile. "My son and I saw the man whipping his little boy in the parking lot after a karate class." He paused. "I decided to teach the man how to manage his anger. He needed a hard lesson."

Oscar looked unnerved by Del's valiant story and the group's aura of respect. "You," he ordered, and pointed to Geena. "You're next."

Trembling, she stood and began to talk. Until recently she had worked as a secretary for Swee Purla of Purla Interiors. Swee, Bigelow's answer to Martha Stewart, was a cold-blooded tyrant. I had been to one or two elaborate parties at her rambling country cottage, and I'd seen her reduce servants to tears.

"My whole dream in life is to be an interior designer," Geena said in a small voice. "I've worked for Mrs. Purla a whole year and never asked for anything but a chance to prove myself. Besides being her secretary, I've walked her dachshunds, done her Christmas shopping, even polished her shoes. She barely noticed I was alive, but . . . but that was all right. I just wanted a chance." She stopped, her throat working, her eyes wet.

"No crying!" Oscar ordered. "Crying is a denial of guilt, and denial leads to uncontrolled anger, and I demand that you control yourself!"

We all glared at him.

Geena wiped her eyes and took a quick breath. "Finally, a nice lady over in Bigelow Estates asked Mrs. Purla if I could help with her lake cabin renovation. We'd become friends on an earlier job, and I'd suggested some colors, so"—she straightened her shoulders—"so Mrs. Purla said yes. I got to work as a designer!" Her face brightened. "I did the whole cabin, and it was wonderful. Mrs.

Purla let me enter my designs in the state decorators' association competition." Her face tightened. "I waited for weeks to hear about my entry, and one day I came into the office, and I heard Mrs. Purla telling a client that the cabin design had won first place!" She paused, knotting her hands in front of her. "I'd won first place! But then I heard. I heard. . ." she groaned. "Mrs. Purla took all the credit! 'Oh, I felt very inspired when I created the look for that cabin,' she said. Well, I just went crazy for a second. After all I'd been through. I . . . picked up a faux Grecian vase off our display counter, and it felt so . . . so well-balanced, I threw it at Mrs. Purla. I didn't mean to hit her, but I did! Right in the back of the head. She collapsed. I was terrified. I'd only stunned her, but she said I'd meant to kill her. I didn't! I only wanted the credit that was rightfully mine."

Geena broke down, sobbing. Rhett, Wolfman, and I got to our feet. Rough rose and leapt ahead of us. "Hey, take it easy," he counseled her gruffly. "You didn't even break any skin. Where I grew up, we got nuns who fight dirtier than that."

"Stop validating her impulses!" Oscar demanded. "She's got to deal with her remorse. Self awareness requires discipline and stamina."

Rough pivoted toward him menacingly. "You just like to make chicks cry."

"Watch what you say! I'm taking notes!"

"Go ahead. My name's Nail Delgado,"

he said in his Brooklyn brogue. "I just moved to Chinaberry last month. Got a trailer on some property my ma left me. Cutie Upton—she was from around here. I got a job at the candle factory. I don't know what it's like to live in the country—hey, I don't know cows from cannoli, see? So my neighbor's cow gets out of the pasture and comes over, and stands in my driveway and has its kid—its calf, whatever— has its baby right there by my truck. So I go out and say, Nice, cow, no hurry, and the baby's just getting dried out, looking for lunch, but the owner comes over, and he's a cranky dude, and he starts waving an electric cow prod like he's gonna zap momma and her little beefcake. And I say, Cut 'em some slack. They've had a long day. So he mouths back at me that they're just dumb animals, and I say they're on my land and it's a cow sanctuary, I just decided. You poke 'em with that zapper and I'll stick it...well, anyway. He got mad at that, and I wrestled him for the cow prod, and when I got it I gave him an electric jab in the rump roast."

So he's Cutie Upton's son, I thought in sad amazement. Cutie had had a hard life and disappeared as a teenager. I looked at her stalwart boy with admiration and then realized everyone else was equally touched by his heroic, breathless, bovine tale. Even Geena stopped crying and studied Nail as if he were a tender cut of steak.

But Oscar's lip curled. "You think cows

deserve more respect than a fellow human being?"

"The cows couldn't fight back. They didn't have an electric people prod."

Oscar snorted. "Give everyone your name, Mister Nail. Your real name."

"Francis Upton Delgado."

"Francis Upton. Not so tough-sounding now, are you, *Francis Upton*?"

"I dunno. Why don't you use my initials, instead?" He paused perfectly. "Just F.U."

I bit my tongue. Glancing at Del Jackson, I caught the twitch of a smile on his lips. The obscene double entendre turned Oscar livid. "You're out of here, jerk! You're out of this class!" He leaned toward Nail, spitting as he shouted. "I'm reporting you to Judge Blakely. How does time in the county jail sound? Better than anger management class once a week? You've got your wish, then."

"Don't you dare," I said evenly.

"Listen to the mayor," Del told Oscar. "She's speaking for all of us."

We all drew closer together, all five of us, bonding in Mossy Creekite defiance. "You'll have to send this whole class to jail," I said.

Geena whispered, "Does F.U. mean what I think it means?"

I lied quickly. "It means *Forget-about-it, You!*" I looked at Del Jackson for support.

He arched an eyebrow. "Yes, it's a Yankee insult."

Wolfman, struggling not to laugh, added, "I think Yankees say it like 'Foo.' As in *Foo You.*"

Geena took a deep breath. "Foo!" she said to Oscar. "Just Foo!"

Nail, speechless through all of this, began to smile. "Hey, if my homies say it, it's true. Foo You."

Oscar looked at us with the white-rimmed eyes of a small, frustrated lap dog, but the slightest twitch began under his beady left eye. He was defeated. Five Mossy Creekites had just declared *All For One and One For Y'all.*

We were The Foo Club.

❧❧❧

"Here's to The Foo Club," I said. The five of us convened at O'Day's Pub after class, sitting in a dark back booth like a merry band of robbers.

"The Foo Club," Del agreed, with a nod of his head.

"Foo!" the others said. We laughed and toasted ourselves. Del and I drank wine, Wolfman and Nail drank beer, and Geena cupped her hands around a soft drink she was too nervous to imbibe. "I just want to say," I told the group, "that I admire every one of you, and I don't think any of you deserve to be in that idiotic class."

There were nods. Del inclined his head

and smiled. "What about you?" he asked in his deep, heartland voice.

I shrugged. "I'm supposed to take an effective stand against the governor's sneaky tactics. What did I accomplish? Nothing."

"Mind if give you a little military philosophy?"

"Go ahead. We're probably going to jail together, so let's share."

"All right. Here's my advice. You need to regroup and attack from a new angle." He smiled, flashing beautiful white teeth. The man was a walking temptation. He made me feel dangerous. And that was dangerous.

"I'll think about tactics in the future," I promised uneasily. "After this class is finished."

Nail hunched his lean shoulders. "None of us are gonna make it through the class at the rate we're going. We got nothing to look forward to. And no way to fight back."

"I meant to be docile," Geena moaned. "I meant to be humble. But now I just feel . . . I just feel . . . mad. And helpless. And wronged."

"Man's got to do, What a man's got to do," Wolfman recited. "Woman's got to do, What a woman's got to do. Right is right, wrong is wrong, Thinkin' that through, Don't take long."

We were silent, all gazing into our drinks like fortune-tellers trying to read crystal balls. "I'm going to get rid of that new welcome sign,"

I admitted. "Somehow."

There was a pause—a silent, collective sharing of fate, pride, and redemption. "I see a fine group of soldiers, here," Del noted quietly. "Ready to help you reclaim your honor, Mayor. And theirs." More nods. I gazed at them in amazement.

"I've got a bulldozer we could use," Wolfman said.

ༀༀༀ

A soft, white, spring fog filled South Bigelow Road and the woods around Hamilton Farm like smoke.

"The fog's here to help us," I said. "My grandmother would say it's a veil of angel wings."

"Don't go nutty on me," Del grunted. "I've heard about you Hamiltons."

I flashed him an evil look, which he didn't notice in the misty darkness. He, I, and the rest of the Foo Club stood in the woods of my farm road, our faces illuminated only by a hissing propane lantern perched on the huge scoop of Wolfman's biggest bulldozer. Behind the bulldozer sat a rented moving van. Del handed out dark ski masks, and we each put them on. I felt like a fool, peering out at the others from inside my mask. Why had I agreed to let Del run this military-type mission? I hadn't. He'd just taken over.

"We all look like yarn monkeys in a craft-show booth," I complained. "Is this really necessary?"

"We don't want to risk being identified."

"No, I certainly wouldn't want to be recognized in 70-degree spring weather wearing a dime-store ski mask. That would add insult to injury."

His blue eyes flashed—what I could see of them, anyway, inside his own wooly covering. "No more wisecracks, Private." He looked at the others. "All right, let's go over the plan one more time. Nail drives Geena south on South Bigelow Road to the curve, lets her out, and she stands behind the crabapple tree on the left roadside, watching for traffic headed north towards us. Geena, if you see headlights, you wave your flashlight at us."

Geena peered at him like a sparrow. "I will, Sir."

"Then Nail drives back to base—that is, the welcome sign and Ida's driveway. Ida gets in his truck, and he drives north on South Bigelow to the top of the hill. He gets out and waits there behind the sweet shrub with a flashlight, ready to signal if he sees oncoming traffic headed south towards us."

"Yeah, I got it," Nail said.

Ida drives back, then hides the truck in the woods behind her grain silo. Then she'll position herself by the silo and watch both north and south for signals from Nail and

Geena. Are you clear on that, Ida?"

"Your wish is my command, General."

"Ida, it's Lieutenant Colonel."

"Lieutenant Colonel, it's *Miss* Ida."

"What?"

"You earned your rank, I earned mine."

He rolled his eyes then pointed at Wolfman. "Wolfman, when the sentries are in place, you drive the bulldozer to the sign, and I'll follow in the van. You scoop the sign up, bring it to the back of the van, then we'll load it and lock it up."

"Man's got a plan, and I understand." Wolfman nodded.

"Good. Let's shake on it." Del held out a darkly gloved right hand.

We each laid a hand atop his. My throat tightened. "Thank you, thank you all. On behalf of Mossy Creek, I make you all a promise. I 'ain't going nowhere and don't want to.'"

"Down with the Swee Purla's of the world," Geena chirped.

"Down with cheatin' house builders," Wolfman added.

"Save the cows," Nail deadpanned.

"What I do for a pretty woman who likes guns," Del said sardonically.

I could feel my face heat under the scratchy mask.

He only smiled.

❦❦❦

We were in position. Wolfman maneuvered his bulldozer toward the sparkling, reflective-green welcome sign that had been installed to replace the one I shot. It was at least four-by-four feet, screwed to two long, steel posts anchored in concrete. Del stood near the sign, gesturing with both hands. I strained my eyes north, then south, checking for signals from Nail and Geena. I held a monogrammed handkerchief in one hand, like a flag.

It was just after midnight, and South Bigelow Road wasn't a major late-night thoroughfare. In fact, the only people likely to be out in this part of Bigelow County at this time of night were Mossy Creek police officers on patrol. I'd discreetly checked Chief Amos Royden's schedules. He was on duty tonight. That worried me. I wasn't certain how he timed his patrol down South Bigelow to the town limits at Hamilton Farm, but I knew he'd make a least two rounds before dawn. Amos, who had come back to Mossy Creek after some stellar years as an Atlanta homicide detective, was disciplined and methodical. Plus his father, Battle, had been police chief of Mossy Creek for thirty years. Amos had inherited the Royden talent for sniffing out trouble. Especially trouble caused by Hamiltons.

"You never told us what to do if a car's

coming," I called to Del over the bulldozer's deep rumble.

He guided Wolfman's scoop to within inches of the sign's bottom. "That part's simple. Run like hell."

"I take it you never won any medals in combat."

Crunch. Wolfman's scoop crumpled the sign's bottom rim. I watched him maneuver levers up in the huge machine's cab. The scoop rose, and the sign shivered. The grassy earth around its steel posts began to tear. I thought the sign might bend and rip up the middle, but it held. Suddenly, its concreted feet popped free. Ham's second brand-new Mossy Creek welcome sign dangled helplessly in the foggy night air. Wolfman used his bulldozer to carry the captured sign over to the van's open door. He and Del lifted the sign off the scoop and set it inside the van. Del pulled the van's retractable door down, locked it, and gave me a thumb's up.

I applauded both him and Wolfman. At the top of the hill to my left, a white, haloed dot of light began to swing wildly. My heart stopped. "Nail's signaling!" I yelled.

Wolfman climbed into his bulldozer cab, gunned the machine's mighty engine, and headed up my driveway through the woods. "Move it, Mayor," Del called, leaping into the van's driver side.

I hurriedly climbed into the passenger

side. "I hate to leave Geena and Nail. They might get caught."

"They'll follow the plan. They'll be fine."

He stamped the accelerator, and we drove swiftly down South Bigelow toward Bigelow and the interstate that would take us to Atlanta. I rolled down my window and hung my head out. Just before Del and I rounded a curve that would hide us from view, I glimpsed a pair of headlights.

I slumped back in the seat. "The chances are good that's Amos, and he's turning around at the silo right now—he doesn't go outside the town limits on patrol—and right this second he's noticing that the new welcome sign is gone."

"So? He didn't see us. He won't see the rest of our gang, either. We did it, Ida!" He drove faster.

Rain began to fall in thick sheets, making it less likely that Amos would do much poking around the site or find any tracks if he did. I glanced at Del. "Maybe this is actually going to work."

"Could be. I'd believe anything, right now." Del pulled off his ski mask, and I removed mine. He grinned. My heart skipped a beat, which it didn't often do. I laughed like a delighted girl. We headed for Atlanta.

We left the sign outside the gates of the Governor's Mansion. By morning, news of it was on all the local stations. It even made the couch-chatter segment on the Today Show. Katie Couric laughed and said she wondered if we had a Hatfield-McCoy kind of feud going on in Mossy Creek.

We're far more inventive than that. Afterwards, I thought of Grandma. Beneath my jeans, I wore pink panties these days. Traditions. I had brought all my family's traditions to bear, and I felt victorious.

I didn't know it at the moment, but my monogrammed handkerchief lay in the grassy edge of South Bigelow Road.

Where Amos Royden picked it up.

❦❦❦

I was sitting at a front table in the crowded banquet room at the Hamilton House Inn, enjoying the scent of the first spring daffodils in the table arrangements and pretending to listen as Chamber of Commerce President Dwight Truman went through one of his rambling, squeaky-voiced luncheon rants about late membership dues. I felt very alive and very self-satisfied—plus slim and sexy in a pale, tailored dress-suit. In short, I was as happy as the cat's meow, which is what old Southern ladies say when a woman has reason to purr.

Until Amos Royden walked into the room and pointed at me.

"Mayor," he said. "You're busted."

❧❧❧

Little Ida asked me tearfully if I was going to prison. She was in tears over schoolyard rumors that her grandmother might end up in striped coveralls, forced to make license plates alongside women nick-named Deadeye and Viper. Robert quietly, wearily told me he wished, just once, I'd ask his advice before I did something that upset the whole family. I apologized and felt ashamed. I secluded myself after that, took no calls, went nowhere, and spoke to no one, including Del, who left many messages. I worked in my gardens at Hamilton Farm, pruning roses. Regret called me to its thorns.

A week later I stood beside Teresa in the packed courtroom down in Bigelow, while Judge Blakely grimaced and shuffled papers behind his tall desk, picking over my record like an old crow nibbling on roadkill. "You committed vandalism and a theft, and you dumped the goods on the grounds of the Governor's Mansion," he cawed, then peered at me above his reading glasses. "Why, Mayor, you're a litterbug, in addition to everything else."

I said nothing. Teresa, red-faced, clamped her lips together.

"But you know what's even worse?" Judge Blakely went on. "You lied to the authorities—to your own police chief, Mayor.

Because only a pie-eyed fool would believe you tore out that sign and carted it down to Atlanta by yourself."

"I've been working out with weights."

He slapped his gavel on his desk and scowled down at me. "Don't you get funny with me again, Ida Hamilton Walker! You've caused enough trouble at taxpayer expense." He held up a letter. "This is a resignation from your anger management counselor. He says he's mentally distressed and blames you for ruining his class."

Oscar had quit because of me? "Your Honor, I don't know what to say. I feel very, well, very—"

"Regretful? Ashamed of yourself?"

"*Proud*. Mr. Seymour was a petty dictator. He was one step away from setting up his own army and taking over a small country."

Teresa groaned. Judge Blakely pounded the desk. "Either you tell this court the names of everybody who helped you steal that sign, or I'll right-now sentence you to two months at a state facility for women, and I do mean women, 'mean women,' not ladies."

"I'll fit in perfectly."

"So be it!" He raised his gavel. Everyone held their breaths—the whole courtroom, the media, the gawkers, my friends and neighbors, Robert, who was sitting behind me, and me. Terrible silence and anticipation spread through the air. Dread thudded in my chest.

Prison. I was going to prison.

"You'll have to send us with her," a deep male voice intoned. "Otherwise, she'll charm the warden and scare the serial killers." The words resonated through the breathless silence. Everyone turned toward the voice at the back of the courtroom. Del, dressed in a handsome gray suit, stood in the center aisle. Wolfman, Nail, and Geena stood with him. Del met my eyes with quiet promise, then looked up at Judge Blakely just as calmly. "Your Honor," he said. "We're proud to be Mayor Hamilton's gang. We helped her steal the sign, and we'd do it again if she asked." He paused, just the slightest hint of a smile cocking one corner of his mouth. "Because we're The Foo Club."

❦❦❦

Down in the governor's office at the state capitol, Ham, Ardaleen, and several advisors listened to a speaker phone on Ham's huge desk. An aide reported directly from the courtroom chaos. "Judge Blakely just ordered a two-hour recess while he sorts this out," the aide said loudly. "Governor, Asia Makumba from Channel Seven just ran by here yelling for her cameraman to set up a live network feed."

Ham punched the console's mute button and said a half-dozen words that could have gotten him thrown out of Bigelow First

55

Presbyterian. "Old Judge Blakely has lost his mind," Ham thundered. "He's let this public scalding get totally out of hand. Mother, you said he'd give Aunt Ida a lecture, add about a thousand hours of community service to her sentence, and let her go!"

"He never promised us," Ardaleen admitted. "The old rummy."

"She got his temper up, and he went right for her hamstrings!"

This unintended pun brought pinched looks all around. "Remember, Governor, no more ham analogies in your vocabulary," coached a red-faced aide.

"Dammit, I did not want my aunt to be put on a pedestal of public sympathy and sent to prison! Can you all see the headlines? 'Governor Lets Activist Aunt Stew In Prison. Ham Fries In Opinion Polls.' Or how about this, someday, when I'm campaigning for President?" Ham stood and spread his hands wide, as if outlining a television screen. "Well, Cokie Roberts, what do you and the other commentators think of Ham Bigelow's message of friendly leadership?" Ham turned to face an invisible person, and his voice rose to a comical female octave. "Why, Sam Donaldson, I just think Governor Bigelow's a big hypocrite because he didn't raise a finger to help his own aunt when she went to the slammer!"

Ham sank back into his plush, high-backed chair.

Ardaleen glowered at him. "We agreed that you should stand your ground and keep a low profile."

"That was before my aunt called in her friends. Her Kung Foo Club, or whatever it is." Ham thumped a page of notes his staff had quickly gathered. "Del Jackson is a veteran. He won medals in the Gulf War!"

Silence. Sticky silence. Visions of Governor Ham Bigelow being accused of a vendetta against military heroes and his own aunt danced like falling poll numbers in the cigar-tinged air.

Ardaleen snapped her manicured fingernails. "Get my son a helicopter," she ordered between gritted teeth. "He's going up to Bigelow and save his damned aunt."

❦❦❦

Ham arrived like some kind of one-man cavalry, telling every camera in sight that he intended to launch a mighty appeal on my behalf. "I don't agree with my aunt's politics," he said solemnly, "but I certainly approve of her courage—and her choice of, uh, patriotic friends. There's been a terrible misunderstanding."

When Judge Blakely reconvened court after numerous aides of Ham's conferred desperately with the old judge in private and promised him god-knows-what, probably an appointment to the state's supreme court, Ham stood up and said, "If my aunt will agree to pay damages for the sign she and her . . . her Foos, Fuchsia . . . "

"Foo Club," Nail called out. "Just Foo, Governor."

Ham nodded. "Thank you, son."

Nail, Wolfman, and Geena nodded back.

Ham cleared his throat. "If she'll agree to cover the damages—" his voice rose grandly— "then I herewith promise to withdraw my well-meaning but misunderstood intentions. In short—no more new welcome sign."

"Agreed," I said instantly.

Mossy Creekites erupted in applause.

I looked at Del and the others with tears in my eyes.

"Foo Club forever," I mouthed.

❧❧❧

"We won," I said to Del softly, in disbelief. He and I sat on the steps of my back veranda in the darkness, with a pair of my grandmother's hand-crocheted pink afghans around our shoulders.

He smiled. "There's strength in numbers."

"The power of Foo." We smiled.

The veranda ceiling lights glowed, along

with the windows of my home. The house was full of people—an impromptu celebration, complete with champagne. Nail, Geena, and Wolfman were all inside, along with the town council and two-dozen neighbors. I heard Robert and Teresa laughing, and from the parlor, the muted sound of Little Ida banging out Fleetwood Mac's Don't Stop Thinking About Tomorrow on my baby grand. "I taught her that," I said.

"I like Fleetwood Mac, too."

"We should get to know each other. Maybe by doing something that doesn't involve stealing road signs."

"I agree. We should talk about a lot of things now that we're going to be seeing each other."

"Seeing each other? Is that an invitation, or an order?"

"Depends on how you take it, Mayor."

"I'll think about it and let you know."

"How long will this thinking take?"

"I'm not sure. I've been using my brain a lot lately. It may need a vacation."

He leaned closer to me. "I know something we can do that doesn't require any brainpower."

"You're going to be trouble, aren't you?"

"Stand up right now if you don't expect to be kissed."

I smiled. "Ain't going nowhere, and don't want to."

❦❦❦

"Mother, you won. Again." Robert stood beside me on the roadside where the sign had been. He sighed, exhaled, then admitted, "You know, I'm proud of you. It's just that I can't be like you. Or like Dad was. I just don't have the imagination."

"You're fine the way you are. I'm proud of you, too." Frowning, I smoothed the grass with my hiking boot. "If I knew a more diplomatic way to keep Mossy Creek safe from the Ham Bigelows of the world, I'd use it. Ham is going to run for President a few years from now. This sign business was just the start. He wants to whitewash anything that might embarrass him or make his family look funny, and that includes Mossy Creek."

The spring wind rose softly, and I gazed up at the old corn silo, then at the mountains I had known all my life. "Do you think I'm getting too old to feud with Bigelows?"

"You? Never."

"A good answer. Maybe I'm not old, *yet*, but I'm like the corn silo. I'm losing my original paint job. Getting down to the real finish." I paused. "I keep thinking that if I can just keep everything in Mossy Creek the same, then nothing can ever change the places and people we love. But it doesn't work that way."

Robert pointed. "Look at the mountains.

They're going to bloom with wild rhododendrons this spring just like they have for years." He pointed to the old silo. "The corn silo will always be right beside the road here. And so will Mossy Creek. Ham isn't going to ruin *anything* about our town. Because you won't let him." He put an arm around me. "So do what you have to do, Mother. And I'll be right behind you, paying your bail."

I lifted my head proudly and couldn't help smiling at a patch of pink clouds that had just drifted into sight above the blue green spring mountains. "Look," I said softly. "there's your Great-Grandma's proud pink butt."

"I hope to shout," Robert said.

And we did.

The Mossy Creek Gazette
215 Main Street—Mossy Creek, Georgia

FROM THE DESK OF KATIE BELL, BUSINESS MANAGER

Lady Victoria Salter Stanhope
Cornwall, England

Dear Lady Victoria,

Things have settled down a little since the sign incident, but there's a lot of talk about the future. Ham Bigelow made it clear he's out to tame our town so we won't cause him any trouble when he runs for President. What can you expect from a man born of a Hamilton and a Bigelow? It's like mixing a wildcat and a Persian: The offspring look good, but you better guard your ankles.

You say you like our town motto? Good. Our grammar's improved, but the sentiment is still the same. You see, Mossy Creekites don't run when trouble comes—except for Isabella and Richard, but that was an extenuating circumstance. Our women are usually the first line of home defense. They have guns, and they know how to use them. They are also keen on keeping their hair nice. Big hair and guns are a Southern tradition, you know. I can't say quite why Mossy Creekite females are fascinated with weaponry, except it never hurts to be armed around Bigelowans. At any rate, I doubt Sandy Crane's

62

shoot-'em-up trip to the beauty shop will ever be forgotten. Read on, your Ladyship.

And by the way, no Chihuahuas were actually harmed in the writing of this story.

Your big-haired friend,

Katie Bell

Sandy

A DAY IN THE LIFE

All I wanted was a haircut. Really.

See, I heard from my brother Mutt in early May that there was about to be an opening in the Mossy Creek Police Department for a dispatcher—Cindy Fuller being seven months along with twins, if you can believe it, and the doctor telling her she needed to start training her replacement now if she didn't want to spend the next two months flat on her back in the hospital (which was probably sounding pretty good to Cindy right about then, come to think of it), not to mention the fact that she was getting so big she could hardly fit behind the desk. The job paid $8.00 an hour, which isn't bad for Mossy Creek, 8:00 a.m. to 6:00 p.m., with an hour or an hour and a half lunch break, depending on how busy they were—which most of the time, wasn't very busy at all. Not much happens in Mossy Creek, Georgia, population 1,700. If you don't count Miss Ida shooting the new welcome sign a couple of months before. Now *that* had been some excitement.

Anyway, I figured working as a police dispatcher would be a lot better than cleaning houses, which is what I'd been doing for the past two years, and before that working customer service at Mountain Telephone down in Bigelow. Talk about your stress. Let me tell you, a couple of drunks duking it out at O'Day's Pub or a mayor shooting the stuffing out of a state road sign is nothing compared to the kind of trouble I used to deal with on a regular basis at the telephone company, which is why I figured I was as qualified as anybody else to take over the dispatcher's job.

Not that I didn't like cleaning houses. Good honest work, as my mama used to say, and I like keeping people in order, freshening up their lives and letting the sunshine in, so to speak. The money's all right, too, especially when the summer people come up and open their big houses. In the winter, though, money gets a little scarce, which is why I recently decided to reconsider my career options, you might say.

My husband Jess, as fine a man as God ever put on this earth, talked about going to work over at the candle factory. But that would mean giving up his part-time job at the *Mossy Creek Gazette,* and it wouldn't leave him any time at all to write his stories, so I put my foot down about that, yes, sir. Jess is going to be somebody with his stories, some day. He writes as good as that Stephen King, and that's a fact. Me, I can't hardly write a postcard without scratching out every other word, but Jess has got a real talent, and that's something the good Lord didn't give everybody. So I figure the least I can do is my part toward supporting the family—which at this point consists of me, Jess, a Ford pickup and two yard cats—until the people at the big publishing houses in New York realize what a prize they're passing up. Besides, I really like reading his stories.

So that's how I happened to be in town that bright May morning, strolling up Spruce Street toward the Goldilocks Hair, Nail and Tanning Salon on Main. I was looking a little ragged around the edges, and plus I heard the new police chief was kind of particular about the hair length of his employees, for which I don't blame him one bit—let's face it, it's hard to be taken seriously by the bad guys when you're a cop with babydoll curls—and I wanted to make a good impression. So I'd made an appointment with Rainey for a cut and blow-dry at ten, which would get me out of there in plenty of time for my interview with Chief Royden at 11:30. I figured I'd dazzle him with my personality and charm for twenty or thirty minutes, pick up a couple of Lunch Specials to-go at Mama's All You Can Eat Café for Jess and me, and be home in time for *Judge Judy* at 1:00. I hoped Cindy had remembered to put in a good word for me.

I parked the pickup down on Spruce because we hadn't gotten around to fixing that broken taillight from where I'd backed into Mama's chicken coop last winter trying to keep from squashing her butterfly bush, and I didn't think it would look right, you know, for somebody that was trying to get a job in the police department to park right out in front with a broken taillight.

I didn't mind the walk. It gave me a chance to see how the Abercrombies' purple petunias were doing on the square this year, and whether Egg Egbert had gotten that sagging front porch of his fixed or not—it was a shame, really, the way he was letting his mama's place run down—and wave to nutty old Millicent Hart, who was probably sprinkling stolen fertilizer pellets around her daughter's roses, and . . .

I slowed my step, the way a cat does when it smells something curious in the air, as I came over the rise and spotted Miss Lorna Bingham's house. It was a sweet little cottage with green awnings and a picket fence, and, at this moment, an odd-looking white car parked in front of it. Well, if you want to know the truth, the only odd thing about the car was that I didn't recognize it. But in Mossy Creek, you don't just walk on by when you see a strange car parked in a neighbor's driveway—especially if there happens to be a strange person prowling through the hydrangea bushes and peeking through the windows at the same time.

I know Miss Lorna. I clean her house the first Thursday of every month. She's a sweet little old thing with diabetes and arthritis bad enough to keep her in a wheelchair, but most times she's just as sharp as a tack in spite of it. I'd met her daughter from Atlanta and her sister from Gainesville, and it was too early for Meals on Wheels to be delivering–besides which, I knew all of them, too. So what do you suppose, I couldn't help asking myself in a real cautious-like way, is that woman in the navy blue pantsuit doing prowling around Miss Lorna's house?

There was only one way to find out. I swung open the gate and called out, "Hello, there! You need some help?"

The woman had pulled up an old paint can, had overturned it, and had climbed up on it to give herself a better view into Miss Lorna's kitchen. She had her face pressed to Miss Lorna's window with her hands cupped around it to shield her eyes, and when I hollered out, she turned around too fast, flapped her arms for a minute like she was trying to take off in a headwind, and then the paint can went out from under her, and she sprawled back on her nether-end into the hydrangea bushes.

Now there are a couple of things anybody who goes to apply for a job in law enforcement ought to know, if you ask me: a) that almost all rental cars are white and b) how to recognize a wig. Now, it was entirely possible that some big-time criminal from Atlanta had rented a car, put on a salt-and-pepper wig and a blue pantsuit, and had driven all the way up here to do some harm to Miss Lorna. Since the wig in question was now sitting noticeably askew, and since I had happened to notice as I passed that the car had Bigelow County plates, I felt pretty confident I wouldn't be shot down like a dog if I rushed to help the woman in the bushes. On the other hand, it doesn't pay to be too friendly until you get all the facts, which might be the third thing anybody who wants to get a job in law enforcement might want to know.

So I hauled the woman to her feet, helped her crawl out of the hydrangea bushes, and waited until she'd straightened her wig before I demanded, in as nice a voice as I could, "What are you doing looking in Miss Lorna's windows?"

The woman, who I guessed to be about fifty, married, from the look of the ring on her finger, and too lazy or too busy to do her own hair every morning, tugged at the hem of her navy polyester jacket, brushed a few dead hydrangea petals off her slacks, worried with the edges of her wig and managed to look insulted and important at the same time as she announced, huffing a little, "I am Clara Dawson from Happy Mountain Home Health Care. Mrs. Bingham is my patient. Who, may

I ask, are you?"

"Sandy Crane," I replied, friendly enough, and extended my hand. I used to be Sandy Bottoms before I married, no lie, which had nothing whatsoever to do with why I married Jess at eighteen. Well, not much, anyway.

The woman hesitated for a minute, then shook my hand. She had a weak, nervous, citified handshake.

"Listen," she was saying, a little breathlessly. "Do you know the woman who lives here? Because I think—"

I said, still real friendly-like, "No, you're not."

She blinked. "What?"

"You're not from Happy Mountain Home Health Care. Lisa Williams is Miss Lorna's nurse, and she comes on Wednesday, not Tuesday. So why don't you just tell me who you are and why you're poking around Miss Lorna's hydrangea bushes before I have to call the police?"

"What?" The woman went bugged eyed. "Aren't you listening to me? I've been knocking on the door, and nobody answers, and this is 418 Spruce, isn't it, Lorna Bingham? I'm going to have to call my supervisor—"

I said skeptically, "You got some kind of card or something from the Happy Mountain Home Health Care?"

"Lisa Williams is on vacation," she told me a little huffily, and pulled out a laminated badge from her shoulder bag. "I drove all the way over here from Bigelow to take her cases, and I'm telling you, I've got a housebound patient in there who doesn't answer the door. Something could be seriously wrong."

I looked at the identification she handed me, and returned it without comment. Rats. I could have really made an impression on the chief if I'd've been able to turn over a felon to him on my way to my interview.

I said, "You probably didn't knock loud enough. Miss Lorna is almost eighty, you know. Sometimes she has a little trouble hearing."

"I think I should call the paramedics. Procedure is—"

I went to the door and banged on it, hard. "Miss Lorna! Miss Lorna, you in there?"

"She could have fallen, or had a stroke— Her record says she has high blood pressure, you know. Or she could be in a diabetic coma—"

I knocked again. "Miss Lorna, are you okay?"

The woman whipped out a cell phone from her bag and started punching out numbers. "The manual says I have to call the paramedics at the Mossy Creek Volunteer Fire Department."

I glanced at her in annoyance, although the truth be told, I was getting a little worried myself. "I don't see any need to do that until we know if something's wrong. Those boys have to get all suited up, bring out the big truck . . ."

She said into the phone, "Hello? Hello, this is Clara Dawson from Happy Mountain Home Health Care, and I'm at 418 Spruce..."

I ran my hand over the top of the doorjamb until I found the key. I inserted it into the lock. "Miss Lorna? Are you in the tub? Because I'm coming in."

I heard the woman say, "Yes, hurry." And she flipped her little phone shut as she came over to me, looking all anxious and flustered. "What are you doing? You're not opening the door, are you?"

I gave her a real patient look. "Unless you've got some other idea about how we can get in?"

"But I'm not allowed . . . That is, until the police or emergency personnel get here, we're absolutely not to enter the premises . . ."

This woman's palaver was getting real old, real fast. "Didn't you just say she could be in a coma?"

"Well, yes, but—"

I opened the door. "Miss Lorna, you okay?"

"Don't you take another step, Missy."

The front door opened right into the main room of the house, which was done up in faded orange chintz and a kind of tea-colored wallpaper. The inside smelled of lavender room spray and talcum powder and, well, old people. I do my best to keep it fresh, but I can only do so much with what I've got.

The curtains were drawn over both windows, making it hard to see too much, but one thing you couldn't miss: Miss Lorna Bingham, sitting in her wheelchair right square in the middle of the room with a 12 gauge shotgun pointed straight at the door. I halted on the spot.

"Miss Lorna, what in the world are you doing?"

"Step back, step back." Clara Dawson bustled past me. "Let me at my patient—"

"You come any closer," said Miss Lorna, "and I'll blow you to Kingdom Come."

It was about that time that Clara noticed the 12 gauge and screamed, flinging her hands over her head.

I heard the Rescue Unit's siren cranking up at the firehouse two blocks away, and I took a couple of steps deeper into the room, squinting a little in the gloom. "Miss Lorna, what are you doing with that gun?"

"I'm defending my property against burglars, that's what!" she declared, jerking the barrel toward Clara Dawson. Clara made a little whimpering sound and raised her hands higher.

"That's not a burglar, that's your home health care nurse! Now you give me that gun before somebody gets hurt."

"I'm not doing it!" Now she swung the barrel toward me. "And she's not my nurse. Lisa's my nurse!"

"Lisa's on vacation. This is the new nurse."

But by now the siren sound was so close that I had to shout, and she cocked her head and yelled, "Huh? What'd you say?"

"I say," I screamed, "this is your new nurse, Mrs.—"

The sirens wound down abruptly in front of the house.

"Dawson," I shouted, because it was too late to find my regular speaking voice by then.

"Well, I don't care if she is a friend of yours," Miss Lorna shouted back, "she tried to break into my house, and I'm going to shoot her dead if she don't get out of here right now!"

There was a clattering on the steps and two paramedics burst through the open door, portable gurney, medical bags and oxygen in tow. They stopped even with me when they saw Miss Lorna's gun.

The lead man glanced at me. "Hey, Sandy," he said.

"Hey, Boo." Boo is my brother, older by three years, and if you think it was bad for me being named Sandy Bottoms, think about how you'd've liked to have been Boo Bottoms back in high school. I nodded to his partner. "Hey, Andy."

"What's going on?" Boo wanted to know.

I was about to explain when Miss Lorna demanded, "Are you the police?"

"No ma'am," said Andy, moving toward her. "We're just here to take care of you. Now why don't you let me just take your blood pressure—"

"You're not taking anything from me, young man! You back up now!" She jerked the gun at him. "Back up!"

Andy looked at me. "What's she mad about? A woman in her condition, she shouldn't get mad like that. Has she been taking her insulin? Could be an insulin reaction."

I said, "She's just defending herself, Andy. She thought this woman was breaking into her house."

Boo looked suspiciously at Clara, who stood trembling with her arms in the air. "Well, was she?"

I shrugged. "She says she's a nurse."

"For heaven's sake will somebody do something?" Clara shrieked.

Andy said, "Somebody ought to get the gun."

Boo looked at Miss Lorna, her chin set and the rifle held high, and then at Andy. He hesitated. "You want me to call the police?"

The mantle clock began its wheezing strike of the hour, and I knew I couldn't hang around here much longer. Rainey just hated it when you were late, and the one thing you don't want is to put a pair of scissors in the hands of a stressed-out hair stylist in a bad mood on the day of the most important interview of your life.

Meanwhile, Andy looked at Boo, Boo looked at Andy, Miss Dawson looked at both of them, and none of us was getting any younger. I said, "Oh, for Pete's sake."

And I marched over and snatched the gun from Miss Lorna's hands.

Andy and Boo rushed over with their official looking blood pressure cuff and important medical equipment, Clara Dawson collapsed into the nearest chair, fanning herself, and I checked the chamber of the shotgun. It was loaded.

"Miss Lorna, are you crazy?" I scolded her. "You could have hurt somebody! What are you doing with a gun like this in the house, anyway? How'd you get it loaded?"

"I always keep it loaded," she replied proudly. "My daddy was in the war."

I emptied the gun of shells and pocketed them. "Well, you ought to be more careful is all I can say. Boo, is she going to be all right?"

"Blood pressure's a little high, that's all. Miss Lorna, did you take your medicine today?"

My watch said five after ten. Blast. I'd forgotten that mantle clock was slow.

"Look," I said, "I've got to go. I'm late for a hair appointment."

"You run on. She's going to be just fine, aren't you Miss Lorna? Tell Rainey I said hey, and good luck on your interview."

I waved my thanks on the way out of the house, and practically jogged the block and a half remaining to the Goldilocks Hair Salon. I suppose I should have stayed and made sure Miss Dawson recovered from her swoon, but, really, I didn't have time.

Rainey was in a state. Her big blonde hair-do looked electrified. She always stuffed herself into a pink smock and tight jeans. She danced from one booted foot to another.

"Lor', child, where've you been? I been calling and calling you. I figured you'd forgot, you'd be surprised how many people do that, you know, no consideration whatsoever for what it does to my schedule. Then I thought maybe you'd had a wreck on your way into town and was laying out in a ditch—"

"I'm only five minutes late, Rainey, and I'm really sorry—"

"Well, you're here now, and that's all that matters, but we're going to have to hurry because I have a perm at ten-thirty, and you know how I just hate to rush. What a pretty sweater, but aren't you going to burn up this afternoon? Supposed to get up to eighty. Just go on in the bathroom and put on this smock. What are you doing with that gun?"

I looked down in dismay. I had run all the way here with Miss Lorna's shotgun in my hands. I was glad the chief hadn't seen that. Talk about your bad impressions.

I stowed the gun in the corner behind the rolling cart, figuring I would return it after my interview, and told Rainey about the adventure at Miss Lorna's house while I exchanged my lavender twin set for her pink poodle smock and she shampooed my hair and tsked a lot.

"Her mind's goin', if you ask me. That sugar diabetes'll do that, you know. It's a ever-lastin' horror on the hair, too. Why, what little hair she's got left won't even take a rinse anymore. Now, what you need, honey, is a few highlights here and there, just around your face, you know, nothing dramatic, not so's your husband will come to bed tonight and wonder who's that sleepin' on his sheets, but just to make your eyes look bigger, don't you know. How much were you thinkin' of takin' off? About four inches ought to do it, right about here, up to your chin."

She spun me around to face the mirror and cupped my wet hair with her hand at the chin line.

"Yes, that's about right, but no highlights today. Jess wouldn't like it, and I've got an interview with Chief Royden about Cindy Fuller's job, so I don't really have time—"

"Plenty of time, don't you worry a thing about it. I'll just get the solution on and pop you under the dryer while I'm doin' my perm."

"No, I don't think so. Thanks anyway."

Rainey was digging around in a cabinet filled with chemical bottles in the back of the room. "You goin' to take over Cindy's job? Well, I just don't think I'd like it. All that sittin' around, nobody to talk to but the boys all day, and I just don't see how Cindy can afford to quit work at all with no more than Lenny makes. But I guess it beats payin' a baby-sitter for twins—and both of them girls, did you hear that? Lor', is poor Cindy goin' to have her hands full! Especially with her mama down in Florida, although I did hear she's comin' up to stay for a month when the babies come. Now, this is what I think—a nice honey-beige cellophane glaze on the bottom layers, to kind of give you some low lights, and then just comb through some Moonlight Mist over the top, make you look just like one of those supermodels. Were you thinkin' of keepin' the bangs?"

"I really don't think—"

"I don't either. I always say, the more of a girl's face you can see, the better. Let's just get some of this length off . . ." Snip, snip and several inches of hair fell to the floor. "And we'll see what we've got here."

"Now, Rainey, that's fine, that looks good. Don't get it too short."

"Don't you worry, you're just gonna love it. That Moonlight Mist is just the sweetest baby-blonde you ever saw, and it'll go just perfect with your eyes. You were a born blonde, weren't you? See, that's what happens when we get older. All that pollution in the air is what I think. Makes the hair darker."

"My hair's not all that dark."

"Lor', honey, live a little. Have an adventure once in a while. You know what I always say, if God had wanted us to look like this, He wouldn't have made Miss Clairol."

Uncertain, I looked at myself—what was left of me, anyway—in the mirror. "Well, maybe just a touch of blonde. But don't cut it too short."

Snip, snip. "And maybe while your color's sittin' I'll call up Mama's All You Can Eat Café and see what kind of pie Rosie baked today. You know if it's chocolate meringue you've got to reserve your piece by 10:30, or there won't be a bite left by lunchtime. If you ask me, I think they ought to give preference to their regular customers, and I told them so, but no siree! You call first, or you don't get a piece. I'm a good mind to just start getting my pie from Ingrid's bakery, but you know, she might have Rosie's Italian cream cake beat all to pieces, but she don't know a thing about chocolate meringue. You want me to tell her to hold you a piece, honey?"

While she spoke, she had been smearing a cold, white, foul-smelling goo all over the right-hand side of my center part. It was burning my eyes, and I coughed a little. "Is that colorin' supposed to smell like a skunk with a B.O. problem?"

She laughed. "You'll get used to it." She turned her head toward a sound from the front room. "Mavis? Is that you, hon? I'll be with you in a minute. I'm running a little behind."

With a harried look on her face, she began to slop more of the goo on my hair. I protected my eyes.

"Now we'll just get you finished up and under the dryer real quick—"

"Maybe Mavis could go for coffee?" I suggested.

But we both realized at the same moment that the racket we were hearing was not coming from the front room after all, but from the street. Rainey frowned, paintbrush filled with goo held over my head, and turned toward the sound. "What in the world?"

"It sounds like someone screaming."

I got out of the chair, and we both hurried to the front door.

We reached the sidewalk at the same time several other people from the other shops on the block did. Dan McNeil from the fix-it shop next door and a couple of women from the dress shop and three customers from the book store were there, and for a minute it was hard to tell what all the commotion was about. Ingrid Beechum, who owns the bakery three doors down, had ripped off her white chef's apron and was flapping it at something while yelling, "Get away! Bob, run!"

Ah, Bob. That explained it. Bob was Ingrid's spoiled-rotten, neurotic Chihuahua.

81

Since he came to work every day with Ingrid, she often let him out on the town square to do his business—which had caused more than one complaint by the merchants on the strip. I figured somebody had finally had it with Bob's careless personal habits and had decided to take the matter into his own hands. Either that, or Pearl Quinlin's pet ferret over at the bookstore had gotten after him again.

Then I heard somebody gasp, "Good heavens, have you ever seen anything like that?"

And somebody else, "Get a camera!"

"Does anybody have a stick?"

"Get a broom!"

In the midst of it all was the most godawful screeching and yipping—not to even mention the wailing set up by Ingrid—that I'd ever heard. This I had to see for myself.

And a good thing too, because I never would have believed it otherwise. I ran down the sidewalk a few steps and edged through the small crowd that had gathered next to where Ingrid was flinging her apron at something on the ground. The something was a bird approximately the size of a lawn tractor, flopping its giant wings and screaming bloody murder. It had Bob's collar in its beak, and Bob himself, who was unfortunately still wearing the collar at the time, dangled about six inches off the sidewalk as the hawk tried to gain altitude.

"Don't let him get off the ground!" someone bellowed.

"Back up, back up! They always go for the eyes!" cried someone else.

It seemed to me that the bird would have been airborne long since if he could have just found the room to take off, so the closer the crowd, the better. But I didn't say anything. I was still trying to figure out how hungry a bird would have to be to come all the way into town to hunt Chihuahuas.

Somebody broke through the crowd with a broom and began to poke tentatively at the hawk. Ingrid snatched the broom from him and started whacking. Feathers flew; the bird screeched; Bob tumbled to the ground and lay there, splay-legged. Ingrid dropped the broom and lunged for her pet. She got hold of the loop end of the dog's jeweled leash, and then the hawk swooped again.

I've never seen anything like it. Within half a second, the Chihuahua was airborne, screaming and dribbling urine all over the sidewalk while the hawk screeched in triumph and flapped its mighty wings, and Ingrid held on to the leash with all her might.

"Drop him, drop him, you damned bird!" Ingrid ordered, tugging at the leash.

"Let go of the leash, Ingrid! You're choking Bob!"

"Somebody call the police!"

"What're they gonna do? Arrest the bird?"

"Betcha he'd let go if you had some rats down here," said Dan McNeil thoughtfully, looking over the situation as though it were an engine with a bad valve. "That's what hawks eat, you know. Rats."

Aha. That explained why he'd gone for Bob.

"Does anybody know where we can get a rat?"

"You won't find any in my shop, sonny!"

Leaning back on her heels, Ingrid gave a mighty pull on the leash. The hawk lost altitude. Ingrid took a chance: leapt for her dog like Michael Jordan making a basket, missed, dropped the leash, and off went the hawk with little Bob in his talons, the leash trailing behind like a streamer on a balloon. Ingrid started running after them, arms outstretched. Maybe four or five people ran along with her, some trying to calm her down, some cheering her on. Other people piled into their cars, yelling something about cutting him off before he reached the edge of town. That was when I remembered the shotgun that I'd left in the beauty shop, and the shells in my pocket.

Now, I'm no dog lover, and even if I was, Bob the Chihuahua barely qualifies as one (I've always been of the opinion that anything under twenty pounds might just as well be a cat). I grew up on a farm where the dogs, like everybody else, had to work for their supper, and I just never have been able to understand people like Miss Ingrid who treat their dogs like babies, or dogs like Bob who think that's a fine way to live. Our old bird dog Sport would have died of embarrassment before he would've let anybody wrestle him into one of those sweaters Bob prances around in on winter days. And let's not even talk about the snow boots and the pom-pom hat.

But Ingrid did set quite a bit of store by him, and she didn't have a whole lot left in her life to set store by. Her son had died in a car accident earlier in the year, and her no-account daughter-in-law had been snooping around for handouts. Ingrid was even thinking about renting an empty shop space next to her bakery to set the girl up with a lingerie business.

You don't just stand back when a neighbor is in trouble—even if the neighbor is a trembly, bug-eyed, nasty-tempered, incontinent dog who is about to become lunch for a hawk. I mean, what a way to go. So I ran back into the shop for the shotgun, chambered a couple of rounds, slid the safety on and barreled down the street with the rest of the crowd, pink poodle smock flopping, gooped-up hair reeking.

Some folks were throwing sticks up in the air, trying to hit the hawk. Dan MacNeil climbed up on the bed of a pickup truck, hoping to snag the leash as it floated by toward the town monument, but the hawk outsmarted him and swung toward a big sycamore tree at the last minute. Off we raced across the square, leaping park benches, clambering over the bandstand. People came out of their shops and businesses, shielding their eyes with their hands as they tried to see what was going on. Some of them ran back inside and slammed the door when they saw; others grabbed their point-and-shoots and their video cameras and joined the parade.

Car horns blared, bicycles swerved, pedestrians jumped out of the way as we ran helter-skelter through downtown. We crossed the Church Street bridge, swung back around over the East Mossy Creek Road bridge, jogged down past the cut-off to the swimming hole, and I've got to tell you, by this time I was sagging. About half the folks who'd started out with us had dropped way behind, and those of us that were left were staggering and wheezing. Miss Ingrid was so red in the face I started worrying about calling out the rescue squad for her. And then, right in front of the Hamilton House Inn, we got a break.

Dan McNeil panted, "There he is! There he is!"

I took a couple more gasping breaths and caught up with the others at something less than a trot. Ingrid had staggered halfway down the cedar path that led through the Inn's famous rose garden, and there she stood, one hand clutching her throat, the other extended helplessly to the sky. Her face was closer to eggplant than scarlet now, and her lips were moving, but the only sound that came out was something I don't want to repeat. I rushed up to her, thinking she was about to have a stroke, and then I saw what she was pointing at.

There, perched on a branch of the Hamilton House Inn's one hundred fifty-year-old spreading oak tree, with a whimpering Bob clutched by the collar in its beak, was the hawk.

I edged a little closer, sighting the distance. Ingrid shook a finger at the bird. The melting goo from my hair was starting to mix with the sweat on my forehead and drip down my face; I blotted it with my poodle sleeve, and shouldered the gun. I slid off the safety.

The murmurs of the crowd died down. Every eye was on me. Then Ingrid got her breath and cried harshly, "Nail him!"

I squeezed the trigger.

ɤɤɤ

No, for all you bird lovers out there, I didn't kill the hawk. I didn't miss and hit Bob, either, although I've got to say the fall didn't do him a whole lot of good. What I did was, I shot the branch right out from under that hawk, which scared him enough to make him let go of the dog. Ingrid caught her baby about four feet from the ground.

Bob is being treated by Dr. Hank Blackshear, our local veterinarian, for puncture wounds, a bruised trachea, and general trauma, but I hear he's going to be okay. Ingrid is being treated by Dr. Champion, our local family practitioner, for nervous stress, but with the aid and assistance of her good neighbors—who haven't stopped bringing casseroles, hot tea and dog biscuits all day—she, too, is predicted to recover. Our forestry service ranger, Smokey Lincoln, came for the hawk. I hear the hawk has an injured wing, which is why he went for Bob in the first place, and why we were able to track him down in the second.

I had to figure it was something like that. I never did know a hawk to fly that low or that slow, even if he was weighed down by a Chihuahua. Smokey informs me that it's against the law to hunt a federally protected species, which the Golden Hawk is. But it's Ingrid he's really after. I understand the fines for battering a hawk with a broom are pretty stiff in Georgia.

So anyway, that's how I ended up going to my interview with Chief Royden in my brassiere and a pink poodle smock, with one side of my lopped-off hair mouse brown and straight as a stick, and the other side looking like a fuzzy, lime-green tennis ball. Apparently, you're not supposed to leave that hair color on for more than twenty minutes, and I think the manufacturer definitely recommends that you don't chase wildlife with a shotgun while applying the treatment.

"It'll grow out," I assured the Chief, plucking at the ends of my green hair. All I could do was repeat what I was told. "I mean, I won't look like this forever. Ask Mutt. I've looked worse."

He smiled at me and tried to pretend he hadn't been staring at my hair ever since I'd walked in the door. He was a really nice fellow, and Mutt loved working for him as an officer. He glanced back down at my application form. "Four years at Mountain Telephone. Now you own your own business?"

"Well," I admitted modestly, "it's just cleaning houses, but that's one way to get to know everybody in town, and a lot of the summer folks, too. And I'm on real good terms with everybody, which I think is important when you're in law enforcement, don't you?"

He agreed that it was. "Of course," he said, "you realize that this dispatcher's job is a lot more than just answering the phone. There are summonses and warrants to be typed, reports to be filled out, even errands to be run. The dispatcher kind of fills in all the cracks in an office like this."

I nodded. "I've got nothing against hard work, and we had to be able to type to get a job at Mountain Telephone. And if you don't mind my saying so. . ." I leaned forward confidentially, "I couldn't help noticing your cleaning service has been letting you down. I'll have this place spiffed up and shipshape in no time."

He nodded, glancing down at his clipboard again. He said, "Pretty fancy shooting this afternoon."

"I qualified as a sharpshooter over at the

rifle range," I admitted modestly. "Well, you know me and my brothers have all been shooting since we were old enough to tote a gun."

Now he grinned. "You ever consider applying for a job on the force as an officer?"

"Well, now that you mention it . . ."

But I didn't get to finish, because at that moment Mutt came into the room. He looked at me dolefully for a moment. "Hey, Birdbrain."

"Hey, Dogface." We always poked at each other that way.

"Rainey do that to your hair?"

"It wasn't her fault."

"Mama's going to have your hide when she sees it."

I bristled. "Well, it wasn't exactly my fault, either."

Chief Royden cleared his throat.

Mutt said, "Sorry, Chief. I came to tell you Jess is here."

"Thanks, Mutt." The chief stood up. So did I.

"Well, Mrs. Crane..."

"Call me Sandy," I said quickly.

"Well, then Sandy, about the job. . ."

"If you think it would be a problem for me working here because Mutt's my brother," I rushed in quickly, "I'll tell you right up front that there's never been any partiality in my family, and Mutt will tell you the same. Besides, Chief, if you don't mind my saying, in a town like Mossy Creek if you eliminate everybody who's related to anybody, you're not going to find anybody to work for you. Or to arrest, either, if you think about it. And after all, your own daddy was police chief. So, uh, hiring family is a good thing, right? A tradition, right? And we're big on tradition around here."

Once again, he seemed to be fighting down a grin. "To tell you the truth," he said, "I think you'd be just about perfect for this place." And just when I was wishing I could throw my arms around his neck, he added, "But you understand, I can't make any decisions before this other business is settled."

I nodded, crestfallen.

He put the key in the lock and swung open the cell door. "Okay, your husband has paid your bond, so you can go on home now." He handed me a folded piece of paper. "This is your summons to appear before Judge Blakely a week from Thursday. Discharging a firearm within the city limits, causing the disruption of a public utility . . ." The transformer on Main Street had blown when some stray shotgun pellets accidentally hit it. "And, uh, threatening the welfare of an endangered animal. I had to put that last one in for the forestry service people."

I nodded unhappily and took the summons. "I know, Chief. You were just doing your job."

I must have looked pretty pathetic there in the jail room with my day-glow hair and my pink poodle smock, because he added, "I wouldn't worry about it too much if I were you, though. Judge Blakely will probably just give you a lecture about firearm safety and throw the case out of court."

I thought about that for a minute, then nodded, grinning. "Probably. He's my second cousin, on my daddy's side."

"Sandy, honey, are you all right?"

I turned around as my big bear of a husband came bursting in. He stopped dead when he saw me, and the look on his face reminded me a lot of the one on Bob the Chihuahua's face when he was up in that tree looking down on us all: horror, disbelief, bone-numbing shock.

I fumbled self-consciously with the ends of my hair. "It'll grow out," I assured him, a little desperately.

He stood there for another moment, just staring, and I swear, I was just about ready to cry when he suddenly moved forward and swept me into his arms in a rib-cracking embrace. It took me a minute or two to get my breath back, and then I tried to wiggle out of his arms.

"You're squishing me!" I choked. But then I realized Jess's shoulders were shaking.

Now my husband is huge, with hands like skillets and shoulders the size of a football field; people are always mistaking him for the bouncer when we go line dancing on country-western night at O'Day's, and I can't tell you how many perfect strangers have come up to him wanting to know what position he played on the football team. (He didn't play any. He was in the drama club.) But he cries at Disney movies and can spend hours lying on his back watching the clouds; he is what you call a sensitive man.

I felt just awful.

"Oh, sweetie," I murmured, patting his back. "I'm sorry I worried you. It'll be okay, really. Don't be upset. I'll get a wig..."

He stepped away from me, wiping his streaming eyes. "I'm sorry," he gasped, laughing. "But you look like—like Gumby!"

I kicked him hard in the shin.

While Jess was hopping on one foot, trying to rub his leg, I turned back to the chief with my sweetest smile. "Oh by the way, Chief, about that job on the force..."

"Good bye, Mrs. Crane," he said sternly, but I could see his eyes were twinkling.

I decided to let it pass. For now.

❦❦❦

Jess wrote the story up for the paper and made me seem a whole lot more important than I was, of course. But the best part was that his boss, Sue Ora Salter, said she was going to submit it for some kind of state newspaper award. How about that?

Ingrid sent us over a cake in the shape of a Chihuahua, and Rainey called me on the phone crying every day for a week until I finally went in and let her cut my hair real short, to get off all the ruined ends, and pour some other goop on it that turned it kind of orange, which is better than green I guess. Jess says it makes me look like one of those leather girls, which he apparently finds very sexy. I'm not complaining. You learn something new every day.

As for me . . .well, let's just say if you ever get in trouble in Mossy Creek, the first voice you'll hear will be mine, saying, "Mossy Creek Police Department, how can I help you?"

So rest easy, Mossy Creek. You're in good hands, this year.

The Mossy Creek Gazette
215 Main Street—Mossy Creek, Georgia

FROM THE DESK OF KATIE BELL, BUSINESS MANAGER

Lady Victoria Salter Stanhope
Cornwall, England

Dear Lady Victoria,

Do you have beauty pageants in England? Well, ours ranks right up there with our dart competition and our softball tournaments for town spirit and excitement, especially when we're up against Bigelowans.

Our pageant is called Miss Bigelow County. That title alone sets our teeth on edge, especially considering the atmosphere in town this year. Mossy Creek girls haven't won a single time in the past few years, though they're the prettiest, smartest, most talented young women ever to twirl a baton or play "You Are The Wind Beneath My Wings" on a banjo. We could always count on Mossy Creek Police Chief Battle Royden to even up the score with Bigelow when he served on the judges' panel, but now that his boy Amos is police chief, we aren't sure what to expect.

I mean, Amos has scruples. Doggonnit.

We've always been quick to celebrate pretty women who have a talent for trouble. As I've been telling you, Isabella Salter was a real looker. Her uncle, Joshua Hamilton, doted on her just like his own daughters. Joshua was none too happy when Lionel Bigelow asked Isabella to marry him and she said yes. Lionel was a good twenty years older than Isabella and a widower with a pack of children already. Bigelow men are good-looking and charming, but folks say they'll always put money ahead of their hearts. Joshua knew that, even then. Isabella was young, and she must have been dazzled. Their marriage would have united both ends of Bigelow County once and for all. But nobody counted on Isabella meeting, handsome Englishman, Richard Stanhope.

By the way, we don't hold any grudges when we lose a contest to Bigelow. At least none we admit until we reload.

Your friend off the runway,

Katie Bell

AMOS

The Prodigal Son

The Bellringer
by Katie Bell
A weekly column of the Mossy Creek Gazette

Boys and girls, wait until you hear this one! Rumor has it that Ham Bigelow, otherwise known as Governor Hamilton Bigelow and honorary board member of the Miss Bigelow County Pageant, has single-handedly wrapped up this spring's pageant title for his beloved Bigelow township by offering the committee an innocent little suggestion. I'm not sure it's going to be that easy. Our own mayor, Ida Hamilton Walker, has a little surprise that will take the wind out of Ham's political sails . . .again. Stay tuned. This is liable to be a barnburner.

Most of the citizenry consider Katie Bell's weekly gossip column amusing. As the chief of police, I consider *The Bellringer* more of a scouting report. Every Friday morning, I walk up Main Street, have my coffee at Mama's All You Can Eat Café, push something resembling breakfast around a chipped china plate, and read the *Mossy Creek Gazette*, Katie's column in particular.

Most Fridays, I push my chair back from the table, feeling mildly pleased that Katie's intelligence network hasn't caught my own sources asleep at the wheel. Today, I resisted the urge to swear as I finished the last sentence. Right there in black and white, in front of God and everybody, Katie congratulated Ida for yet another quiet coup against pork-belly politics. Whatever Ida'd done to Ham this time would probably cause me as much trouble as it would cause her nephew.

Ida didn't seem to care that I was wearing a trail to her door. She had a strong set of small-town values that didn't necessarily reflect the worldview required of a law officer. Policing Mossy Creek was an experience akin to sliding down a rabbit hole and into the Twilight Zone.

After reading Katie's column, I knew it was going to be a rabbit hole day. All morning, I felt the hairs inexplicably rise on the back of my neck way too often; I had to use every ounce of self-control I had to keep from looking behind me—a talent I developed while on the force in Atlanta. I even debated checking the back of my shirt for a target.

By noon, I stood in the town square,

honestly considering hauling a few individuals down to the county jail and booking them on suspicion of "something." First in line for jail would've been the always-too-helpful Pearl Quinlan, who owns Mossy Creek Books and What-Nots. I looked at the book she pressed into my hand and tried to give it back, but she was already making her escape.

Pearl might be a very nice woman. And she might run an excellent bookstore. But she'd lost her mind if she thought any self-respecting chief would intentionally be caught dead walking through the town square with a book like this. Much less be caught reading it. The dust jacket was covered with nubile young women wearing tiaras. A splashy, neon-red title proclaimed *Venus On The Runway*.

I already knew everything I wanted to know about beauty pageants in general and the Miss Bigelow County Pageant in particular. I appreciated beautiful women as much as any red-blooded American male, but I wanted no part of the local pageant. I'd sooner wade into a bar brawl between hardened criminals than referee a name-calling match between stage mamas and contestants for Miss Bigelow County. A smart man didn't take sides, place bets on the winner, or lie to mothers about their homely daughters' chances.

I like to think my daddy didn't raise a fool.

There were fools aplenty in Mossy Creek

during the month of May. Every armchair judge had an opinion, a favorite and a pageant story to tell about past Mossy Creek beauties. Except me. And I had no intention of acquiring an opinion, a favorite or a story. Most especially, I did not want to endlessly debate whether baking a cake, twirling a baton on your nose, and line dancing to Rocky Top—all at the same time—constituted a talent.

My position regarding pageants was no secret. So, why had Pearl gone out of her way to hustle into the square and give me the book? What in hell was I supposed to do with it?

I got no help or sympathy from Mac Campbell, who was well within conversational range when Pearl foisted the book on me. He'd managed to avoid hooting some pithy comment by staring at the ground until Pearl turned away. Now Big Mac lifted his eyes from the fascinating patch of concrete sidewalk at his feet and began to smirk. Openly. And with great satisfaction. If we'd been thirty years younger and on the playground, the smirk would have been cause for rolling in the dirt-- me telling him to take it back and him refusing.

But we weren't younger. We were thirty-five, and I doubted I had a prayer of winning a wrestling contest with the mountain of muscle in front of me. The man had been my friend more years than I could count. My lawyer for the last few. I knew him well enough to know the smirk meant he was about to say something I didn't want to hear. I cut him off at the pass.

"Don't start with me, Mac. Today is not the day."

"Might as well tell me not to breathe."

"Don't breathe."

Call me an optimist; I thought it might work. It didn't.

"Amos . . . Amos . . . Amos. Something's going on here. Inquiring minds want to know: *What's up?*" He plastered a look of disbelief on his face. "You're beloved all of a sudden. After months of people complaining about you enforcin' the rule of law around here. Why the change? You been lettin' the speeders off with a warning? You walkin' all the old ladies home from bingo the way your daddy did? What?"

I didn't answer. He didn't expect an answer. Hank was on a roll.

"That's the fifth person who's stopped you to chat, invited you to O'Day's for a beer, or told you to drop by for a little homecooking. And now they're givin' you things!"

"You done? Pearl gave me a lousy book. Let's not make a production out of this. Ida's probably preparing a beauty queen defense for her next crime spree and wants to be sure I understand the psychology involved." I scanned the familiar square as the last of Pearl's pink tennis shoe disappeared into her bookstore across the way. "Doesn't mean anything. I talk to people in the square every day. Just like now. When I do my job and make the circuit."

I walked off. He followed, fell in beside me and made noises I can only describe as chortling. I tried to ignore him and concentrate on exactly what had changed in Mossy Creek.

There were always plenty of people in the square. Zeke and Eleanor Abercrombie perennially planting petunias. Moms moseying along with baby strollers. A couple of the twenty-something workers grabbing rays during lunch. I knew the square regulars. They knew me. During the lunch hour, I made a habit of walking the circuit. Partly from my need to get out of the office—away from Sandy so I could run my own life for thirty minutes— and partly from the conviction that a town that "saw the law, kept the law."

Unfortunately, the people who stopped me today weren't square regulars. Nor were they tourists hitting the trails to enjoy the wildflowers. The odd collection of folks toadying up to me were business owners, the kind who probably hadn't left their shops unattended during lunch in years. Pearl was the fifth shopkeeper who'd broken longstanding habits to put herself in my path.

Not that I was about to enlighten Mac on that score.

This information was on a need-to-know basis, and Mac didn't need to know. He and his wife were already far too interested in my re-adjustment to life in Mossy Creek. Living my life under a small-town microscope again was uncomfortable as hell for me. It wasn't a feeling I thought I'd ever really get used to.

I couldn't tell Mac that either since it begged the question of why I'd moved back to Mossy Creek if living here felt uncomfortably like living in a goldfish bowl.

A breeze pushed a few stray grass clippings up against one of the vacant park benches as I turned back. "I'm their cop, Mac. *Their* cop. People are supposed to want to talk to me."

He snorted. "Since when? Your daddy was their cop. Same way my daddy was their lawyer before he was their judge. That doesn't make us anything but the unproven prodigal sons of legends. We're both on borrowed grace."

"Thank you for pointing that out. That changes everything. God only knows how I survived all that time on the streets of Atlanta without you. Now, why don't you go deliver subpoenas or something before I'm forced to arrest you for loitering?"

"Subpoenas?" He shook his head sadly. "That's the best a big city cop can do for tough talk? Subpoenas? And loitering? I'm disap-pointed. Plain damn shattered, in fact. You *have* changed, Amos, my man. You've caved in to the subliminal need to be liked."

I narrowed my eyes and gave him my best Clint Eastwood look. "Make my day. Go back to your office, where tearful soon-to-be-ex-wives are no doubt waiting in some vain hope you might actually know what you're talking about."

"Clients are waiting for me morning, noon and night whether I'm ready for them or not. You'd be surprised at the business a lawyer can do in little ol' Mossy Creek. Especially when their only other choice is to make the trip to Bigelow."

I glanced down Main Street to the usually filled parking spaces in front of his office. Not only were the parking spaces empty of client vehicles, I didn't see the heap of rusted 4x4 that Mac called a pickup truck. "Where the hell are you parked, anyway?"

He hesitated.

Watching Mac Campbell try to lie is a lot like watching the progress of a tall truck that hadn't quite cleared a bridge. There's a brief moment of panic in the driver's eyes and then the horrible squeal of metal scraping against concrete. "What, Mac? Don't remember? You double-parked and don't want a ticket?"

He mumbled something I couldn't quite catch. I thought he said Pine Street. Not that *that* made much sense.

"Pine! Why would you park over on Pine? Nothing over there to interest a lawyer except maybe the funeral home. . .ah. The light dawns."

He looked at me sourly, checked his watch and waited for the inevitable.

I'm proud to say I resisted the urge to needle Mac—well, for about five seconds. "So. I guess you'll be playing the dirge for another Piping-Our-Pets-To-Heaven service? Got your instrument all tuned up?"

No answer. He was clearly considering a roll in the dirt and telling me to take it back. I smiled. "How *are* those bagpipes, Mac?"

Finally he spit out the explanation he'd given at least fifty times since the first critter's funeral. "The bagpipes . . . were. . .Casey's idea."

Casey was the wife of Hank Blackshear, our local veterinarian. The critter funeral itself had been Hank's idea, but Casey embellished. Oh, how she had embellished.

I didn't bother to hide my amusement at his very careful distinction. "But you're the one *playing* the bagpipes. Folks are in awe. The kilt is a nice touch. Takes guts. Honoring your Scottish heritage like that. Means a lot to folks around here."

"Don't start with me."

"Might as well tell me not to breathe. They're still talking about your knees down at the Goldilocks." I nodded toward Rainey's hair salon. "I understand she offered you a free leg wax." I shook my head in wonder. "Heck, over at Mama's Café, they've got a new fried bologna sandwich called Under-the-Kilt."

Mac stoically waited for the rest. I obliged. "They wrap the bologna around a little weenie."

He opened and shut his mouth twice, then gritted his teeth as he moved silently off toward Pine. Just when I thought I'd finally gotten the last word for the first time in our history, Mac stopped. By the time he turned back, he was sporting that irritating, patient smile we had traded over the years. He had a few thoughts to back it up.

"I'm goin' to tell you this one more time, Amos, and then I may have to begin pummelin' you. That whole thing—the whole critter funeral—was Hank's deal. The man's a vet. The rabbit was the library pet. The reading group kids needed closure. I'm not really happy about the fact Hank started a fad for pet funerals. But he was right about those kids needing closure. And I'm beginning to believe the same thing about you."

"Excuse me?"

He stopped smiling. "Closure. You're in Mossy Creek because you're looking to prove something to your old man."

He didn't wait for a reaction or look back as he walked away. He'd scored a direct hit and knew it. He hadn't given voice to the familiar Southern truism, but it rang in the air nonetheless. In the South, you're not a man until your daddy says you're a man.

Or maybe until your daddy's town says you're a man.

Mossy Creek had been Battle Royden's town. He'd owned it—every man, woman and child. Body and soul. He'd been *their* cop for more than thirty years. Had been their chief for most of them. Revered for all of them.

They trusted him. They knew him. And us. They realized the old man and I had had our differences. They remembered that Battle hadn't ever quite gotten around to pronouncing me a man in the true Southern tradition. He had never introduced me as his "son." It was always, "Come over here and let me introduce you to my *boy*."

My boy. Didn't matter how proud his voice had been or how hearty the slap on the back. The actual words were what mattered. I was Battle Royden's boy.

Folks around here didn't care that I came to the job of chief as a fifteen-year veteran of the Atlanta Police—a detective by the time I left. Didn't matter that I was a good two inches taller than Battle in his prime. Didn't matter that I had managed to finish my degree in criminology or that I was thirty-five years old. They gave me the job, and the benefit of the doubt, as a posthumous favor to Battle.

One thing I learned at the old man's knee was to live with reality. You can hate a Southern truism. You can scoff at it. But you can't escape it any more than you can escape death and taxes. I had known full well what I was getting into when I pinned Battle's badge on my shirt. But damned if I could resist the job when Ida offered it to me.

Mac had the right of it.

Cussedness or stubborn determination had made me Mossy Creek's new chief of police.

"Whatcha readin', Chief?"

Zeke and Eleanor Abercrombie, each carrying a flat of petunias, had crept up on me while I was lost in thought. I blinked at the two grinning old gardeners and then scowled down at the silly book in my hand.

A painfully underdeveloped part of my intellect wanted my old man's town to admit that I'm more than a chip off the old block. That I'm a man in my own right.

Carrying *Venus On The Runway* through town was probably not a good way to accomplish that goal.

ごごご

Hiring Sandy Crane had been an easy decision. The job was more clerk than true dispatcher. Lack of experience hadn't been a problem. Of course, her application failed to mention one tiny problem. No one really *managed* Sandy. You just grabbed hold of a handful of the back of her shirt and did your best to slow her down. She had been as good as her word about making sure the place was clean. It had taken a few weeks before she was satisfied with the results.

Somewhere during the cleaning process, she'd adopted me as a project. I got "the eyebrow" if I had nothing more than chips and canned chili from the Piggly Wiggly for lunch. Sandy had no problems with my patronizing the local businesses, but she had particular ideas about what *her* chief should eat. I was personal property in much the same way the department offices were now her personal property.

God love her, she thought the mirrored sunglasses our two patrolmen had taken to wearing were a new addition to the uniform. Truth was that after enduring a particularly bad patch of sunny days, the boys had gotten sunglasses to cut the glare from the office's newly scrubbed, blindingly white counters and walls. No one had the heart to ask her to stop cleaning, especially since she did it all while digging her teeth into the clerical job like a territorial junkyard dog dispatching trespassers.

Word got around. It always does.

The county sheriff down in Bigelow hinted about taking her off my hands every time I ferried a prisoner to the county jail for lock-up. I always smiled, thanked him politely and declined. Two weeks into her tenure, I had decided to take my chances with Sandy and wasn't likely to change my mind. Battle always said, "Better the devil you know than the one you don't."

My devil scrubbed ink marks off the wallboards with a cotton hair scrunch soaked in motor oil.

All the same, the sheriff still checked to be sure I was happy. Just in case I decided we really did need to start grooming a bonafide dispatcher after all. We didn't, and besides, Sandy was an asset to the department in other ways. The woman always seemed to be plugged in to the nuances of life in Mossy Creek. I was hoping that particular talent would pay off in regard to Pearl's strange behavior.

The moment my foot crossed the threshold of the office, Sandy put down the phone and bounced up from her desk. We reached the counter at the same time. I slid the book across to her. "A gift from Pearl."

She glanced at the title and made a "huh" sound that was part delighted surprise and part satisfaction. A half-beat later, she shuffled the four pink slips of paper in her hand. Not a good sign.

"Those are my messages, I assume?"

"How do you want them?"

The first time she'd asked me that it had thrown me. By now I was used to her system. I could have them sorted by time, caller urgency or *Sandy's Picks*—which meant she'd priori-tized them. Of course the offer of choice was merely an illusion. I'd learned early on to trust Sandy's judgment. "Fire away."

"You need to hot-foot it out to Hamilton Farm. Miss Ida wants to discuss something with you. Stop by Disney Halbeck's on your way back into town. He wants you to talk some sense into his boy, Mickey."

"You've got to be kidding."

Sandy looked up. Her hair had grown a bit since the disaster at Rainey's hair salon, but it still fought for its independence, making her look like one of the plucky dandelions along Mossy Creek's roadsides. "Why would I be kidding? Mickey's sixteen and thinks he's immortal. Somebody's got to knock some sense into the kid before he kills himself skateboardin' on these roads."

"Point taken. Next?"

"Hannah says someone's moving books in the library again."

"And the last one?"

"Bud Esterhaus thinks someone's trying to kill him. Says someone shot at him. Twice. He wants you to find out who it is."

The day just kept getting better. "Someone's reporting a murder plot, and yet it's number three on your list of calls I should make." I rubbed my temple, carefully keeping both the amusement and the irritation out of my voice. "You didn't radio me, so I'm guessing Bud is still in one piece. The person missed, and you've solved the crime."

"Well, not missed. Not exactly."

"Of course not. Continue."

"The black satin sheets on his clothesline took a couple of rounds." She formed a gun with her hand and aimed. *"Kapow.* Flat and fitted sheets—matching holes in the lower right corners. Bud's about as mad as I've ever seen him. Those sheets cost him sixty dollars." She sighed. "It's a real shame. Apparently he has fond memories of those sheets."

I reached for the messages. "I'm a little more worried about Bud than the sheets."

"Why? He's safe as a baby's butt in Pampers."

"Okay. I'll play. You know this. . .how?"

"I sent Mutt over to take Violet Martin's gun away. He radioed back and confirmed she'd done some shooting today."

Forget any personal quest in being the chief of Mossy Creek. I'd have taken the job for sheer entertainment value alone. "How do you know who's shooting at Bud if Bud doesn't even know?"

"I doubt she was shooting at Bud per se. His backyard meets her backyard. There's about a six-foot privacy fence separating them."

Apparently, my blank look conveyed my confusion. Sandy barely stopped herself from rolling her eyes. She despaired of me at times, but there wasn't a quitter's bone in her body. She gamely jumped in to play our version of

Name That Crime.

"Garden? Scarecrow? It was windy earlier today?"

"Ah. . .the edges of the sheets—black sheets—kept flipping up in the air. She thought the flapping sheets were crows."

"Exactly."

Sandy beamed. "Violet's about seven hundred and four years old. Her eyesight's been terrible for centuries. She thought the crows were swooping in to clean out her bird feeders again. I told Mutt to get her an air horn to scare off the crows."

I nodded, resigned. "Of course you did. In fact, anything less would have been disappointing."

"Thanks, Chief!"

"If Ida calls again, tell her I'm on my way." I paused for a second before pushing open the door. "And, Sandy. . .someone did let Bud know he's safe, right?"

The stricken look on her face assured me that I had one or two weeks left before Sandy could run the department single-handedly.

❦❦❦

You have to respect a woman who cleans her own guns. Ida Hamilton Walker was that kind of woman. Today's gun happened to be a Mossberg shotgun—my own personal choice in a shotgun since it holds an extra round. You have to wonder about a woman who cleans her guns when she's expecting company. Ida was either trying to soften me up or intimidate me. Gunsmithing paraphernalia was scattered over the top of her desk, although I was certain each item was exactly where Ida wanted it. Most things in her life were exactly where she wanted them to be. She was that kind of woman, too.

She didn't put the gun down to extend her hand, but she lifted her gaze. "Amos."

"Ida." We took a moment to size each other up. It was a habit we'd developed, although I wasn't sure whether the habit came from the need for a good defense or a quick offense. Ida never seemed personally in need of either. Nor did she seem to mind that I'd dropped the Miss in front of her name.

Arresting a person was the quickest way to break down social barriers. To my surprise, she hadn't held a grudge over the welcome-sign incident. There'd been no indication of revenge. . .so far. Unless today's events were her way of getting even. I feigned innocence. "What can I do for you?"

"Not for me." She gave a particularly stubborn spot on the barrel an extra pass with a chamois cloth. "For the town."

"Last time I checked, you were the town."

Her eyebrows shot up, and she smiled. "You're learning, but if you don't already know why you're here, you aren't the chief I was hoping for when I hired you."

"I'd have to have been deaf, dumb and blind to miss the clues people have been dropping about the pageant. But you still won't get what you were hoping for when you hired me. You were hoping for Battle. I'm not Battle. I thought you had that figured out by now."

Her genuine laughter filled the room. "I hope to shout! I knew that when you arrested me in March. I'm not sure Battle could have done it. Actually hauled me off to jail, I mean." For a minute, her eyes actually. . .twinkled. "It might have taken him a while to work it all out, but he would have figured a way around it."

"Or he would have let you talk him out of it." It wasn't a compliment.

"But not you." It wasn't a question.

Ida simply stated the fundamental difference between Battle Royden and "his boy" Amos. The cost of avoiding a speeding ticket wasn't a pot roast dinner. A bowl of homemade grape sherbet and a game of pinochle didn't make it okay to disturb the peace. A mayor who vandalized a road sign wouldn't escape the consequences simply because she was just about as sexy at fifty-something as she had been twenty years earlier, when every teenage boy in town, including me, daydreamed about her.

"Like I said, I'm not Battle."

Ida smiled again. If she hadn't had a

shotgun in her hands, I'd have called it a *reassuring* smile. Instead she reminded me of one of those smart, flamboyant dinosaurs from *Jurassic Park.* A predator practiced at distracting the victim while she eyed the jugular. Mesmerizing me as she shook her head.

"No, you're certainly not your daddy. He was two-hundred-plus pounds of good ol' boy with a soft spot for a pretty face and anyone in need. Maybe he didn't have your college degree, but Battle Royden knew how to run a town."

I clenched my teeth and ground back the flare of frustration. "Am I the only one who noticed that he'd broken every marriage vow by the time my mother died? Or that he ran his town by looking the other way and playing let's-make-a-deal every day of his life?"

"That he did. But you and I know his real sin was he never gave his kid the leniency he gave his town. God knows I wish I hadn't been so hard on my own son after my husband Jeb died. Robert's much too serious and intense because of me. Because of what I wanted for him."

She dropped the chamois and placed the shotgun carefully across the desk before delivering the gut kick. "Of course, that's all most parents ever really want for their kids...for them to be better than us. It's certainly what Battle wanted—for you to be better than him. He loved you and your mother. He was just lousy at expressing it."

Ida Walker had an uncanny ability to get at the truth, to identify the needs of her townsfolk. I wasn't certain whether she was a sly witch or just a shrewd mayor. Probably six of one, half a dozen of the other. *One* of those women, I admired. Damned if I knew which. Or maybe I admired both. It was easy to see why people were drawn to her.

At Battle's funeral, Preacher Hickham hadn't closed his Bible good before she'd offered me the job as chief. "It's what Battle would have wanted," she'd said. That simple sentence will always be one of the great ironies of my life. I hadn't cared what Battle wanted in more years than I could count. Until then.

Everyone hates the completely useless epiphanies that come as you're putting a coffin in the ground. What earthly good did it do me to finally understand why Battle pushed me so hard as kid? As a man? I really hadn't wanted that little bit of enlightenment. But I got it anyway. Courtesy of Ida Walker, who'd never met a truth she didn't feel compelled to quietly share when the occasion warranted.

She stood up, lightly dusting her hands together as if finished with that portion of the interview. I wondered whether she realized she always lifted her left eyebrow the tiniest bit as she shrugged into her mayor persona. I also wondered exactly when I'd begun separating the "woman" from the "mayor." She was twenty years older and my boss. I wasn't supposed to notice that she was a woman. Especially since it gave her a subtle advantage I wasn't at all certain I liked.

Only a fool would spot Ida Hamilton Walker points in the game of life or politics. I was still pretty certain my daddy hadn't raised a fool. I let the silence spill out. Let her struggle with how best to get to the issue that had brought me there today.

I'd known what Ida wanted from the moment Sandy shuffled the messages. But politeness and strategy demanded I wait for the formal request before declining.

"Chief," she said, "I'll make this quick and easy. I'd like you to be one of the judges for the Miss Bigelow Pageant."

"No."

Her right eyebrow rose to join the left. "I think...*yes*. Consider it a civic duty."

"More like torture."

"Good." She rounded the desk and casually propped a blue-jean- clad hip against the edge. "Then you understand civic duty."

I struggled with the smile that tugged insistently at the edge of my mouth. "I understand how not to get my butt in a sling. I've got a town to run. Maybe not the way Battle ran it, but that's what you hired me for, all the same."

"I did hire you, didn't I?" She managed

to make the sentence echo with meaning without ever raising her voice.

This time I let the smile loose. "You won't fire me over refusing to be a judge."

"Of course not." She waited, completely unconcerned.

As the silence gathered, I realized my mistake. Realized one more thing I had forgotten about Mossy Creek, but it was too late now. Ida was about to nail my hide to the wall. She let her own smile loose. "Amos, I don't care which pageant you judge. Miss Bigelow...Mrs. Bigelow. Whatever. Your choice."

The only thing worse than the free-for-all of Miss Bigelow County was the backstabbing lunacy of *Mrs.* Bigelow County. The disappointed teens and twenty-some-things would actually go back to college eventually, but I'd have to wave to, talk to and purchase food from the unhappy Mrs. Bigelow County contestants forever.

Ida was very well aware of that fact. The choice was really no choice at all.

"Why me? You know I hate these things."

"If you want to be their cop, Amos, it's time to get in the game."

"Ida." It was as close to a warning tone as was wise to use with your boss, but my instincts were nudging me hard. Ida was reeling me in, using that damnable insight of hers to get what she wanted. This wasn't about my finding my place in Mossy Creek. At least not completely. "What aren't you telling me?"

"The truth?" she asked, just as innocent as a five-year-old standing next to a shattered vase. When I nodded, she said, "There is a distinct shortage of Mossy Creek cleavage this year."

When I laughed, she glared. "I'd rather eat dirt than lose the crown four years in a row. I need a man Mossy Creek can count on because he won't be blinded by Bigelow boobs!"

I finally sobered, spreading my hands to call a truce. "You're actually serious."

"As a heart attack. I'm playing to win this year, and Ham knows it."

"Then you've got the wrong man for the job. I'm not Battle. I don't look the other way. I don't make deals. If you insist on my judging, you'd better understand that my contest vote's not for sale to the highest bidder or to settle accounts. Or even for Mossy Creek pride. You can't count on my vote. The rest of Mossy Creek can't count on my vote."

"I'm not counting on your vote. I'm counting on *you*. Right after we voted down Ham's judge and the committee ratified your name, Ham said we're wrong if we think you can get past the cleavage issue."

I held up my hands. "So that's why Katie Bell wrote a column saying you've pulled a fast one on the governor. That's why you're looking like you've just swallowed a small songbird."

"Because I know the one thing that Ham Bigelow hasn't figured out yet." She folded her arms across her chest, quite pleased with herself for getting a step ahead of Ham. "You aren't Battle. Cleavage isn't enough any more. I think maybe cleavage will never be enough, for you."

Ida waited. She knew the moment I'd accepted my fate. Her smile was the kind of smile you hope to see in bed. . .after. "Welcome to the game, Amos."

❦❦❦

Suddenly, more pairs of eyes than Ida's were focused intently in my direction. I'm talking more than the usual intensity reserved for eligible bachelors in a land of married men.

I won't deny that there is a certain amount of pleasure and irony in being dog meat at sixteen and catnip at thirty-five. Of course at sixteen, there were plenty of eligible males for the womenfolk of Mossy Creek to choose from. And plenty of jocks who could hit a softball out of the park for the glory of Mt. Gilead Methodist Church. A lot can happen in twenty years.

Women apparently like a man with a little edge. My body had finally caught up with my height, and my softball skills had improved with age. But more importantly, I was the guy who was about to hit one out of the park for the glory of Mossy Creek. Or so they believed.

Amos Royden, damned good catcher. . .complete hypocrite. That's one helluva epitaph for a Mossy Creek headstone.

But true.

Consider the plight of contestant Josie McClure, from the isolated Bailey Mill community just outside town. The poor girl was so shy she had trouble facing herself in the mirror. Her chances of winning Miss Bigelow County were astronomically low. Especially when you factored in her talent--napkin folding, accompanied by a deadly accurate Martha Stewart impression. But her mother honestly believed Josie stood a chance of taking home that sparkling tiara. Of course, Mrs. McClure's belief might have something to do with the fact that she revered Martha Stewart and could bake chess pie that made grown men weep.

I was on my third one.

God help me, I'd even gone so far as to give Mrs. McClure a conspiratorial wink when she delivered number two. It didn't matter that I'd told Mrs. McClure that she shouldn't waste her time making pies for me. I *winked*. That's not something you can take back or pretend you haven't done. Not when Miss Bigelow County is on the line.

The road to hell is surely paved with

chess pie.

When my conscience pinched me awake at night, I ended up pacing the long dogtrot hallway in my house as penance for falsely raising a mother's hopes. The pacing always ended in the kitchen, at the table, with another slice of pie and the knowledge that I was no better than Battle after all. Maybe worse. At least if you gave Battle the third chess pie, you knew exactly what you were getting.

Mutt and crew were ecstatic over the constant buffet of food that appeared at the office, and more than a little awed by the bevy of beauties from around the county who stopped in to chat. Sandy eyed me with beady intensity, and every time I reminded her that I would be voting fair and square—food and celebrity be damned—she made the *huh* sound and continued to take note of the parade of beauties who came through our door.

Even willowy Sissy Truman, who was destined to follow her father, Chamber of Commerce president Dwight Truman, into Mossy Creek politics, developed a sudden and unaccountable interest in law enforcement as a career. Mutt actually tripped in his rush to welcome Sissy. Sandy didn't seem much impressed by Sissy's devotion to all things police, but she did reach for her much written-on and crossed-off list of contestant names that looked suspiciously like a racetrack handicapping sheet. I didn't ask for specifics. She didn't volunteer.

I assured myself that lots of people make lists and keep up with their favorite candidates when they watch beauty pageants. Logically, a woman who prioritized mail messages according to a mysterious system couldn't resist listing and shuffling the local beauty pageant entries as well. *Right?*

Too bad, a quiet voice in my head--one that sounded like a suspiciously amused Ida Hamilton Walker—kept whispering, *All the signposts on the road to hell read "Denial."*

I consoled myself with the fact that Josie McClure—one of our own local girls, since the Bailey Mill community is considered a suburb of Greater Mossy Creek—was still dead last on Sandy's list of likely winners. That made me feel marginally better about whether accepting the chess pies had raised hopes where I shouldn't have. All the same, I resolved that pie number four would be declined.

So, with a semi-clear conscience, I donned a tux and prepared to do moral battle at the Bigelow High School Auditorium. As I waited for the pageant to begin, I smiled and nodded and tried not to wince when the high school's concert band tuned up. I had honed the phrase, "ThankyouGladtobehere" into the perfect generic response to almost any comment.

"Great tux!"

"Good to see you!"

"We appreciate you stepping in!"

"We're so happy you came back to Mossy Creek!"

"Cheer up. It'll be over soon."

"ThankyouGladtobehere."

Worked like a charm until Dwight Truman shook my hand. "I won't forget how you helped my daughter out," the chamber bigwig said.

Since I hadn't helped Sissy Truman with career plans or anything else, I'm sure my stare was as blank as my mind. "Beg pardon?"

"Well, now, that disappoints me. Yes, it does. I thought you were a quick one. I didn't think I'd have to spell it out for you." He looked furtively over his shoulder to be sure he wouldn't be overheard. The man looked like a guilty Ross Perot. "Surely you were aware that Battle and I always came to an understanding about these things?"

I had better manners than to call him a liar, but liar he was. Battle would sooner have made a pact with the devil than Dwight Truman. Not because Dwight's grandmother was a Democrat turned Republican. Not even because Dwight sold insurance and sucked up to Ham Bigelow, Georgia's newest governor. Battle had a much stronger, if less concrete, reason than any of those.

I remember joining him inside the voting curtains as a kid. He hesitated over the lever with Dwight Truman's name for city council before finally flipping a different one. When I asked him why he changed his mind, he said, "Don't matter how much sense he makes. You can't vote for a man if you honestly think he's capable of drowning a bag of kittens."

Staring into Dwight's sunken-cheeked face, I decided Battle had a very good point. If I were a betting man, I'd guess Dwight had bullied small children for lunch money as a kid. He was about to shake me down as well. Or try. This would be interesting.

Dwight sighed. "Look, Amos, I kept hoping the pageant would turn out as a landslide victory for Sissy, and that we wouldn't be having this conversation. But I'm nothing if not honest. Point of fact—this race is too close to call. That means you and I need to come to a little agreement, so we can make Mossy Creek and Sissy happy."

"Chances are that's not going to happen in this lifetime."

His eyes narrowed. "You don't get it, do you? I'm the budget chairman on the council. I don't mind tellin' you that we've got to make some cuts this year. That means that Sandy Crane's job may well be on the casualty list. You're going to be coming to me asking for a favor about that clerk of yours, boy. You'd best think about that."

"Oh, I'm thinking," I assured him. Being the chief of police didn't make me immune to violent impulses. Right now, I wanted to deck the weasel and haul him out of the auditorium by his ankle like the trash he was. But I had a contest to judge, so I clamped down on my temper and smiled at him. Must have been a miserable attempt, because he backed up a step as I answered.

"What I'm thinking is that you're going to find a seat and be very glad that I'm reluctant to embarrass your daughter by arresting you for trying to blackmail a judge.

"When this pageant is over, I suggest you sharpen your budget pencil and find the money for my dispatcher. Otherwise, Sandy'll be working for the Bigelow County sheriff, and you'll be explaining to Miss Ida how that happened. Are we agreed?"

Truman never got to answer. Ida did that for him. "Oh, I think we understand each other."

I stiffened and wondered where the hell she'd come from. *Sly witch. Shrewd mayor.*

"Now, run along, Tru. I need to speak to our chief."

We watched him go and carried on a conversation without looking at each other. "The answer is the same for you, Ida."

"Yes, but you have to admit that my technique is vastly superior."

"Agreed, but you're Southern and a woman. I believe that constitutes an unfair advantage."

"Why so it does." She waved at her son

Robert and daughter-in-law Teresa who were holding her seat. "You know, Battle would have handled Tru the same way. Made that same deal to avoid haulin' him off to jail."

"I think I know that. And I'm sure if he were here, he'd have had an *I told you so* for me." As the house lights began to dim, she looked at me finally, that slow, confident smile tipping up the corners of her mouth. "No. Battle would simply say we picked the right man for the job. Welcome home, Amos."

I smiled as the lights dimmed around us in the auditorium. "Thank you. Glad to be here."

The Bellringer
by Katie Bell
A weekly column of the Mossy Creek Gazette

...Put away your guns. Stop egging the chief's car.

Some days the best you can hope for is a tie with Bigelow. That's exactly what we had last Saturday night when the dust settled at the high school. Despite being contenders, Bigelow and Mossy Creek both lost with equal style and grace. And just as publicly.

Bigelow's Tiffany Clarkson showed plenty of "physical fitness" in the swimsuit competition. Our own Sissy Truman shined in the talent portion. (All bias aside, I'd have to say that girl picks a guitar and sings like a Dixie Chick.)

But the evening gown competition was won by Rhonda Clifton from Yonder. Not only was she stunning, but she'd designed and sewn the dress herself.

Three events. Three front-runners.

There hasn't been tension like that in the high school since. . .well, there's never been that much tension. It came down to the all-important interview question.

I don't mind telling you that my sources report that first-time judge Amos Royden looked a bit unhappy most of the night. A lot of us think he had an easy job. That his vote should have been a slam-dunk for one of our Mossy Creek girls. But I've been giving this a little thought. Can you really blame the man for handing Rhonda Clifton the crown?

Think about it.

When asked to name the television character she most admired, the clever Rhonda promptly replied, "Andy Griffith, because you've got to admire a man who's strong enough to take on a whole town. Even when the folks put him into the worst situations, he always cared about them and seemed glad to be there for them."

Personally, I think if she can think that fast on her feet. . .maybe it was time to send the crown out Yonder's way.

The Mossy Creek Gazette
215 Main Street—Mossy Creek, Georgia

FROM THE DESK OF KATIE BELL, BUSINESS MANAGER

Lady Victoria
Cornwall, England

Dear Lady Victoria,

Like I've told you before, once you dip your toe in Mossy Creek, our magic claims you, and sooner or later, you come back home—unless Bigelows have put a price on your head, the way they did with Isabella and Richard. But more news on that as I get it organized.

Anyway. . .about a year ago Dr. Hank Blackshear's daddy died and Hank took over the Blackshear veterinary clinic. Hank's young—only in his late twenties—but he's already got a brand of Jimmy Stewart 'aw, shucks' kindness and wisdom about him. Used to be a real loner, a little homely and shy, wonderful with animals, but didn't know how to fit in with people. Our librarian said when he was growing up he read *Catcher In The Rye* so many times she had to order a new copy.

The last thing anybody in Mossy Creek expected was that he'd marry Casey Champion. Casey is a real looker and used to be the best athlete in the county. Most popular girl at Bigelow County High, daughter of Mossy Creek's family doctor, Dr. Champion—a golden girl, you know? Not the bookish type, like Hank. If she ever read anything other than *Glamour* or *Sports Illustrated*, I don't know it.

Didn't matter. They fell head over heels in love, but life's handed them a pretty tough road to share. That road brought them both home to Mossy Creek. You've heard that saying, "It takes a village to raise a child?" Well, around here we like to say, "It takes a town to remember a child's dream."

And this year, we tried to help Hank and Casey remember theirs.

Your friend,

Katie "Play Ball" Bell

Casey

Casey At The Bat

We had a dry summer in Mossy Creek the year I turned fourteen, and the leaves were coloring early. The woods would soon look like they'd been splatter painted with deep reds and bright yellow. Above the Blue Ridge Mountains, the September sky was so blue I wanted to swim in it. I didn't know it then, but that afternoon my life was about to follow a path that would change it forever.

I threw my head back and filled my lungs to bursting with the private joy of the moment. As I ran along a hiking trail up in the mountains just north of town, I felt a blinding rush of excitement. My legs took flight. I was Mossy Creek's finest girl athlete, the best softball player anyone could ever remember. People were already predicting I'd make a college team someday, and maybe even the Olympics. "Here I come world, ready or not," I shouted, and felt the breeze snatch the words right out of my mouth, erasing them before they'd been given sound.

That's when I plowed into Hank

Blackshear, the son of our local veterinarian. He loved the hiking trails, too. I tripped him just well enough for him to go headfirst down a slope covered in head-high, thorny blackberries. I scrambled down after him and gasped in horror when I found him laying face down, covered in small red scratches. I thought he was dead. The headlines of the *Mossy Creek Gazette* flashed in my mind: *Local Doctor's Daughter Found Guilty Of Murder.* I knelt beside him.

"I'm so sorry! I didn't see you," I babbled. "Are you hurt? Can you walk? I'll help you down to the road. I've got a bicycle. Maybe you can sit on it, and I'll push you into town."

He untangled himself, stood up, and grinned. "Thanks for the help, kid, but I'm leaving for the university this afternoon. I'm fine, honest I am."

That's when it happened. As sappy as it sounds, I knew what *love at first sight* meant. Of course, we'd grown up in the same town, so I had seen him over the years. But suddenly I was on the verge of womanhood, and Hank looked different. I started to smile in return. I couldn't help it. This tall, lanky seventeen-year-old wearing skimpy running shorts simply looked at me, and my heart melted.

"You're leaving town?" I said.

"Yeah, kid, I am." He looked happy about it.

Kid? Here I was falling in love with a boy who had eyes the color of that September sky, and he was looking at me as if he thought I was some pony-tailed teenybopper.

Didn't matter. At three o'clock on a Friday afternoon, on the side of a mountain overlooking Mossy Creek, my life changed forever. I fell in love with Hank Blackshear.

"Doesn't matter," I said, "I'll wait."

He gave me an odd look, ruffled my hair, climbed back up the slope, and jogged away.

❧❧❧

Looking back on that day, I don't know why I ever thought it would be simple to catch up with him by the time I was old enough to earn more than a pat on the head. But then, I'd never let common sense stand in the way of my dreams. I was Casey Champion, daughter of Mossy Creek's beloved family doctor, Dr. Chance Champion, who had once played minor league baseball. Since Daddy loved baseball, when I was born he talked Mama into naming me Casey, after "Casey At The Bat," the famous baseball poem. Someday, I was going to be chosen for the Olympic softball team and make Daddy proud. And someday I was going to marry Hank Blackshear.

A few years later, about the time I graduated from high school, Hank received his undergraduate degree from the University of Georgia. His father had a mild heart attack, and Hank returned to Mossy Creek to help out at the Blackshear Veterinary Clinic all summer. I fell even more madly in love with Hank. But he was busy and worried about his father and the struggle he'd gone through. He planned to enter veterinary school at the university that fall. He still saw me as a little girl. Nothing had changed.

Didn't matter. I followed him around, anyway. He was very patient, explaining that he was too old for me, too poor compared to a doctor's daughter, and he had a lot of hard work in his future. No time for dating. He didn't say I looked like a high-maintenance kind of girl, but I'm sure he thought it. He finally gave up being Mr. Nice Guy and bluntly told me I was a distraction he didn't have time for. My heart was broken, but I still didn't give up on him. For the first seventeen years of my life, I'd gotten everything I wanted, except Hank. And I wasn't done yet.

With a name like Casey Champion, it never crossed my mind that I wouldn't accomplish what I'd set out to do. After all, I'd won a softball scholarship to the university. I had the Olympics in my future. Hank wouldn't ignore me when I wore a gold medal around my neck.

That August, I packed my belongings and drove down to the university in my new convertible—a graduation present from my father. I was a college freshman, now. Not a kid, anymore. Away from Mossy Creek, Hank would see me differently. I was sure of it.

But Hank was busy in vet school classes and working the part-time job he needed to pay his tuition. He headed the other way every time I got close to him. All right, so I'd get his attention on the softball field. By the time I was a sophomore in the school of education and he was a second year vet student I was making a name for myself playing fast pitch ball for the UGA women's team. I was a star.

Hank remained oblivious.

Then, one morning at the university track, fate stepped in. I was out for my morning run, head down, going full steam. You guessed it. I ran into him, again. I took him down like an NFL tackle. I fell on top of him. He was wearing running shorts and no shirt. I noticed.

"I'm so sorry," I said, planting my hands on either side of his bare chest. "Are you hurt?"

"You again?" he said. "I don't believe it."

"I didn't plan this. I swear."

He closed his eyes and let out a sigh. "I give up. I can't avoid you, and I can't forget about you."

"It's about time." I caught his face in my hands and kissed him.

He laughed helplessly and kissed me back.

From that point on we were together—and wildly in love. The next year, Hank accepted an internship with Angel Memorial Hospital in New York City, where he'd specialize in research and surgery. My coach recommended me to an Olympic scout. It was May. The world was in bloom, all pink and white and sweet.

That's when I proposed.

"Hank, let's get married."

"We will," he promised.

"I mean now. Tonight. You know Mother will want a big wedding, and that will take weeks. Since I'm going to be trying out for the Olympic team, I may not be able to finish my classes early and graduate along with you. And I'm not going to let you go to New York without me."

"Look, I know you say I'm too practical-minded, but I'm right this time. You stay in school and play on the Olympic team. I'll go to New York, and we'll make it work out. Then we'll have the big wedding and all the trimmings. I love you, Casey. I want everything in our lives to be solid."

I knew he was smart, but I refused to give up. "Dr. Blackshear, there are three things I want in my life: I want you. I want to see the world, and I want to play on the USA Olympic Softball Team. I'm scared something will happen if we wait. Let's get in my car, find a place that allows quickie weddings, and get married tonight. We practically live together, anyway. Think of the money we'd save."

"I'm thinking of you being Casey Blackshear," he said gently. "I'm thinking that just once I'm going to do something that isn't practical. Because I can't think of anything I'd rather do than marry you right now."

I kissed him and cried. "See? Just listen to me, and we'll both get everything we want."

"I've got you," he said. "That's everything I need."

The justice of the peace who performed the ceremony was late for a dance at the American Legion Hall and rushed through the service. It was simple. It was quick, but it was glorious. Hank and I couldn't have been happier in a fine chapel with a thousand guests watching.

Mentally, I marked off the first of my three life objectives—marrying Hank. Moving to New York took care of another dream. All I had left was the Olympics, and that was straight ahead.

On the way back to the university, we put the top down on my convertible and let the sweet scent of honeysuckle fill the air. The world was ours—until Hank swerved to avoid a deer that dashed across the highway in the darkness. He lost control, and the convertible shot off the road into a grove of oaks. I remember him flinging one arm out to hold me, but too late. My side of the car slammed into a tree. I wasn't wearing my seat belt. I was thrown from the car.

The doctors told me I was lucky to be alive. I didn't feel lucky. When they told me I'd never walk again, Hank blamed himself.

My Olympic dream shriveled up and fell into a black hole. Hank's internship at Angel Memorial slithered into the same deep abyss, though the admissions director promised he could apply later. I never blamed Hank for the accident; I should have buckled my seatbelt. I knew he would never intentionally hurt any living creature, including me. That's why he is such a good vet. We don't talk about it any more, but I know he still lives with his guilt.

For the next year, he alternated weekends between working for his father, who'd had another heart attack, and riding his motorcycle to Atlanta, where I was in a spinal rehabilitation center learning to live without the use of my legs. If I hadn't fallen in love with Hank the summer I was fourteen, I would have during that year.

The doctors fitted me with braces that made it possible for me to stand, but I spent most of my time in a wheelchair. Two days after I was released from the spinal center, I attended Hank's father's funeral. I'll never forget the pitying looks people gave Hank and me, though there was plenty of support and love in Mossy Creek, too. I just didn't recognize it yet. Hank graduated from vet school, and we moved into the rambling Blackshear homestead beside the vet clinic. Hank intended to put his father's house and clinic up for sale.

"You and I never had a honeymoon," Hank told me one day. Then he handed me two airline tickets. "We're going to the Bahamas."

"You'll have to carry me everywhere, or push me in the wheelchair."

"I don't mind," he said.

I cried.

We were in the Bahamas when Hank told me we were nearly broke. He didn't have the money to pay off his student loans as well as his father's large medical expenses. The old Blackshear Clinic showed no signs of selling. That's when Hank confessed: He had given up hope of interning at Angel Memorial. He'd decided to take over his father's practice in Mossy Creek. He said he did it for me, so that I could stay close to my doctors in Atlanta, and my family. And this way he'd have time to take care of me—I'd always be right next door to the clinic, at the old farmhouse.

There was only one problem. He didn't ask me if that's what I wanted.

I didn't. I'd forever given up my dreams of the Olympics, but I'd expected New York, the theater, museums, sports. What I was getting was a husband and a new life in the very town I'd wanted to escape, a town where I believed people loved the glorious Casey Champion, not the crippled Casey Blackshear. A town whose motto seemed to predict a terrible future for me. *Ain't Going Nowhere and*

Don't Want To.

But I had trapped Hank in that future alongside me. I owed him every bit of loyalty in the world. "I think living in Mossy Creek is a fine idea," I lied. "We'll be happy, there."

❧❧❧

Hank tries everything he can think of to get me out into the community. But other than picnics with him in the mountains and weekly dinners with my folks, the only activity I've done is volunteer at the children's hour at the library. I liked telling the children stories. They soon forgot about my wheelchair. I even asked if there was an opening for an assistant librarian.

"I'm sorry, Casey, but we don't have the budget to hire you," Hannah Longstreet, the head librarian, told me. I could hear the regret in her voice.

"I completely understand," I said cheerfully, then went home and sobbed.

I hate feeling worthless. I can't help out much in Hank's practice; I'm afraid I might fall down while trying to stand with my braces and hold a cat or dog on the examining table. Other than answering the phone for the clinic when Hank's receptionist is at lunch and sending out a few bills, I have nothing to do. In short, I've spent our first year in Mossy Creek being bored, depressed, and mad at the world.

Today was one of those days. We were heading into the Fourth of July, and the weather was sticky hot. The mountains baked under a bright-blue sky. I sat in my wheelchair by the bedroom window fanning myself with a magazine. The antique clock over our fireplace started to chime. It reminded me that Hank was showering, getting ready to report to the new softball field with his friend, Buck Looney, who coaches down at Bigelow County High. Buck played four seasons of pro football for the Green Bay Packers thirty years ago, and he's never lost the burly attitude of a gorilla in shoulder pads. He's coaching the Mossy Creek Twelve-and-Under Softball Team as if they're hard-boiled linebackers. Buck is big and stalwart and gruff, but he tries his best to help out with the kids' teams in Mossy Creek. Every kid in the town is in awe of him. After the little girls' practice session, Buck, Hank, and our police chief, Amos Royden, planned to practice with the Mossy Creek adult co-ed team. I insisted that Hank join the team.

As the chimes came to an end, the bathroom door opened and Hank emerged in a cloud of steam. He was already dressed in a faded teeshirt, cutoffs and his baseball cap with the bill turned backwards. His *Let's Cheer Up Casey* smile was planted hopefully on his face. "Ready, Case? I told Buck we'd be at the ball field at two-thirty. I put your glove and bat in the van."

I stared at him. "Why?"

"You might get the urge to play."

"Is that a joke?"

"No, it's a hope. At least, you could coach from the sidelines. Buck has no clue how to deal with little girls."

I shook my head. "Neither do I—not when you're talking about coaching softball. Why would they listen to me? I can't demonstrate much. I can't get up and run. I'm useless."

"No, you're still a world-class softball player."

I groaned. The world doesn't look at me and see an Olympic contender, but Hank still does. My wheelchair and Hank know how worthless my body is. The wheelchair doesn't talk, and Hank won't. He doesn't say so, but he thinks I'm a coward. He's right. Reading stories to children at the library is one thing. Helping girls hit, run and field, is another thing all together.

"Those girls need you," Hank coaxed.

"Any summer league that would give a little girls' softball team to an ex-pro linebacker who used be nicknamed *Jawbone* deserves what it gets."

"That's why Buck needs help." Hank laughed. It was a good laugh. There haven't been many of those lately. My heart still melts when I hear it, it just takes longer now.

"You're talking little girls who have one

foot in their childhood and one foot in their teens. If Buck Looney makes the little girls cry with his harsh methods, I'd say you need a new coach."

"It's too late, now," Hank admitted. "We're set to play Bigelow in the Fourth of July tournament and the Twelve-And-Unders are scared to death. Please, Case, I really need your help. Buck thinks that if you'll just give them a little pep talk, Mossy Creek has a chance of winning the All-Star Tournament for the first time in years."

"What exactly is their record?"

He squinted at the ceiling, thinking. "This is the ninth year they've held the county play-offs since you were on the team. Bigelow has won eight of them."

"You've got a softball team with a record of 1 and 8, a coach named Looney, and now you want to add an assistant coach in a wheelchair?"

"I'm counting on the Casey magic." He took my face between his hands. "I'm counting on the Casey who never gave up."

Hank always got to me. I would follow him forever, even though I'd send us both tumbling. I shook my head and tried to smile. "Okay, Blackshear. Let's go see who I can knock down this time."

🐛🐛🐛

There are two categories of natives in

Mossy Creek: the people who've been here all their lives and those who've left and come back. As one of those who left and came back, Hank appreciates progress but knows why Mossy Creek is special. He's beginning to see what Ida Hamilton Walker and the rest of the older generation have been trying to preserve. I hate to admit it, but I'm beginning to understand, too. I feel safe, here.

Hank was even persuaded to run for the city council and was given the parks and recreation department as his responsibility. The job should have been easy; it would have been for anyone else—there was no recreation department. But my Hank takes his duties seriously. So do the other Mossy Creekites. As we drove to the ball fields outside town, I noticed all the *Beat Bigelow* signs in shop windows and on bumper stickers.

I unfolded a copy of the weekly newspaper and saw that the *Mossy Creek Gazette* had gotten into the mood. Even the front page touted the Fourth Of July All-Star Play-Offs. Hank hadn't told me that Katie Bell's *Bellringer* column confided that I'd agreed to help the Twelve-And-Under girls, but Sue Ora Salter made sure I got a copy of the *Gazette* every week. Sue has a big heart, but she's as big a meddler as Katie. She's just more subtle about it.

When we arrived at the practice field, it was painfully obvious that Buck Looney took all the hurrah as a mandate to win. Though the older girls' softball team was a shoe-in to win the All-Star tournament, and the co-ed team, on which Hank was the pitcher, looked great, the Twelve-And-Unders were, well, they were a *big* question mark.

With his ball cap pulled firmly down over his head and his stopwatch in hand, Buck had all the players lined up behind first base. They looked as nervous as paratroopers ready to make their first jump. Hank parked the van, came around to my side and opened the door. I heard Buck bellow, "We may not have much experience, girls, but we sure are fast. So we're gonna run Bigelow into the ground. Kill 'em. Stomp 'em. I'm going to clock your speed. Are you ready?"

The girls simply looked at him.

"Trust me," he barked. "We'll make those Bigelow sissies throw the ball around, and when the dust settles, we'll win. Little Ida, you're first. I want you to hotfoot it to second base, as hard as you can. Go!"

Ida Walker, the granddaughter of Mayor Ida Hamilton Walker, took off toward second, running as hard as her spindly legs could carry her. She was ferocious, but only eight-years-old.

"Go to third!" Buck yelled, swinging his arm in a furious circle. "Faster!"

Little Ida glanced back, lips narrowed in determination. "Yes sir!" That's when she caught her right foot behind the base bag and tumbled into left field.

"Oh, for. . ." Buck let out a sigh and started toward her. "You're not hurt, Little Ida. Get up."

Ida lay there for a minute, then sat up. One knee had turned into a raw scrape. Her lips went from firm resolve to impending tremble. Buck came to a stop beside her and frowned. "Be tough, Little Ida, like your grandma. Ball players have to suck it up!"

I didn't have to be told that Little Ida had been compared to her tough grandmother all her life. She burst into tears. I glared at Buck. The idiot. Buck Looney might know how to coach burly, knot-headed teenage boys for our county high school, but it was obvious he had no clue how to deal with little girls.

"Hank, get me to the field!" I said, disconnecting my seatbelt.

"You sure?" Hank asked slyly. "What do you plan to do?"

What did I plan to do? Hell, I. . .I didn't know *what* I could do. "Gimmie my bat and my wheelchair, and I'll show you!" I'd figure it out when I got out there.

I refused to acknowledge Hank's broad *I told you so* grin as he helped me into my chair and rolled me down the path to the field. "You aren't going to hurt Buck, are you? We need him on the co-ed team."

"Possibly, but first I'm going to restore

Little Ida's confidence. Push me out there." I pointed at the third base dugout, where Little Ida sat hugging her wounded knee. Hank parked me beside her.

"Hi, Little Ida, I'm Casey. That was a real Michael Jordan move you made! Where'd you learn how to do that?"

The child stopped her sniffing and looked at me with eyes as big as robin eggs. "Michael Jordan? You mean Bugs' friend?"

"Bugs? Eh?"

"The commercial with Bugs Bunny," Hank whispered. He straightened and grinned at Buck. "Hey, Coach. Casey decided you were right. These ladies can use a woman's touch."

"We need more than that," Buck grumbled. "Need a stack of hankies for everybody to boo-hoo into every time I look at 'em wrong."

By this time, Little Ida was standing wide-eyed beside my chair, skinned knee forgotten. "Are you going to be our coach?"

"Of course not, silly," one of the other ballplayers said. The team gathered around my chair. "She can't walk."

"You don't need to walk to play great sports. You have to use your brain." I nodded somberly to Little Ida. "Michael Jordan uses his brain. And he'd be impressed with the way you run bases."

"Little Ida's no Michael Jordan," another girl said. "The only reason she's even on the team is because her grandmother is the mayor and her daddy's the president of Hamilton's Department Store. They're donating the uniforms. She's too little."

I saw pain watering Little Ida's eyes again. She blinked to remain stoic, but I could see disaster in the making. Nothing ruins a team as quickly as hurt feelings between the players. And Buck was making no move to nip it in the bud. I took Little Ida's hand. "From now on, no one makes mean comments about any other player. That's my rule. Okay? Now, does this team have a name?"

Little Ida sighed. "No, ma'am. We're just the Mossy Creek Twelve-And-Unders."

"Well, if we're going to use our brains, the first thing we have to do is think up a name. A name for the team—and good names for each other, too. We'll only worry about player names, for now."

"Whatcha mean?" the dissenter challenged.

"Well, you know. The players on television always give each other nicknames. If we want to be tough, let's think like them. Now, I'm Casey. My name is really Cassandra. But I'm named after a very famous ball player who once struck out. He was known as Mighty Casey of Mudville." They nodded. They'd heard the poem in school. "My daddy told me not to worry whenever I struck out. I might have missed that time, he said, but with a nickname like Casey I'd be famous one day."

"That's true," Hank added. "And she was. Before she got hurt, she was being scouted for the Olympics. Her accident changed that dream, but she's still Casey. She still knows how to play softball."

Little Ida smiled and ignored my wheelchair completely. "So what's my nickname going to be?"

"Hmmm, I can't say yet. Why don't we practice our running for the coach, and we'll think about it." I looked at the rest of the girls. "Coach Looney doesn't expect you all to be a fast rabbit like Little Ida. He's just trying to help you find a way to confuse the other team into making mistakes. The Bigelow team doesn't expect Mossy Creek girls to run well and they'll get so shook up at our gooney bird speed they'll miss their throws, and we'll get on base."

"Huh," Buck grunted. "All right, whatever. I guess I don't need the stopwatch. Let's just start over and see what we can do."

The girls obediently lined up again at first. I started to wheel myself off the field when Buck put his hand on my chair. "Why don't you stay out here, so you can get a good close-up look at the girls? That way you can help us come up with their nicknames."

Two hours later, Buck and I knew we had four real runners, four tippy-toes runners, and four who would always be just slightly faster than turtles. "I thought this was the All-Star team," I whispered to Hank.

"Sorry, babe, we only had four teams, and some of the best girls weren't eligible for the play-offs."

"Why not?"

"We got a lot of girls from Look Over, Yonder, Bailey Mill and Chinaberry. They don't live inside the city limits of Mossy Creek, so the league doesn't consider them eligible to play. All the girls on the Mossy Creek All-Star Team have to live inside Mossy Creek. Just like the Bigelow All-Star team lives inside Bigelow's city limits."

"But Bigelow's *huge* compared to us. There are 10,000 people in Bigelow. That's not fair."

"I know. But the Bigelowans control the league's board of directors. Buck says they pushed through the rule change a few years ago." He sighed. "We broke that rule just by signing the county girls up for regular season play. We did it, anyway. But our team will be disqualified from the play-offs if we include any girls outside Mossy Creek."

I growled under my breath. It had been a long time since I'd played summer sports, but nothing had changed. Everyone seemed to forget that the playing ought to be fun. Maybe it had been once, but the adults found out that losing wasn't fun. So they began to make rules to keep everything equal. Or in the case of

Bigelow, to ensure that Bigelow always won.

"Okay, ladies," Buck called as the sweaty little girls downed water from a cooler. "Practice again tomorrow at 3:30. Okay?"

"Is Casey coming?" a chorus of small voices asked.

Hank looked at me. Buck looked at me.

"I don't know," I said. "Hank has appointments. I might not—"

"I'll come and get you," Buck said quickly.

I glanced at the parking lot, where the only other vehicle was Buck's red pick-up truck. "The last time I rode in the back of a pick-up truck was the Miss Bigelow County Parade."

"I'll leave my truck with Hank, and we'll drive your van."

Before I could shake my head, Little Ida put her hand on my arm. "Please?"

I looked at her, then at the rest of the girls, and made a decision I never thought I'd make. "I'll come, Buck. And don't worry, I can drive myself."

"Are you sure, Case?" Hank asked as we drove home. "I know I pushed you into helping Buck, but if it makes you uncomfortable, I'll understand. I just thought it would give you something fun to do."

Not that I could teach them anything, but that it would give me something to do. That hurt, even though I knew he didn't mean it that way. I didn't try to explain. Today, I just didn't want to go there. I remembered Little Ida's hopeful eyes. "Of course, I'm uncomfortable. But they're uncomfortable too. I'll help them get ready, but I'm not going on the field on game day. Coaching from a wheelchair while a stand full of people watches me is not my idea of fun."

In the next week, with Grandma Ida offering encouragement, Little Ida became known as "The Rabbit," flying around the diamond like a demented bunny. All the other girls demanded their own nicknames. Soon, Buck was teaching Killer, Slayer, Boom Boom and Slick how to slide. My job fell somewhere between cheerleader and mom. The All-Star team was coming together. And, to my surprise, I was enjoying myself.

The next thing I knew, Hank was dragging me along to practice with his and Buck's adult team, the Mossy Creek Mustangs. He failed to tell me that this team was also entered in the playoffs until I was appointed assistant coach and team scorekeeper. I was now an official member of the team. Not only did I have to watch the others play *my* game, I had to record it.

I smiled and pretended that didn't hurt, either.

🐰🐰🐰

The Fourth of July dawned clear and hot.

The mountains sucked up the air, and the sun couldn't even find a cloud to hide behind. Hank was up early, making his rounds, feeding and treating his boarders at the clinic, then getting on the phone to reassure parents about the girls' chances of winning in the play-offs. I couldn't believe this comfortable small town veterinarian was the same man who'd been determined to join the Angel Memorial veterinary staff as a surgical intern. He'd turned into his father, and the transition had come so easy to him. For me, it was harder to find my place in Mossy Creek society.

"Ready, Case?" Hank called out from the clinic door as I was washing the breakfast dishes at a special tub I set up on the porch of the farmhouse.

"Ready for what? It's too early."

"We need to get into town. I want to check on the ball field."

There was no delaying him. Already dressed in his playing shorts and numbered tee shirt, he'd become a ball player with his toe on the pitching mound. I might as well get ready.

When I rolled myself out to the van, I found a package on the passenger seat. Hank had bought me a team shirt. The name on the back read Mighty Casey. And the number was the same as the one I'd worn in college—number 6.

"Like it?" Hank asked quietly.

I looked at him with tears in my eyes and

nodded. "I don't know what to say—"

A soft, whickering sound stopped me. I froze as I looked across the van's front seats at Hank. "There's something in the back of this van," I said in a low voice. "And it sounds like a horse."

"That, my sexy wife, is not just a horse. That is a miniature *mustang*."

He opened the van's side doors. I gazed at a tiny brown pony tethered inside a crate full of hay. His white mane and forelock were so shaggy I couldn't see his eyes. "Looks like a pony who needs a haircut, to me."

Hank laughed. "Well, for our purposes, he's a wild, miniature mustang. He's our team mascot. From now on, the Twelve-And-Unders are the Lady Mustangs."

I couldn't help laughing.

❧❧❧

In town, red, white and blue banners lined the gazebo. The fireworks started early when someone tied a bunch of balloons to the sword of General Augustas Brimberry Hamilton of Jefferson's Third Confederate Division. The pigeons that normally rested on his broad-brimmed hat protested the distraction and retaliated by puncturing the balloons one by one.

Around the grassy square, booths had been set up where handmade leather goods, artwork and hooked rugs were offered for sale. Barbequed pigs and chickens were turning on spits. And deep iron pots of bubbling grease were frying catfish. A mountain of yellow corn was shucked and ready to be boiled. Later, there would be watermelon and pie-eating contests.

When we arrived at the ball field, Hank led the pony into our dugout and tied him to the chain-link fence beside a bucket of water and a pile of hay. As soon as the girls got there, they surrounded the pony with squealing delight. "What's his name?"

"Uhmmm. . .Homerun," I said. "Yes. Homerun. We can call him Homer, for short." "Homer, Homer!" they chanted.

"Oh, Casey, he's beautiful," Little Ida said. "He'll bring us good luck. Thank you!" I looked at her glowing eyes and those of the other girls, then met Hank's gentle gaze. "Girls, I have to tell you that this whole idea was really—"

"Okay, okay, the hat was my idea," Hank said.

"What?"

He pulled a pony-sized baseball cap from his back pocket. It even had special holes cut in it for the pony's ears. He fitted it on Homer's head. The knee-high fake-wild mustang peered out at us through mounds of white mane. Homer looked like a sheepdog. Plus, he was now wearing a turquoise baseball cap with the name Lady Mustangs embroidered across the bill. "And look what our sponsor, Hamilton's Department Store, has for everybody else." Hank opened a long canvas tote bag. Beautiful turquoise softball shirts tumbled out.

The girls cheered.

I rolled a few yards away, wiping my eyes. Hank followed me. "And, by the way, Case, you're on the team program. Buck put you down as a coach. He figured you deserved it." I swallowed hard. I had a uniform, and I was on an official roster of two softball teams— the Mustangs and the Lady Mustangs. I never expected that to happen again. The lump in my throat refused to budge.

The girls' game started at noon under a broiling sun. Excitement was high as the turquoise-uniformed Lady Mustangs of Mossy Creek took the field. The stands were full, the girls optimistic. But at the end of three innings, the Bigelow Baronettes led the Lady Mustangs by five runs.

"Look, little ladies," Buck said, more patiently than I'd heard him speak before, "we're ready to put in our secret plan. I want you next two batters to bend your knees and look like you're going to hit it out of the park. Grit your teeth. Get mean!"

I took the floor. "Then, just squat there."

"You mean you want us to *Wait on the pitch*, don't you?" the player nicknamed Killer asked, lowering her voice to mimic Buck's.

I nodded. "Yes. Wait until the next inning, if you have to! But this inning, don't, under *any* circumstances, *swing*."

Puzzled but following orders, Killer got set. Knees bent, arms up, she waited as the first pitch came in high.

"Ball one!"

The next pitch was a strike. Killer squirmed.

Buck called time and whispered into her ear.

She squatted lower.

The next two pitches were balls followed by another strike. "Full count now," the umpire said, "Three balls—two strikes."

Killer squatted lower.

"Ball four."

Buck turned to me in the dugout. "Well, I swear," he whispered. "I wouldn't have believed we could get that to work if you hadn't told me."

I grinned. The team managed to put two runners on base before the first out hit the scoreboard. Boom Boom, our best hitter, was up next. I whispered instructions to her.

"What'd you tell her?" Buck asked.

"Secret girl stuff," I said.

The whole team was standing now in the dugout, fingers grasping the fence like woodpeckers hanging on to tree bark. The pitch came. Boom Boom hit the ball. It went over the right fielder's head and rolled to the fence. As Boom Boom rounded second, our two base runners crossed the plate. The ball came in to the Baronettes' rattled second baseman. Just as I had hoped, she threw the ball over the third baseman's head and Boom Boom crossed the plate at a placid jog.

In the dugout, everyone, except me and Homer, of course, jumped up and down. Even Buck. I burst out laughing.

We scored two more runs that inning.

The Lady Mustangs held steady for the next couple of innings before the Baronettes went ahead by a run, then we caught up. The score was now Baronettes 6, Lady Mustangs 6. Soon we were down to the last inning. As the home team, we had the last bat. All the Baronettes had to do was keep us from scoring, and the game would go into extra innings. Our team had been lucky, so far. If there were extra innings, our luck would probably run out.

The Lady Mustangs' first two batters popped out. Finally, our girl Slick hit a low line drive and made it to second.

Little Ida was next at bat.

"I'm The Rabbit, I'm The Rabbit," she chanted as she went to the plate. Following my instructions, she took her stance and squatted so low she looked like her nickname. All we needed was a hit or a mistake by the other team. As she crouched there, I could feel the tension. For not once—either in a practice session or any game—had Little Ida Walker actually hit the ball.

Even Homer seemed to be holding his breath.

Strike one. Strike two. Ida narrowed her eyes and leaned forward. The pitcher threw the ball a third time.

"Now, Rabbit, now!" I yelled.

For the first time all summer, Little Ida hit a ball. She slammed it. The ball dribbled straight down the right field line.

"Let it go foul!" the Bigelow coach yelled to his first baseman.

"Run, Bunny...uh...Furry...uh...Rabbit!" Buck screamed, swinging his arm in a circle toward first base.

Little Ida, too surprised to move, simply stood there.

"Run, Rabbit!" I cried. "Use your brain and your feet! Show them how fast you are!"

She launched herself toward first base like a turquoise whirlwind. The ball rolled to a stop about halfway from first plate—still in fair territory. The catcher and the first baseman darted toward it at the same time, tripped each other, and sat down hard in the dust cloud Little Ida made as she flew by them. Slick headed for third. The catcher scrambled to her feet and threw wild to the surprised pitcher, who flailed at the ball hopelessly. It bypassed her glove and rolled between the shortstop and the second baseman as if it had eyes. They collided over it.

"Run!" screamed Buck.

Slick raced toward home. The Barronette second baseman finally picked up the ball and threw it to the pitcher. When the dust settled, Ida was safe at first base.

And Slick had scored the winning run.

"Home team scores," the umpire called out. "That's the game."

Little Ida started to cry.

I rolled my chair to the field and grabbed her. "You did it, Rabbit. We won the game. You got the winning RBI."

"But I didn't get to run around the bases."

"Doesn't matter. You hit the ball. The Lady Mustangs scored. You're a hero."

The stands were screaming. The teams gave each other high fives. Then with Little Ida in my lap, the Lady Mustangs rolled my wheelchair around the diamond chanting "Rabbit! Rabbit! Rabbit!"

It was a miracle. Homer neighed with excitement.

"You did it," Hank said, grinning as he loped over and kissed me.

I shrugged. "I just used my brain."

"Well, use it some more. Come on." He wheeled me to the next ball field, where the adult teams were warming up. I stationed myself and my wheelchair in the dugout of the Mossy Creek Mustangs with a lap desk and a scorebook. I penciled in the line-ups and told myself this was as good as the day was going to get. I'd accomplished a lot. I could bear to watch my friends, my neighbors, and my husband play softball without me.

We take our softball seriously in Mossy Creek. Things got tense right away when three Bigelow Baron batters, including the first woman to hit, got on base. Hank's pitching was, to put it mildly, interesting. "Sort of looks like he's winding up to swat the back end of a cow," I heard one of our teammates say. Everyone chortled.

I chewed on the end of my pencil. The next Bigelow batter, the right fielder, a shapely blonde, picked up a bat and sauntered to the plate, setting off a chorus of wolf whistles. "That's Swee Purla's younger sister," someone said. "Interior decorator. Just like Swee. Mean as a snake in silk."

She hit a hard line drive that careened off Hank's foot toward Little Ida's dad Robert, the first baseman. Robert scooped it up and stepped on the base. Next, the Bigelow catcher popped up. Two outs, bases still loaded. I pushed a sweaty strand of hair away from my forehead as a Bigelow banker about the size of Rush Limbaugh popped a short fly over the head of our wiry shortstop, Nail Delgado. The Barons scored their first run. Their pitcher, a woman, hit a dinger over first, and a second run scored.

Out in center field, Sandy Crane chewed

a wad of gum, squinted with deadly intent, and crept forward. Her determined look said, *No dingers are getting past me*. When Hank let the next pitch go, I knew we were lost. We all watched in dismay as the Bigelow batter slapped the ball over Sandy's head. The ball rolled all the way to the fence. The Barons' runner held at third. The next batter struck out. We were lucky to be only three runs behind.

That's where it stayed for four innings. Bigelow 3, Mossy Creek 0. League rules had set the game at an hour and twenty minutes time or seven innings unless the score was tied. Our team finally scored two runs in the fifth. The crowd behind our home-team dugout went wild. I could hear the Lady Mustangs screaming in excitement. Little Ida's voice carried across the other fans when she yelled, "Go, Coaches!"

But the crowd went silent when the Barons scored another run in the bottom of the fifth, putting us two runs behind. Nail Delgado went down with a pulled hamstring in the top of the sixth and Chief Royden—our catcher—got a phone call and had to leave the field.

"Two fender benders out on West Mossy Creek Road," he said as he gathered his gear in the dugout. "Sorry. We're short-handed during the holidays. And I promised Mutt he could have the Fourth off."

Mutt ducked his head in grateful

acknowledgement. He had a new girlfriend in the stands.

"Chief, I'll go," Sandy called. She wanted to be a full-fledged police officer in the worst way. "I can write up a ticket! I can make notes about the dents and the tire marks! I can take people's statements and yell at 'em for speedin'! Lemme go, Chief, uh, please?"

Amos Royden didn't bat an eye. "Only one little problem. You're not a police officer. It would be illegal."

"Picky, picky, Chief."

He shook his head in amazement and left.

We were out of substitutes and almost out of time. Tension gripped the field like a tightly clenched fist. Olympic tryouts couldn't have been more serious. In the bottom of the seventh, we were still two runs behind. Sandy, our first batter, hit a grounder that bounced over the shortstop's head. Hank managed to get to first on a well-hit ball to right. When Regina Regina, our double-deck-named cocktail waitress over at O'Day's Pub, popped up, things looked grim. Then we got a break; the Bigelow pitcher walked Mutt, the next batter.

One out and the bases loaded; we still had a chance. Behind me, in the silence, I heard a low murmur. Buck Looney, our most dependable homerun hitter, was up. The crowd's applause rose and took on a cadence. Buck glanced toward the stands, cocked his head for a moment, then nodded. "Casey," he snapped, "Get a bat. You're up." He turned to the umpire. "We're putting in Casey Blackshear for Buck Looney."

My mouth fell open. "Me?"

"You. Everybody on this team plays. It's one of my rules."

"But I'm not really on the team, Buck."

"Oh yes, you are. Once your name goes on the roster, you're official. Besides, your fans are calling for you."

The crowd noise grew louder. I could hear the Lady Mustangs. "We want Casey. We want Casey. We want Casey."

"Buck, don't be foolish. I'm a score-keeper, not a player. I can't bat. I can't walk."

"I'm not asking you to walk, Casey. I'll push you out to the plate. You stand up and bat."

"I can't do it." He couldn't know how badly I wanted to stand up and swing a bat again. He couldn't feel the shaft of pain in my heart, or he wouldn't keep on asking. By this time, every eye in the park was fixed on me.

"Remember Mighty Casey," Little Ida called out.

"Yeah," I growled under my breath. "Mighty Casey struck out."

Hank walked down from first base. "Go for it, babe. You're a champion, remember?"

I looked up into my husband's adoring eyes and wanted to disappear. *He's helped everyone back you into a corner, I told myself. Your parents and everybody else in Mossy Creek are watching. If you don't try, the Lady Mustangs will think you're a coward. But if you do get up there, you'll strike out and maybe cause us to lose the game.*

The chant grew louder. "We want Casey. We want Casey."

I knew what I had to do. What I wanted was unimportant.

By refusing to try, I'd make myself a quitter before my Lady Mustang team. *My team.* When had it become my team? When Little Ida tripped over the base on the first day, that's when. Slowly, I rolled forward and picked up my bat. "Get my braces out of the van, Hank."

Hank gave the umpire the signal for time out.

The crowd hushed as he ran up the hill to the van.

The umpire moved over to the dugout to confer with Buck for a moment. "Batter Up!" he called out, resuming his place behind the Bigelow catcher.

I rolled my chair into the batter's circle and took a couple of practice swings.

The umpire reached out to help push my chair to the plate. I shook my head. I'd do it on my own, or I wouldn't do it. Studying the plate, I positioned my chair so that as I stood my feet would be in the right place. Hank made it back to the field with my braces and strapped them on. He loped out to first base and stood there on the plate, watching me urgently.

"How much time have I got, Ump?" I asked as I released my wheelchair's foot rests, leaned my bat against the side of the chair, and firmly set my feet on the ground.

"Three minutes," he answered.

I drew in a shaky breath and pushed myself up. There was a gasping sound, as if the crowd had inhaled at the same time. I made certain that my feet were balanced, then motioned for Buck to move my chair away. Casey Champion Blackshear lifted her bat one more time.

The chant picked up again, growing louder as all the fans joined in. From the expression on the pitcher's face, I knew he was worried. Not worried that I'd hit the ball—worried that *he* would hit *me*.

"Throw it in here, Pitch," I called out. "You're holding up the game."

He gave me a weak grin and threw a high, slow ball so far outside that he might have been trying to walk me.

I forced a grin in return. "Throw me a strike. You know I can't walk."

He took me up on the taunt. The next ball had a perfect arc, straight down the middle of the plate. I swung—hard. And missed. And fell. I sprawled across the plate like a side of barbecued ribs flopped on a plastic platter.

"Casey!" Hank started toward me from

first base.

I gave him a look that froze him in his tracks. When they'd fitted me with the braces in the spinal center, I'd fallen—lots of times. They even taught me how to get up.

"Casey!" Little Ida called out. I could hear the tears in her voice. "You don't have to bat, Casey. We love you anyway."

I positioned my legs so my feet were pointed toes out, then reached for my bat. Marshaling every ounce of strength in my upper body, I clasped the bat and began to ratchet myself up, dragging my feet forward. Now I had to do something I'd never done in public—push myself erect without losing my balance and falling over in another humiliating display. Inch by inch, I moved the bat toward me and I straightened my body until I was standing.

The crowd roared.

I wiped my forehead on my sleeve and pulled my turquoise cap lower.

The pitcher threw the ball. I drew my bat back and swung. The bat connected with the ball with a clang like an old-fashioned dinner bell. I raised my gaze, hoping, praying. As if it were in slow motion, the ball rose and shot across the sky.

The crowd was on its feet, cheering. The ball seemed to hover for a moment, then fell—just inside the centerfield fence. I simply stood and watched. Then I heard the thunder of feet.

Our three base runners had to touch home plate, and I was blocking it. I couldn't reach my chair and I couldn't walk.

I had to walk.

Like a mummy in a bad horror movie, I leaned on the bat and inched forward. Sandy reached the plate and danced around me. Mutt pranced across the plate next. Hank, not the fleetest-footed member of the team, was running like he was being chased by the hounds of hell. He tried to miss me. I tried to get out of the way. Neither of us succeeded. It was a déjà vu all over again.

With a crunch, I went down. Hank fell on top. I grabbed his hand and planted it squarely on home plate. The crowd went wild. The impossible had happened. Mossy Creek had defeated Bigelow twice in one tournament. A home run on an Olympic team wouldn't have been as sweet.

Hank rolled over, turning me with him. "Are you okay, babe?"

I looked down at him and smiled. I was fourteen and falling in love with him at first sight, again. "Oh, yes."

If I could coach and play on a softball team, I could get myself back to college and finish my degree in education. If I could teach Little Ida to play softball, I could teach other children. And maybe I could help Hank out in the clinic. And maybe. . .well, there were a lot of maybes. They'd just have to get in line.

That evening, as we sat on benches around the town square listening to the Mossy Creek band play *It's a Grand Old Flag* and watching fireworks, I leaned against my husband and knew that today's victory was more than just winning a game. It was a victory of the heart.

Mighty Casey didn't strike out.

FROM THE DESK OF KATIE BELL, BUSINESS MANAGER

Lady Victoria Stanhope
Cornwall, England

Dear Lady Victoria,

All right, I admit it. We Mossy Creekites—past or present—are fools for love.

Now, where was I? Oh, yes. Isabella was pledged to marry old Lionel Bigelow. She began to suspect Lionel might be more interested in her Mossy Creek land-owning connections than her own sweet self. Her uncle, Joshua Hamilton, was suspicious of Lionel's plans, too, so he hired the finest land surveyor in the South—your great-great-great-great grandfather, Richard—to survey the land in Mossy Creek. Just in case there were any squabbles with Lionel Bigelow over the old land deeds.

Richard Atworth Stanhope—now if that's not a dashing Englishman's name, I don't know one that is! Legend has it that Richard wore a diamond collar pin. He'd barely settled into a room at the Hamilton House Inn before his collar pin was pilfered by Amarinth Hart Salter, a nutty aunt of Isabella's on the Salter side. Amarinth said she needed the collar pin to work a love spell on Isabella's behalf. Nobody in the Hart or Salter families seemed at all embarrassed when she was caught. They just returned the pin to Richard and promised it wouldn't happen again. He was gentlemanly enough to let the matter drop.

In the South we don't hide our odd relatives—we get them out and show them off. Mossy Creekites are natural show offs, but there's more to it than that. We believe the sweet truths of life can be found in the least likely places sometimes, hidden inside peculiar ways and wistful memories.

Relatives of Amarinth made news just last month in Mossy Creek. Of course, the real story is that Maggie Hart and her mother Millicent realized they were hiding the sweet truth of life from themselves and each other. As you're about to see, all it took was a natural force of nature to help them remember where they put their hearts.

Sentimentally, your friend,

Katie

Maggie

The Hope Chest

To my way of thinking there was no prettier month in the year than August in Mossy Creek. My dahlias, zinnias, and daisies turned their cheerful faces toward the golden summer sunlight and nodded sleepily with the soft mountain breezes. I smiled as I clipped a sunset rose from the bush at the corner of the veranda and dropped it into my basket. My lush gardens provide baskets full of herbs and fragrant blossoms for the soaps and toiletries and potpourri I make, perfuming the Victorian house I call home. I live just a block off Mossy Creek's town square, but my house—which is also my shop—could be a cottage in a fantasy painting.

I guess I'm still a flower child at heart. Nearly thirty years ago, I really *was* a flower child, but not for very long. Just my first couple of years at college down in Atlanta. I was going to be the first attorney in my family. But I was a Mossy Creekite girl, born and raised. Set me free in a big city, and I look for adventure.

My freshman year I met Bea, my college roommate. Beatrice Starling Williamson. Her parents had sent her to law school in hopes she'd follow in her father's legal footsteps, perhaps even to become a judge like him. Bea immediately discovered the hippies who hung out near the campus. Within days, she renamed herself Petunia, then swapped her Villager skirts, and sweaters, and Weejuns for a tie-dyed t-shirt, ragged bellbottom jeans, and sandals. A fashion rebellion looked like fun to me. I went right along with her.

Petunia made a perfect hippie, but I never did, not really. Oh, I perfected the look, the long straight hair, the granny boots and peasant skirts and incense sticks, but I didn't have the rule-breaking heart of a truly shocking social rebel. I mean, a person can never forget Sunday School lessons at Mossy Creek Mt. Gilead Methodist, where little girls had to wear white gloves and hard patent-leather shoes and were expected not to burp after drinking a Coca-Cola. Oh, I burned my bra and dated a guitarist in a rock band and changed my name from Maggie Hart to Moonheart, but that was about all.

Petunia and my guitarist ran off together, and I, brokenhearted, dropped out of college to find my way in the world of natural living. Maybe I wasn't a flower child, but I wasn't a lawyer either. Eventually, I wandered back to Mossy Creek, the way almost all expatriot Mossy Creekites do. I opened my shop and hung out a sign that named it Moonheart's Natural Living, though no one in Mossy Creek called me Moonheart. I started out selling natural products I purchased from suppliers in California, but gradually began to make my own candles, soaps, cosmetics, teas, and other organic, nontoxic items.

Becoming Mother Nature's business manager was the best thing that ever happened to me—unless you ask my mother.

My mother, Millicent Abigail Hart, is one of Mossy Creek's more outrageous characters. She considers herself an everyday, run-of-the-mill, meatloaf-and-marriage kind of woman, though Daddy disappeared on us when I was just a baby. Mother's been waiting all these years for me to give her a son-in-law and grandchildren to redeem the Hart female pride in Mossy Creek. Yet for obvious reasons, she's wary of men, and has never liked my taste in potential mates.

I can't help but agree with her. The men I chased when I was younger didn't want to play husband. The ones who chased me wanted to play caveman. I seem to be irresistible to the world's truck-driving, deer-hunting good old boys who wear white socks with their dress pants and love a woman who smells like a warm meadow full of does. It must be my flower scent.

Having never outgrown my rock-guitarist phase, I've dated one free spirit after another. Disillusionment has always followed love at first sight–or first twang on the guitar, or stroke of the paintbrush, or quatrain of iambic pentameter--and the pickin's are getting slimmer.

Recently I looked in the mirror and saw a fifty-year-old woman. Pretty, sassy, still sexy, but fifty. I decided to stop falling in love with grown men who haven't found themselves yet. No more hippies. No more musicians. No more poets. And no more artists.

So, I've devoted myself to running my shop and keeping track of my mother, which is no easy task. You could say her phone calls to reality are all long distance, now. Some people think I phone home on a loose-screw connection, too. Even my fellow Mossy Creekites—who are very open-minded in their own way—are whispering about me since I started expanding the shop. I've added a New Age book section, health foods, and a few swami-psychic-goddess trinkets. I still attend Mt. Gilead Methodist. But I admit the Mossy Creek Unitarians have been courting me.

Mother is convinced I'm a witch, but not beyond fixing. "You're not too old to renounce this nonsense, find a nice young man, get married, and have some children," she says. She neglects to remember that I just turned the half-century mark. Or maybe she *can't* remember. Her memory ebbs and flows just as rhythmically as the eddies that dapple the edge of Mossy Creek. In her lucid moments, she plots ways to make me marry Mossy Creek forest ranger Bradley "Smokey" Lincoln. "He's really dull," she says, "But you'll never run out of firewood." She doesn't even like him. Bradley was nicknamed Smokey as a rookie ranger after he set the forest on fire. He and I have been friends for years. I've occasionally considered the idea of a romance with Smokey, but it just didn't feel right. Like dating your brother. Not that Smokey would like to hear that.

As I pondered such circumstances in my life on that hot, beautiful August day in Mossy Creek, I cut my last rose and walked back up on my veranda to return to the cool sanctuary of my shop. I heard a car pull into my little gravel parking lot and turned around in time to see police chief Amos Royden getting out of his blue-and-white patrol car.

I froze. "Morning, Amos. Pretty day, isn't it?"

Amos nodded. I could see he was uncomfortable about something. "Come on in," I added.

He entered the shop behind me. "This place always smells good."

"Thanks. I think so." I floated my roses in a big cut glass punch bowl and turned back to him. I was procrastinating. A visit from the chief always meant one thing. "Smokey told me about the lost little boy and the skunk."

Amos nodded. "Smokey found him in the woods before I got there." Amos was procrastinating, too. "Followed a skunk too close. Got lost and got sprayed. Whew, what a smell!"

"Ah, the life of a forest ranger. Smokey brought him home in the park service Jeep, then had to fumigate it. I gave him some lemon-rosemary spray to use."

Amos smiled.

I sighed, and gave up. "So, what's Mother done this time?"

"She's been on a little shopping spree at the new shop by the theater."

"The sculptor?"

"I don't know what he is, exactly. She stole a tiara. You know." He gestured vaguely toward his head, and frowned. "A tiara."

"A tiara? In a sculptor's studio?"

"Yeah. The sculptor's ex-wife was an actress, and she left a crate full of her old costumes behind when they got divorced. When your mother snatched the tiara, he followed her next door to the theater and cornered her in the director's office. He was nice to her. But you know your mother. She doesn't like to be caught. He didn't understand that he wasn't supposed to notice when she pilfered something."

"How much was the tiara worth?"

"Garner says about a hundred dollars."

"Garner?"

"Right. Last name is Garner. I'm on my way over to the theater now. I knew you'd want to go with me."

I didn't. Boy, how I didn't, but I couldn't see that I had any choice in the matter. Mother had promised to behave after the last incident. She was getting bolder in her old age. She'd swiped Julia Ledbetter's twin-seat stroller. I'd returned it laden with two of my finest hanging baskets of moss roses, as an apology.

"Let's go," I said wearily.

I placed my closed sign on the door. Weekday mornings in August didn't usually bring in brisk traffic, so I wouldn't lose much business. There weren't many tourists in town, and the locals would come back later.

"Oh, Mother," I said under my breath.

❧❧❧

The Mossy Creek Theater was very small and anchored the southwest corner of the square with a small marquee that advertised the Mossy Creek Players' soon-to-premiere production of *Oklahoma!* Nestled right beside it, in a small, turn-of-the-century storefront that used to house a shoe shop, was Tag Garner's sculpting gallery and studio. His sign said, Figuratively Speaking. I hadn't met him yet and gaped at his work. His shop windows were full of rugged, manly looking sculptures, some of marble and some in bronze, mostly of athletes or wild animals butting each other and snarling.

That worried me.

Amos and I walked past the shop and into a side door at the theater, then down a narrow hallway to the office. A well-built man with a streak of iridescent blue hair that began at his temple and ended in his graying ponytail rose from a chair near the director's desk. He looked as if he'd been in a barroom brawl and lost. His shirt was ripped, his nose was bleeding, and his left eye was swollen nearly shut.

My mother was nowhere to be seen, which was more than a little worrisome. "Where's my mother?"

"Probably wrestling a bear," the stranger said dryly.

"My mother is a genteel little old lady—"

"Genteel?" He sat down again and pointed to his shiner. "I got hurt less playing football."

"I'm real sorry about the attack and the theft of your tiara, Mr.—"

"Garner," he confirmed. "Tag Garner. Victim." Without his newly acquired bruises, Tag Garner would have been a handsome, brawny man, even with the funky blue streak in his hair and the ponytail. The door opened behind me and our theater director, Anna

Rose, walked in carrying a plastic baggie filled with ice. Anna grinned. "Your mother's performing her own brand of experimental theater these days, Maggie."

"She's been obsessed with tiaras since this spring's Miss Bigelow County Pageant. Pearl Quinlan loaned her a book about beauty pageants. It had pictures of tiaras in it."

"Somebody ought to give her a book on manners," Tag growled. He held up his right arm. I saw a perfect set of my mother's denture marks on his forearm. "She bit me."

I dropped into the chair opposite him and waited while he pressed the ice bag to his eye. "Did you see which way she went?"

He laughed darkly. "I thought I had her trapped in here, but she faked me out and ran like a linebacker."

"My mother is an elderly woman with health problems."

"Health problems? Has she had her shots? I could get rabies."

"Now, wait just a minute, Mr. Gardner—"

"Garner," he corrected. "Tyler Adams Garner—Tag, for short—bloody but unbowed, at your service." He held up his bitten arm, again. "I'll probably turn into a werewolf at the next full moon. When I do, you can still call me by my human name."

"Well, Tag, I am very sorry—very—for everything my mother's done, but if you don't quit making jokes about her I'll—"

"Punch me and bite me? Get in line."

"Settle down, both of you." Amos stepped to my side. "Let's start over. Let me introduce you. Maggie Hart, Tag Garner."

I tried to smile but failed miserably. "Pleased," I muttered.

"And, I'm just as pleased to meet you, Mrs. Hart, as you obviously are to meet me."

"I'm not married," I corrected absently.

"So the werewolf line stops with you?"

I glared at him, all the while wondering if my mother was admiring her looted tiara on a park bench beside one of Mossy Creek's pretty little bridges—only a short walk away, and her favorite spots after a crime spree. Mother had no sense of guilt, so she never ran for cover. I looked at Amos. "We've got to go and look for her. She may have hurt herself, this time."

"She seemed fine when she was sucker punching me," Tag Garner intoned. He stood up, becoming an even more imposing sight— over six-feet-tall and big-shouldered. "Look, she has a problem. I understand, I really do. But she needs to be corralled before she attacks somebody else. Wouldn't she be happy stealing bedpans in a nursing home?"

"My mother isn't ready for a home. She's just crazy." Nobody can imagine how difficult those words were for me to say. Mother's condition was hopeless. "I'll be happy to pay damages—"

"No, save your money. Spend it on a doctor for your mother. Get her some help."

His patient tone infuriated me. "Listen, Mr. Garner, my mother is a Mossy Creek institution. People around here don't mind her little quirks. She just needs to be left alone. If you don't like the way we do things here, then leave."

Tag, still holding the ice bag to his eye, squinted at our police chief for help.

Amos shook his head. I could tell he was observing the stalemate unhappily. He had one of his grim *Thankyougladtobehere* expressions.

Tag sighed. "Chief, I don't intend to press any charges. But I do want to go on record—I don't like being rolled by little old ladies."

Amos nodded and looked at me. "Maggie, I'll let her off the hook this time, but you've got to do something. We're getting more and more new people around town—and they don't know her. If this rumor about Ham Bigelow running for President is true, over the next few years we'll be swarmed with visitors. Someone will press charges, and then there'll be real trouble for her. You don't want her to end up in Judge Blakely's courtroom, do you?"

I sagged. "No. You're right." I faced Tag. "I apologize again, and I swear she won't steal anything else from you. I'll find the tiara and return it."

"Listen, she can keep the tiara. I was

planning to donate it to the theater. My ex-wife wore it when she was in a touring company of Cinderella."

"Oh, your ex-wife played the starring role?"

"Nah, she was one of the evil stepsisters." He smiled. "Typecasting."

"I'm sorry."

"I must attract crabby women who like tiaras."

"Are you saying my mother is evil, too?"

He feigned fear and held up a hand to protect himself. "Please, Daughter of the She-Werewolf, don't twist my words. Let me live."

I walked out.

I spent some time wandering the town, looking for mother, but didn't find her. When I got back home, my beautiful yard roses didn't seem nearly so lovely. The hot sunshine felt cold. Entering the shop, I breathed deeply, inhaling the fragrance of vanilla, cinnamon, lavender, and roses. The scents in the shop usually had a calming effect, but they did little to help today.

I walked to the stairs. "Mother! Are you up there?"

No answer. I didn't really expect her to be back yet. When she went on one of her little shoplifting expeditions, she didn't usually come straight home. That was the strangest part of her hobby. I never found any of the items she took. Over the years, there had been a toaster, a fancy garter from the Mossy Creek Bridal Shoppe, a golden heart necklace, a pair of lace gloves, and even a small, decrepit trunk from the Up The Creek Flea Market. How could she steal something as big as a trunk and not be seen? Even Battle Royden, Amos's legendary father and police chief, had never been able to ferret out Mother's stolen treasures. And, believe me, for years I had searched the entire town myself.

I made a cup of tea and settled down to meditate for a few minutes. All right, I admitted it: My mother might be a Mossy Creek institution, but now she needed to be put *in* a Mossy Creek institution. I thought of Magnolia Manor, our nursing home. In her better days, Mother had done a lot of volunteer work there. She had known most of the staff and residents all her life. Unfortunately, they knew her, too. Just recently, she'd stolen a flower arrangement from the lobby.

I heard a sound outside and jumped up.

"Mother?" I called and swung the door open. It was Smokey. "Hi. Come on in."

He leaned down and gave me a peck on the cheek. "Howdy, Mags. What's up?"

I smiled at him. Tall and lanky with beautiful brown eyes, so comforting, so comfortable. There were times when even I didn't understand why he didn't make my heart race. "It's Mother. She went AWOL, again." I told him what had happened.

"Anything I can do? You want me to go look for her?" Smokey knew her habits almost as well as I did, maybe better. "I could radio the smoke tower and—"

"No, that's real nice of you, but unless Mother sets herself on fire, I don't think your idea will help."

Smokey looked crestfallen. I patted his arm distractedly. "But thanks."

"You okay, Mags? You want a hug, or something? You always get this faraway look in your eyes when we talk. Sometimes I think you need your hearing checked."

For some reason, I was thinking of Tag Garner, wondering why a man like him would set up a studio in a small town like Mossy Creek. He belonged down in Buckhead, Atlanta's ritzy art district, where rich socialites and country clubbers would quickly pay a small fortune for his work. And what had he said about playing pro football? I rubbed my forehead, trying to remember anything other than the color of his eyes. They were the softest gray.

"Mags?"

"Huh?"

Smokey sighed. "Deaf, again," he muttered.

"I'm sorry."

"Look, I know about this Garner guy. About twenty years ago, he played football for the Atlanta Falcons."

Omigod. Now I understood why Tag Garner was vaguely familiar. Despite my flower-child roots, I loved rock 'em, sock 'em sports in general and Falcons football in particular. Smokey watched my face closely. "You want me to go have a man-to-man talk with this smart-alecky Garner? I hear he has a streak of blue in his hair, now. He's an insult to American sports. He's some kind of Communist, I bet. I wouldn't mind punching him if I had to."

"Don't you dare. This problem is something I have to work out myself. I'm just trying to take care of Mother. At the moment, in fact, I'm just trying to *find* Mother."

"You know, hmmm, uh, Margaret—" he stumbled over his words as he put a hand over his heart—"if you married somebody, uh, like me, uh, I could help you keep her in line."

"I appreciate the offer, as always, but you and I aren't even dating."

"We could. Uh, date. How's about we take in the new kickboxing movie down at the Bigelow Big Cine-Plex? Or go to dinner and then stop by that big sports outfitter's place at the Bigelow Mall? We could look at the new deer rifles."

It suddenly dawned on me that life was full of compromises, I mean, it really dawned, not in the way we mull over thoughts like reciting a quote of the day, but in the stomach-twisting way of long, hard experience and grim reality. I needed help with Mother. I was fifty years old. I needed to start compromising and learn to take my blessings where I found them. I looked up at Smokey with a little twist of defeat in my heart. "You know, I'll think about going out with you, I really will. Ask me again, soon."

"That's a yes!" He grabbed me by the shoulders and kissed me on the forehead. "Hot damn, we've got a date!"

My door chimes tinkled. Amos walked in. "Hi, Smokey. Please tell me Maggie's mother chased a skunk and you found her, too."

Smokey grinned. I heard another car pull up outside. I looked through the window but didn't recognize the classic Corvette. I did recognize the driver. Tag Garner. He didn't look happy. "Uh, oh. Here's trouble with a black eye and Mother's denture imprints," I said.

Tag took my steps two at a time and crossed the veranda quickly. He opened the shop's door so hard my little chimes jangled violently. "Mommie Dearest came back," he announced flatly. "And stole Cinderella's glass slippers." I groaned. He gave me and my shop a sardonic once-over, then added, "Would you tell her that nobody in her right mind wants my ex-wife's size ten shoes?"

🐞🐞🐞

Tag and I sat on my back porch swing and sipped herbal tea. I fought back tears. I'd sent Smokey and the chief away, so they wouldn't see me cry. But I owed Mr. Garner some waterworks. I suppose I hoped he'd feel sorry for me and forgive Mother. I felt sorry for myself.

"Don't cry," he ordered. "I have a syndrome called, hmmm, Active Sympathetic Knee-jerk Boo-Hoo Condition. I cry automatically when women cry. There's no cure."

I wiped my eyes and couldn't help smiling. "Tell me something. Why the heck did you dye a blue streak in your hair? I mean, if you were a twenty-year-old punk rocker, I could understand—"

"When I hit fifty, I decided to do whatever appealed to me. And I like blue." He paused. "When I was twenty, I was too busy trying to become the greatest football player ever. I missed out on just being goofy."

"You're not goofy." I paused perfectly. "Dopey, I think. Or Grumpy. But not Goofy."

He threw back his head and roared, then sloshed blackberry tea on himself and laughed some more. He nodded toward the shop. "I like this place. Smells great. Brings out the worst in me."

"I'll take that as a compliment."

"I'm going to buy some of your potpourri."

"Are you gay?"

He laughed, again. I warmed up to him. I couldn't help myself. The only time I'd offered Smokey some potpourri he'd asked me what kind of soup it made. "I'll mix you a custom bag," I told Tag. "I see you as a thyme-rose-mint kind of man."

"Oh? Most women see me as a smelly socks-tequila-burrito kind of man. But only when they're being polite." To the sounds of my laughter, he added, "Okay, okay, thyme-rose-mint, then." He picked up a candle off the windowsill near the swing, and sniffed it like a wine steward sampling the aroma of a fine Bordeaux. "Muskadoodle berry. My favorite."

"There's no such thing as 'muskadoodle berry.' That's vanilla you smell."

"Ah, vanilla. Smells just like muskadoodle. My shop will smell like an ice cream cone. Got any chocolate sprinkles?"

I led him inside and packaged up a candle and some potpourri. "Here, let me give you this, too." I handed him a fragrance ring I'd soaked in orange oils. I couldn't believe I was having a conversation about fragrances with a former professional football player who had a blue streak in his pony tailed hair and a sense of the absurd that made me want to tickle him just to hear him laugh. He twirled the fragrance ring around a forefinger. The delicate scent of citrus perfumed the air between us. I found myself smiling at him with giddy enjoyment. "I love oranges," I said.

His eyes warmed me. "Call me sometime, and we'll squeeze a few." I laughed, blushed, then stopped smiling and gazed at him wistfully. He returned the scrutiny and leaned closer. "I don't know any other way to say this, Maggie Hart, but are you and Smokey engaged or something?"

"Engaged? No, we're...well, you see, we..." How could I explain an inexplicable relationship? One I didn't understand myself. "I guess the best thing to say is that we're comfortable with each other."

"Comfortable? Hmm. Doesn't sound very exciting to me. Want to be *uncomfortable* with a man?"

"I could stand it," I said in a small voice.

"So what about tomorrow night?"

Red danger lights flashed in my head, warning me against beginning a relationship with another artistic type. But this man was different. Tag was an artistic-*ex-footballer* type who let my mother beat him up.

"Tomorrow?" I breathed.

"How about I take you to dinner some place?"

"What time?"

"When can you leave?"

"Pretty much anytime. I own the shop. I can let myself off early."

"Great. I'll pick you up around four." He plucked a rose from the water bowl I'd arranged that morning. With a smile that sent the summer heat rippling through me, he tucked it behind my ear, then grinned and walked out. I closed the shop's glass door behind him and watched him through its Victorian curlicues until he climbed into his Corvette, waved, and drove off. I walked back to my roses and stared into the bowl. What in the world had I just agreed to?

Mother needed stability. If I encouraged Smokey, I'd have a husband. If I gave Mother a son-in-law, maybe her nutty perspective on life would calm down. Maybe she stole things to make up for having no son-in-law and no grandchildren. There wasn't much I could do about the latter.

For the first time in a long time, I wanted to talk to Mother about life and love and stealing joy.

I wandered into my shop's office and sat down, staring at a poster of an ivy trellis in a French courtyard. Tangled. Relationships could get tangled so quickly. One date with Tag could insult Smokey and end our potential future together. Maybe I should cancel my date with Tag. That way, everything would remain the same, and I wouldn't be agonizing over this.

The shop's front door opened, interrupting my waffling. I darted out of my office. Mother sauntered in, humming quietly. She was a staunch old lady, looking deceptively delicate in white cotton pants and a flower-embroidered t-shirt. "Maggie, dear, I'm home."

"Mother, why did you beat up Mr. Garner and steal his tiara?"

"Because I was testing him! And he passed! I like him! He's kind to old ladies even when they bite him!" She settled on a wicker lounge among baskets of dried flowers, and smiled. "I think he's the perfect man for us."

I didn't have the heart to ask where the tiara was.

🐞🐞🐞

Tag picked me up in the Corvette, top down, and whisked me away. We drove north, crossed the North Carolina state line, and climbed into mountains so high and rugged they take a person's breath away. I guided him to a picnic site overlooking miles of mountains and coves. We munched on yummy fried chicken, made by Tag himself, potato salad, and iced tea while we watched a glorious Appalachian sunset. I honestly believe I've never seen a more stirring sight. The mauves, golds, and blues were magnificent. Then we marveled at the clarity of each star as it twinkled into view above us. "Can you see?" I asked Tag, studying the way he squinted with his bruised eye.

He smiled bravely. "I can't quite make out the dip in the Big Dipper."

I pointed skyward. "There, One Eye, there it is." We leaned close together, our faces nearly touching as we gazed up at the night sky. My heart raced. "You smell like roses," I said. "That's wonderful."

"Ah hah! The bait works!"

What a great evening it was.

By the time we returned home, I realized that some men just know the meaning of a romantic date and others don't. Tag did. The light kiss he brushed against my lips left me wanting more. He whistled happily as he went down my veranda steps and then turned to smile. What a smile! What a handsome face—in spite of his black eye.

"Maggie," he began and then hesitated. He looked as if he were in a mental feud over something. "Aw, hell." He bounded back up the steps and took me in his arms. Before I could whisper his name, his lips claimed mine in the most sensuous kiss I can ever remember. When he drew away to look down into my eyes, I was gasping for breath. It was as though my entire body molded itself against him involuntarily when he kissed me again.

"You taste good," he said.

"You smell good."

"This time, roses. Next time...muskadoodle berry."

I burst out laughing. He grinned as he drove away.

There was clearly something lacking in

my life. Emotions that had been dormant for years sputtered to life. Leaning against the veranda's railing for support, I tried to decide what to do next. I couldn't go in, not yet. Going in would mean returning to reality, and I didn't want reality intruding on feelings I had yet to identify. I settled into the veranda swing and pushed off, letting the swing lull me back into the sweet memory of the evening. I hugged myself and sighed deeply.

All is right with the world, I thought. *At least until Smokey finds out about Tag.*

❧❧❧

Oklahoma! opened the next night. Mother and I always attended premiere performances at the Mossy Creek Theater. I nodded at her excited chitchat as we waited for the curtain to rise, but my mind was anywhere but on the play. Tag waved at me from a row nearby. Mother pretended not to notice.

At intermission, Tag stopped me as I went to the concession stand for drinks. Like a schoolgirl, my pulse raced, and I could hardly speak. He leaned close and, for a moment, I thought he might kiss me.

"You should stop by and smell my studio," he said.

"So you like the scent of muskadoodle berry?"

"Makes me positively giddy."

I pointed to his eye. "Your shiner looks much better tonight."

"I put the orange fragrance ring on it."

Tag walked me back to my seat, though I warned him that he'd run into Mother. I was wrong. She wasn't there at all. I soon spotted her sitting with Ida Hamilton Walker. Mother appeared to be talking Ida's ears off, while Ida listened patiently.

"Would you like to sit down?" I asked Tag, knowing Mother wouldn't return. Ida had the best seats in the house.

He looked at me wickedly. "Are you sure you can stand the public scandal of being seen with someone other than Smokey?"

"I'll manage."

So he sat. From that moment on, I don't know how the show went. For all I know, the actors could have been naked. Tag's arm, tucked comfortably behind me, was all I could think about. I desperately wanted to rest my head on his shoulder, but resisted. No matter how I felt, I really didn't want to deal with the gossip. Not yet.

During *Oklahoma's* famous dream sequence Anna Rose—playing the part of Laurie—snagged her beautiful wedding gown on an uneven board on the stage's old wooden floor. Fortunately, the dress's lace hemming didn't rip. Anna gracefully bent down and released it before continuing the scene. "That dress is one I donated," Tag whispered. "My ex-wife wore it in the wedding scene for a dinner theater production of *The Sound Of Music*. She was such a bad singer that old people threw breadsticks at her."

"But the dress is gorgeous," I whispered back. I glanced at Mother. She was on the edge of her seat, gazing at the dress greedily. *Oh, no you don't,* I thought. *That one's going to be locked up tight. I'll make sure Anna Rose knows you're eyeing it.*

Too soon, the show was over, and the lights came up. Tag and I rose with the rest of the crowd for the standing ovation, then filed out into the lobby. I searched the crowd for mother but couldn't find her. "You look worried," Tag said.

I glanced around furtively. "Everyone's staring at us."

"That's just because I'm so good looking."

"I have to take this seriously."

Tag sighed. "All right. I'll see you later." He squeezed my hand and left me there alone. I dodged the curious stares in his wake and spoke innocently to people as they drifted by. Ida waved goodnight as she went past. Where was Mother?

"Ida!" I called and hurried after her. "Ida! Wait up a minute."

"What is it? It was good to see you sitting with Tag Garner tonight. I like to know our new residents are getting a personal welcome. I knew when I leased the shop space to him that he'd fit in. Confess, now. Are you dating him?"

"I'm not sure what you'd call it. Where's my mother?"

Ida frowned. "She said she was going to meet you outside the lobby."

I hurried outside and spotted Amos.

"Amos, have you seen Mother?"

"Not since intermission. I thought she was with Ida."

"She's disappeared."

"I'll radio Mutt. He's on patrol tonight. He'll keep an eye out for her."

"She's probably walking home or something. Maybe she went over to the café for a cup of coffee and some pie." I followed the theater crowd up Main Street to Mama's and peered through the curtained windows. Mother wasn't there.

Praying she'd headed home, I started that way. Halfway across the square, I spotted her near the statue of General Hamilton. "Mother!"

She spun around and nearly fell, but caught herself on a bench. "Oh, is that you, dear?"

"Mother, where have you been? I've been looking everywhere for you."

"Obviously not, or you would have found me." She turned to hurry on her way.

"Where are you going in such a mad-dash hurry?"

"Home. It's late, and I need my beauty rest."

For an eighty-year-old woman she moved remarkably well. It was all I could do to keep up. I frowned at the statue. She spent a lot of time there, sitting on a bench. I'd never thought that unusual, before. You see, my father's family had been in the granite business when the statue was erected, back in the late 1800s. Great-Great Grandfather Hart designed and built the base. We had a sentimental attachment to the statue. Or at least to its base.

"Mother, walk more slowly, will you? I'd hate for you to trip over something and break a hip." I caught her arm, and we sauntered along together the rest of the way.

"Did you enjoy the show, Maggie?" she asked.

"Yes, did you?"

"Yes. Especially after I saw you sitting with Mr. Garner."

"He's a nice man who has forgiven me for my mother's life of crime."

Mother laughed merrily.

That worried me.

❦❦❦

Needless to say, I slept little that night and finally dozed around dawn. A banging on the door woke me. "What now?" I asked myself as I dragged on a bathrobe and rushed to see who could be dumb enough to knock on a Mossy Creek door before the breakfast biscuits were in the oven.

Through the ornamental glass, I saw Smokey. Though the glass distorted his image, I realized he wasn't his usual cheerful self. I twisted the key in the lock and pulled the door open. "Smokey, what a surprise."

"I heard you went out with Garner. And I'm mad."

"Listen, I'm sorry I didn't tell you. Tag and I—"

"I can smell like roses if I want to. I can grow my hair long and put a blue skunk streak in it. I'd get fired from the forestry service, but still—"

"Smokey, it's not that. It's just—"

"You don't have to explain. I saw him on this veranda just a minute ago."

"What?" I glanced around. There was a package on the swing. Holding my bathrobe tightly around me, I retrieved the package. "He only came here to deliver this."

"I can smell like roses and deliver packages."

"Smokey, please—"

"We're finished, you and me."

"We never started."

"Well, uh, oh, never mind." He scowled, stomped down the veranda steps, got into his Jeep, and roared away.

I went back into the house and settled onto the sofa in my office. Morning sunshine poured through a window as I opened the box. Inside was the rhinestone Cinderella tiara and the big glass slippers, sparkling in the light. I read Tag's note. *Your mother, aka "Swifty," left these on my doorstep during the night. I want you to give them back to her, or wear them yourself. I never thought of myself as anybody's Prince Charming, before, but for you, I'll try.*

I smiled. Not a cultured, pretty smile, but a big old dumb uncontrollable smile, the kind that just bubbles up when you least expect it. It was going to be a great day.

I was wrong. A few minutes later, Anna Rose showed up at my front door. "Maggie! God, I'm glad you're up."

"Great show last night."

"I thought so, too. Until this morning."

"What happened? I know it can't be a bad review. The paper isn't out until Wednesday."

"I wish. The wedding gown is missing."

"What? How is that possible?"

"I don't know. I just don't know. Nobody remember seeing it after the show last night. I need that dress back right away, Maggie. There's no way I can get another one before tonight's show."

"Let me put on some clothes." I raced upstairs to change. I looked into Mother's room but found the bed made and the room empty.

Anna and I went over to the theater and searched everywhere. The dress was definitely gone. I wanted to cry. "Anna, did you see Mother last night?"

"No."

"Could she have gotten backstage after the show without anyone noticing?"

"Sure."

"Where would the dress have ended up after the actress took it off?"

Anna took me to the wardrobe storage room, which was right beside the theater's back exit. I opened the door and walked outside in a small parking lot behind the building. "Ah, hah." I bent and picked up a tiny white seed pearl. A few feet farther I found another. The trail led around the corner of the building, up the side, and onto the sidewalk fronting Main Street. Anna and I stood there, looking across at the square. "Let's go."

We picked up seed pearls all the way to General Hamilton's statue. I stood there looking at the base. I began to run my hands over the large, square granite stones and the bronze plaques that listed Mossy Creekites who had served not only on both sides of the Civil War, but in every war since. "What are you doing?" Anna asked.

"Trying to see whether an old story in my family is true or not." Feeling around the edge of one of the bronze plaques, I gasped. My fingers found a hidden groove behind the plaque. I slid two fingers inside and touched what felt like a metal lever. I pushed down on it. The bronze plaque opened like a door. "Look!"

"What?" Anna asked, peering over my shoulder.

There was the wedding dress, folded neatly across the stolen flea market trunk and a pile of other pilfered items from years past. I stuck my head inside the opening and looked around. The hidden space was large enough to hold much more. Was Mother only getting started?

"I see you found my stash."

I banged my head as I spun around to face my mother. "I always thought the stories about Great-Great Grandpa building a secret compartment into the statue's base were a joke."

"No, your daddy knew about it. When we were dating, he used to leave flowers and notes and little boxes of candy for me in there. It was our secret. We called it our hope chest." Tears filled her eyes. "After he deserted you and me, I couldn't bear to leave it empty."

I sagged. "But why did you steal the wedding dress, Mother?"

"It's for you." She cried and touched the statue's base with trembling fingers. "I had to make a hope chest for you, too."

Now, we were both crying.

❦❦❦

Mother and I sat on a park bench looking across Main Street toward Tag's studio and shop. She placed the box containing the tiara and the slippers between us. Mother ran one hand over my hair, a gesture I'd loved many times as a little girl. "I was so afraid you were going to start dating Smokey," she said. "I couldn't let that happen."

"So you deliberately provoked Tag, just so I'd meet him?"

"Look at it this way, dear. I got you two past all the preliminaries right up front. I saved you months or maybe even years of beating around the bush."

"Okay, Mother, but he and I have just started getting to know each other. Don't get your hopes up."

The choice of words made her smile wistfully. "At least you know where I store them, now. In our hope chest. And we *do* have hope."

I smiled, but she was right. There was something different about the way I saw Tag, about the way I felt, already. Too many times, I'd fallen for the wrong kind of man. Now, maybe, thanks to Mother, I would fall for the right one.

"There he is," Mother whispered.

Tag walked out of his shop, a broom in

hand. He started to sweep the sidewalk, then spotted us and halted. The expression on his face settled somewhere between a cocky smile and a worried frown.

"Go for it," Mother urged. "I may be crazy, but I know a good man when I steal from one."

I took a deep breath and stood. I put the tiara on my head and slipped my bare feet into the oversized Cinderella slippers. A huge smile burst across Tag's face. The summer sun warmed my face, and the sunshine of Tag's smile warmed the rest of me. Today was a brand new day. The air was scented with flowers and possibilities.

Hope blooms forever, with a little help from a thief of hearts.

The Mossy Creek Gazette
215 Main Street—Mossy Creek, Georgia

FROM THE DESK OF KATIE BELL, BUSINESS MANAGER

Dear Victoria,

Let me tell you, you English folk haven't got us Mossy Creekites beat when it comes to neighborhood watering holes. We've got O'Day's, the only true Irish bar in this whole part of the state. The people down in Bigelow say the pub is just more evidence that Mossy Creekites can't bear to be completely respectable. *We* say we're just honoring a fine tradition of social libations.

Let me explain. The farmers around here used to earn their spring seed money by selling illegal corn liquor. We called it "moonshine" because most of it was made in backwoods stills by the light of the moon. When Lionel Bigelow declared war on Mossy Creek, the first thing he did was bust up all our liquor stills.

I don't think we've ever forgiven him for that!

Me? I'm a soda fountain kind of gal. I like my drinks with a scoop of ice cream floating on top and an extra splash of vanilla flavoring. By the way, (don't tell my husband Leo) but Michael is a good-looking, unmarried Irishman with dark blue eyes and a sense of humor that'll warm a woman's body *without* a toddy. But the first annual Mossy

Creek dart contest at his pub was serious business, and yet another battlefield where Mossy Creekites and Bigelowans duked it out for the greater glory of town pride.

I hope you get the point.

Yours in pun,

Katie O' Bell

Michael

Your Cheatin' Dart

As they say on TV: There are a thousand stories in the naked city. And then we have Mossy Creek, where there're at least a thousand and one.

My name is Michael Conners. When I moved to Mossy Creek five years ago, after working and tending bar in the big city suburbs of Chicago, I thought I'd seen everything: from gang bangers, to mob wannabes, to crooked politicians (are there any other kind?). I'd had enough of the crooks and criminals in the world. Mossy Creek seemed like a green oasis, settled between the sturdy arms of the mountains, protected from the ever more daft world outside.

But there's daft, and then there's *daft*.

I'm a native Irishman, you see, with all that entails. We recognize daft in its many forms.

There's an old joke that goes, "God created whiskey so the Irish couldn't rule the world." Whiskey runs in our family, you might say. Not as a vice, although I've been known to down a dram or two, but as a living. My father owned a pub in Chicago like his father, who owned one in County Cork. Now I was the proud owner of O'Day's in Mossy Creek—named after my sainted mother's family for good luck, since they were all legendary drinkers, too.

Not difficult to find, O'Day's is right next door to the town's tiny city hall. Coming into a small, protestant Southern town in a dry county five years ago had been a challenge to political correctness, but to my surprise the Mossy Creekites welcomed me with open arms. "We're always amenable to the right new ideas," the mayor said—after I poured her a drink of the best whiskey I owned.

The fine citizenry voted a liquor ordinance into law as quick as you please, and my business became the first and only Irish pub in Bigelow County. I rented myself a handsome brick shop that had once been the Mossy Creek General Store. It's a place of fond memories, the locals tell me—games of checkers and cards up front, a little homemade liquor in the back room. And best of all, it's located, like I said, right beside city hall. I figure the best place to sell liquor is to those who need it most in order to sleep at night—lawyers and, without a doubt, politicians.

We Irish have an uncanny knack for

finding our place in the world. Unfortunately, that place is rarely situated in Ireland herself, although we love her dearly. And in Georgia, from the earliest times on, the Irish have moved in and set up shop giving upstanding Bible Belt cities like Savannah and Atlanta an excuse to have a drunken parade on St. Paddy's Day. Faith, we even named one city in the southern part of the state *Dublin* in honor of our blessed homeland. We Irish have our moments. But on the whole, if we're not too busy drinking whiskey, then we're busier selling it.

There had yet to be a St. Paddy's Day parade in Mossy Creek, though I was working on it. I had learned quickly that Mossy Creek had its own traditions, and a bunch of drunken pseudo-Irishmen had nothing on Mossy Creekites in a lather. Did I mention. . .daft?

"We'll give you Labor Day," the mayor told me. "See what kind of happy trouble you can make out of that."

Now, an Irishman can make trouble out of nothing, so I founded the All-County Mossy Creek Labor Day Dart Competition.

For quite some years, there's been a dart contest held in the back room of the Steak and Mug restaurant down in Bigelow. Always in November, a time when the weather, rainy and cold, forced folks inside for their amusements. Always held on Saturday night—which gave year-round residents an excuse to turn off the

TV, come out and have dinner, then settle down to some serious competition before the official start of the holiday season.

Did I mention the word, serious?

I've been around serious contenders. Men who might have a potbelly and a bald head but who can whip you at golf with one club tied behind their back. Or women who don't hesitate to slide tins of freshly baked chocolate chip cookies into the hands of a priest to make sure their sons serve as altar boys for Christmas Midnight Mass. But I've never seen anything like the rivalry between these two towns—Mossy Creek and Bigelow.

It amounts to civil war on a different level, and there's nothing 'civil' about it. I don't really know all the whys and the wherefores. . . Suffice it to say, when I moved to Mossy Creek I was informed that anyone from Bigelow was suspect and most downright untrustworthy. I stepped right in the middle of the feud with my Labor Day dart contest, pre-empting the annual Bigelow event's thunder and upping the ante in the bad feelings competition.

Who am I to argue? A transplanted Irishman whose own family holds its share of brotherly grudges? Oh yeah, did I forget to mention the other thing we Irish are famous for? Fighting.

But as I told Police Chief Royden, it wasn't me who started the fight which broke up the first All-County Mossy Creek Labor Day

Dart Competition. And I tried my damndest to make Buddy Daily put his clothes back on.

But I guess I ought to start from the beginning.

It was a dark and stormy night. . . Oh, sorry, that's more of my Irish blarney showing. All the nights in Ireland seem to be dark and stormy.

Now where were we? Oh yes, in my pub, O'Day's, on a Monday in the first week of September. Just a hint of fall in the air, the days still hot but the nights cool, the dogwood leaves starting to blush red. I'd been setting up all day for the holiday crowd, had to rent extra chairs and hire one of the local men, the aforesaid Buddy Daily, to help pumping beer.

In order to put the perfect head on Irish stout, a certain amount of time is involved. With the added customers the event would bring, I knew I wouldn't have time to finesse each glass to the perfect ratio of one-third head, two-thirds brew. Buddy, who in the past had more experience downing drinks than serving them, proved adequate with a little training. And as he said, he needed the work. He'd been staying in a cheap monthly hotel in Bigelow but wanted to get a good job and live in Mossy Creek. I can't fault the man for wanting to improve himself.

Did I also mention that we Irishmen are good listeners? I'd been nicknamed "Father Michael" for the multitude of drunken confessions I'd heard over the years.

But let me get back to this particular story. The first round of championship darts was to begin promptly at eight o'clock. The six finalists had already been culled the week before at the Bigelow VFW hall. Two teams for doubles and two for the individual title, divided equally between Bigelow and Mossy Creek. Around seven, the crowd began to trickle in, filling the seats closest to where the action would take place. The tables immediately behind the dart line had reserved signs on them for players.

By seven-thirty, I had begun to notice a pattern. The spectators had divided into two distinct groups—Bigelow on one side, Mossy Creek on the other, and I could see some wagering going on. Such gambling should have worried me, but at the time they were ordering pints as fast as I could serve them, so I ignored the observation in lieu of counting my profit in my head.

The more the merrier.

But they didn't get merrier. By the time the first team stepped up to the line, every seat was filled and the room had grown smoky and watchful. Someone had even unplugged the jukebox in the corner.

"Gentlemen, and ladies. . ." John D. Hayslett, a fine auto parts salesman if there ever was one, who was acting as the MC for the night, nodded toward the scant females scattered throughout the crowd. "Welcome! Our first competitors are from our own hometown, Mossy Creek—"

A chorus of cheers rose from the left side of the room, combined with a smattering of boos coming from the right. John D. patiently waited for order before continuing. After all, the contest was being held in Mossy Creek, and being a hometown son, John D. must have come to the conclusion he could handle the crowd any way he saw fit. And, if the blessed Bigelowans—"Big-e-loads," as we call them around the bar—didn't like it, they could always forfeit.

A man with an Irish heart, I thought proudly.

"Jimmy Partain and Will Stewart placed in the top five All-County down in Bigelow for the last two years and won the coveted Golden Dart for team play two years before that." Another round of applause halted John D., but only momentarily. People seemed anxious for the action to begin.

I took myself to the end of the bar in order to have a better view, leaving Buddy to handle the slowed requests from our one cocktail waitress, Regina Regina. Earlier, Buddy had painstakingly written down the numbers of each table in order to be more helpful. I didn't see any need for him to know which table got what drink—that was up to Regina—but I've always admired individual initiative.

"The second team is Dan Graham and his wife Laura. From Bigelow."

It could have been my imagination, but I thought I heard a slight hesitation in John D.'s voice, like even saying the name Bigelow out loud put a strain on his sensibilities. I learned later that John D. had visited the Grahams recently with the sole purpose of talking them into moving to Mossy Creek. They were too nice and too good at darts to be trapped in a sorry town like Bigelow. I never heard the exact offer, but whatever it was, Laura's mother lived in Bigelow, and Laura intended to see her children through the county high school down there before pulling up stakes.

The crowd reacted to this introduction in reverse—applause from the right, silence from the left. The dearth of boos demonstrated how badly the Mossy Creekites wanted the Grahams in *their* town and on *their* team.

"The rules for this evening are as follows: The game is 20-20, round robin, first out wins. Start when you're ready."

The players went through the rituals of checking the height of the new board on the paneled wall, pacing off the eight feet regulation distance, and discussing rotation of the horsehair. (Dartboards are made of horsehair.) I wasn't worried. I'd gone to great trouble to make sure the dart 'field' was regulation, even going so far as to install a chalkboard for scoring. If my adopted hometown was unhappy with the outcome of the tournament, I, at least, was determined it wouldn't be because of the facilities. My dad always said, "Don't do anythin' to get betwixt a man an' his drink, or between a man an' his darts."

The coin toss went against Mossy Creek, so Jimmy and Will had their work cut out for them. That along with the fact that Laura Graham seemed to be able to throw double twenties all night long. It was sad, really. I felt for the men, but the draw and follow through of Laura's throwing arm was something to behold.

In short order—that's less than a half hour in dart time—the Mossy Creek team was eliminated, and the Grahams had been crowned the champions. My brand-new Mossy Creek Labor Day Dart Competition trophy would go to Bigelow to be displayed in the window of Dan's Uncle Shorty's Ford Dealership. To add insult to injury, anyone in Mossy Creek who needed a new or used pickup truck would have to go to Shorty's for it and walk past the well-polished symbol of their shame. That or make the trip all the way to Atlanta.

In the break between games as wagers were being paid and another round of drinks were being ordered, I was forced to get back to work.

Now that the team competition had been decided, everyone's attention focused on the highlight of the evening: the individual event between Randy 'Punch' McPherson, who worked over at the Mossy Creek furniture factory, and William 'Tell' Chesney, a bank teller from the Bigelow National Bank.

As you might surmise from the nicknames, these men were serious darters, the real deal, although I believe Punch had acquired his name by virtue of the job he did at the factory rather than his darting expertise. He did have the size to do some damage as a pugilist, but he seemed to be the peaceful sort. That aside, facing anyone with the moniker "Tell" would be a challenge.

Both men had brought a table full of people for support, including their wives and, in Punch's case, his mother Miss Alameda McPherson. A regular at O'Day's, a dedicated scotch drinker, and a sports fanatic, Miss Alameda would cheer on two ants in a race for the sugar bowl if no other competitions were available. All in all, it was a rowdy crowd and getting rowdier with every downed beer and shot. I noticed police officer Mutt Bottoms at a table in the back of the room and felt a little easier about my furniture not getting smashed to smithereens if a dispute arose.

When the time came for John D. to introduce the competitors he had to shout to get everyone's attention. Last minute bets were being hurriedly placed as he spoke: "From Bigelow, we have last year's All-County champion William Chesney."

Someone from the Bigelow side yelled out, "That's *Tell* Chesney!"

John D. held up a hand in apology, "Like I said, William 'Tell' Chesney."

"And from Mossy Creek, our hometown favorite," he paused for effect, "Punch McPherson!"

Boos and hisses sounded from the Bigelow side of the room, and a few of the heavier drinkers banged their pint glasses on the tables like a bunch of drunken Vikings at a woolly mammoth feast. Miss Alameda shouted something over the din that sounded like, "Oh, can it!" But, I couldn't be sure.

That's when Tell began to unpack his darts.

The room fell silent. This time I could hear Miss Alameda's cry as loud as a banshee's wail.

"Those are Hammerheads!"

"They're made of titanium, too," Tell informed her and the onlookers in a smug tone.

Later, I would learn that he'd been sponsored by the Bigelow Women's Club, who'd put on three spaghetti dinners and two bake sales to buy him those darts.

"That's cheating!" Miss Alameda declared. "Those darts have retractable points!"

Half the Mossy Creek side vocally

agreed with her.

John D. was given the unenviable task of delivering bad news. "We have no rule in place to disqualify any type of legal dart."

"Those aren't legal! They're titanium, for cripe's sake!" Miss Alameda hated to see her son at a disadvantage, especially when she had fifty dollars wagered on the outcome.

The rest of the Mossy Creekites agreed with her.

"There's nothing I can do about it," John D. confessed, although I could see by the expression on his face that next year the Bigelow darters would be facing Mossy Creek titanium if he had to buy the set himself.

Miss Alameda stood to her full height of four foot nothing and faced Tell. "Well, you had just better keep your toes behind that line. I'm gonna be watching you. We don't like cheaters here in Mossy Creek."

Whether it was sarcasm or belated good manners, Tell simply replied, "Yes ma'am."

After a few more huffing breaths and an evil eye that would make most men shuffle their feet in a hurry to leave, Miss Alameda settled back into her seat. Then she dug in her purse until she found her glasses and put them on.

The coin toss went in Punch's favor, but Miss Alameda still demanded to see the coin herself, with her bifocals. Regina, the cocktail waitress, hurried over to deliver a new round of drinks to Miss Alameda's table in hopes of lowering the old lady's blood pressure and blunting her killer instinct.

The first round was even. Both men hit three twenties. The room, held to an uneasy murmur during the actual throwing, erupted into cheers and shouts of certain victory. The Mossy Creekites composed a cheer of, "Titanium or not, Punch is hot!" and repeated it until John D. called for quiet.

Punch, smiling at his friends in the audience, picked up a new, full pint to salute them before taking a long pull. He wiped his mouth on the back of his hand to the cheers of his compatriots, but then he frowned. He raised the glass and looked at it.

"There's something wrong with this beer," he said in a room suddenly silent enough to hear the foam rise to the top of a stout.

Now, those are simple words. Words that wouldn't alarm anyone—except a bartender. I suddenly felt the ulcer I'd had five years before begin to warm up. I watched with a sinking feeling as Miss Alameda demanded to taste her son's brew.

After one gulp, she turned her beady eyes toward the bar. "There's bloody Irish whiskey in this," she proclaimed, and I had no reason to doubt her. After all, she'd been a regular at O'Day's long enough to prove she knew her way around a bar and the many spirits therein. "What are you tryin' to do?

Spike my boy's beer to get him drunk?"

When a person's life is in danger, a strange phenomenon happens in the mind. Time slows, possibilities waver, and most of all, you realize what you're going to miss in life. Right then, I missed the solid ash, major-league baseball bat I used to keep under the bar I ran in Chicago. I'd given it to the new owner when I left, thinking I was escaping the need to use it by moving to a calmer, more civilized place. Watching the growing amazement and anger on the faces of the crowd filling my pub that night, I knew I'd made a fatal error in leaving the bat behind.

"Let me taste it," I demanded, holding out my hand for the mug. There was always the slim possibility that Punch's sainted mother was wrong. Beyond that, I needed time to think.

Miss Alameda marched over and shoved the glass at me across the bar. I tasted it.

Jesus, Mary, and Joseph, she was right.

"Now, wait a minute," I said. "I had nothing to do with any spiking of drinks."

Miss Alameda just crossed her arms and scowled at me. A Mossy Creek fan sitting at the bar was a little more descriptive. "How about you step outside with me for a little dance in the parking lot," he said, pushing off his stool and bracing both hands on the bar.

"Hold it!" Regina shouted. "Michael didn't pour those drinks—" She pointed her finger at my temporary bar help, Buddy. "He did."

That was the instant I decided to give Regina a job for life. The crowd turned as one toward Buddy. He cringed back into the corner near the dish sink, hoping, I suppose, that no one would breach the sanctity of the bar itself.

Everyone seemed to freeze, except for Mutt Bottoms. I saw him slide from his seat and go to the pay phone on the wall. I prayed he was calling for help because right then, it looked pretty bleak for Buddy. And for my stock of expensive cognac he was splayed against.

"Give him over, Michael," one of the men at the bar said.

"Now, gentlemen," I put on my best blarney smile. "He's new. Tonight's his first night. Surely, he made a mistake, but—"

"They paid me to do it!" Buddy shouted, pointing directly at Mr. Tell 'Titanium.' "He said they always did it that way in Bigelow."

The leprechaun was out of the bag, so to speak. Before I could remember any vocabulary that might stop a lynching, three men shoved up the bar hatch and dragged Buddy out into the room. I looked at Mutt. He looked back at me. Then, he tried to block the troublemakers, but they dodged him. The best weapon I could find behind the bar was an industrial sized flashlight, so I picked it up. I made the sign of the cross, silently muttering an old Irish prayer, *May you be in heaven before the Devil knows you're dead*, and vaulted the bar to meet Mutt on the other side.

"What should we do with him?" One of the men asked the angry crowd.

Miss Alameda pushed her way to the front of the onlookers. "In the old days we woulda' tarred and feathered any cheatin' varmint from Bigelow!" she shouted, shaking a bony finger at a wide-eyed Buddy.

"Yeah! Let's take him over to Mossy Creek Paving And Grading. They've got tar!" someone in the crowd yelled.

"Now, Miss Alameda," Mutt said in a softer, slower tone, probably aimed at buying some time until reinforcements arrived. "Chief Royden wouldn't go for no tarrin'."

Miss Alameda seemed to consider that hitch before walking back to her table and picking up one of the dozen or so darts that belonged to her son. She returned to the center of the fray and held up the dart.

"How about just featherin'," she said with an evil smile. She ran one finger along the feathered shaft, and the three men holding Buddy tightened their grip.

"I say we finish the competition, but instead of hangin' the target on the wall, we hang it 'round this varmint's neck."

The crowd erupted into hooting and arguing. Depending on which side of the room, some thought it only fair; the rest were dead against it.

The men holding Buddy began pushing him towards the wall which held the target. "Somebody get some duct tape," one of them ordered.

Mutt had to raise his voice to be heard. "I can't let you do this!"

The men stopped.

One of them, Jerry I think his name was, faced Mutt and gave him a choice. "It's either this or we take him outside and make him sorry he ever stepped over the Mossy Creek line."

Mutt considered the options for a moment. He also glanced at his watch. In the interim, someone slapped a roll of duct tape into Jerry's hand. Finally Mutt nodded, not permission so much as recognition that something had to be done. Being taped up would cause less damage and take longer than a trip outside.

Jerry and his assistants pushed a terrified Buddy up against the wall, took down the target and placed it in the temporary bartender's hands.

Miss Alameda sauntered up to Buddy and pursed her lips. "I think we need to turn him around. I won't be responsible for puttin' out an eye, even in a Big-e-load cheater."

Buddy looked somewhat relieved and turned on his own. But when the duct tape wouldn't stick to his shirt properly, a new tragedy befell him.

"Take off your shirt," Jerry ordered.

Buddy didn't move right away, but when Jerry reached for the buttons himself, Buddy complied.

That's when a female voice somewhere in the crowd shouted, "Make him take off his pants, too!"

Over the roar of male laughter, Jerry ordered Buddy to comply.

Now it just isn't right to strip a man of his pride that way. Even though I had my own grudge rights, seeing that Buddy almost got me beaten to a pulp in my own pub, I still didn't think the punishment fit the crime.

"Don't do it, Buddy," I said.

All the men closest to the action turned at my words. I tightened my grip on the flashlight in my hand.

"It isn't right," I added.

Jerry and his friends took a few seconds to size me up. I'm not a giant by any means, but I'm big enough to inflict some damage in a fight. And, with four brothers, I'd had plenty of practice. I faced them, ready to give as good as I got.

Finally, Jerry said, "I'll give him the choice then." He turned to Buddy. "It's this—" he held up the target, "—or the parking lot. Which do you want?"

Buddy dropped his pants.

As soon as they had the target taped to their human backboard, the competition resumed. I remained in the front of the now standing-room-only crowd and watched each dart fly.

Buddy, left with only his socks and jockey shorts for decency, was shaking so badly the competitors were literally firing at a moving target. In the following round, each man hit the mark and the competition remained tied.

"Man, these guys are good." I heard someone say behind me. And I was forced to agree. At this rate, Buddy wouldn't have to worry about an inch of sharp steel, or titanium as the case may be, sticking into his back.

The next round was under way when there was a commotion at the front door. I turned to look over the heads of the crowd and saw Chief Royden, sweaty and looking ominous, pacing toward the center of the room with another uniformed officer at his back and Sandy Crane right behind them, trying to look official.

That's when the fight started.

From somewhere in the crowd, and I had a good suspicion where, a rogue dart was thrown toward the target. It hit Buddy almost dead center in his nether-end. A small dot of blood appeared in the cotton of his jockeys as Buddy let out a howl. Spinning around and ripping the tape away, he slugged the closest man to him, who happened to be Jerry.

♥♥♥

It took over an hour to straighten out the aftermath. Chief Royden threatened to clear the place and take everyone involved to jail. That announcement quieted the room, because everyone wanted to stay to see what the official ruling on the dart competition would be. Buddy was treated for his puncture wound and Jerry for a split lip by Dr. Champion's nurse, who happened to be in attendance, while each participant recited his or her side of the story, so to speak.

The best excuse came from Miss Alameda. "Why Chief, didn't you ever play pin the tail on the donkey when you were a kid?" she asked with an innocent air. "I used to be real good at it."

This confirmed my suspicion about the origin of the rogue dart.

"Miss Alameda," Chief Royden said in a long-suffering tone, "you don't play that game using a person for the donkey."

"Well in this case," Miss Alameda sniffed, "that *ass* deserved it. He's a cheat; he admitted it. He was helpin' Tell Chesney steal the trophy as sure as I'm standin' here. Ask anybody."

When half the room agreed and the Bigelow contingent remained suspiciously quiet, the Chief went on. "Who won?"

"Nobody yet. It was a tie when I—when we got interrupted," Miss Alameda answered.

Chief Royden drew himself up to his full

227

height, standing a good head taller than the rest of the crowd. He rested his hands on his hips like he was addressing a bunch of third graders on the ball field. "This competition is the start of a new tradition in Mossy Creek, and you've acted like a bunch of children," he said, sounding thoroughly disgusted. "I'm shutting it down."

"But what about the trophy?" someone in the crowd asked.

The chief looked from one competitor to the other. "The trophy will be shared this year. Six months in Bigelow and six months in Mossy Creek. I officially call this competition a draw."

A chorus of groans and muttered curses echoed through the room, in anticipation of having to take back the many wagers that had been placed on the outcome, no doubt. A few looked glad they didn't lose any money, at least.

"Now, I want you all to be sure you pay your bar tabs before you leave."

"And please don't forget to tip your waitress," I added helpfully, as I winked at Regina. "We'll meet back here next year for a, hopefully, more civilized event."

Chief Royden looked at the erstwhile Buddy and said, "Buddy, you can put your clothes back on now."

❧❧❧

As I said before, there are a thousand and one stories in Mossy Creek, and, for my part, I hope I never again have to bear witness to Buddy Dailey's nakedidity.

Next Labor Day, I think I'll hire a bouncer or put Chief Royden at a reserved table on the front row. That way he can keep an eye on Miss Alameda. And I won't have to invest in a new baseball bat.

From the Desk of Katie Bell

Dear Victoria,

Since the Labor Day brawl, we've all been laying low. I swear every time we see a stranger in a dark suit these days we think it's some spy of Ham Bigelow's.

By now, you've figured out that everybody in Mossy Creek knows everybody else's business. It's just an accepted fact that our news flies faster than a chicken being chased by a cat. It used to be that we could just pick up the phone and ask the operator what we wanted to know, like, "What time is it?" or "Who was that at dinner with so-and-so last night?" or "Ask Chief Roydon if he fixed my parking ticket yet, and tell him I'm bringing the homemade fruitcake over in the morning." That would have been Amos's ol' daddy, Battle, not Amos.

But every now and then, something still comes along that surprises us all. Until last month, if you wanted coffee in Mossy Creek you perked it yourself or stopped in at Mama's All You Can Eat Café for a jolt of plain ground Joe that could scald the grease off an axle. That was before Jayne Austin Reynolds came along. Named after your very own Jane Austen, see? We worried she might not like us if we didn't drink our brew with our pinkies raised. We are not uncouth people—we like our touches of elegance. After all, we were

willing to fight for Isabella's elegant Englishman!
But it turned out that Jayne's problem with us was
right next door, in the form of Ingrid Beechum. You
remember Ingrid? Bob the Flying Chihuahua's
mother? Ingrid's had a bad year, and I won't pass
judgement on her.

I'll just let the facts do that for me.

Oh, by the way, just disregard the Gazette's
reference to Jayne's trouble with the nursing
home. No charges were ever filed. You'll appreciate the prank, being English and a tea drinker. In
the end, it all worked out. It always does, in Mossy
Creek.

Your friend with the upturned pinkie,

Katie

Jayne

The Naked Bean

I arrived in Mossy Creek in late November, possibly the worst time of year to open a new shop. The tourist traffic is sparse then, and the locals hunker down for the winter holidays. Icy rain soaked my new hometown, and fog rolled in from the mountains. Half the citizenry went into hibernation the week I arrived, and I felt alone in a ghostly world. I looked at my name on the shop's lease. "That Jayne Reynolds must be an idiot," I said aloud, as if someone else had signed the paperwork. Indeed, I didn't know who I was anymore. My husband had died only two months before, after a long illness. I was only 34 years old, but felt ancient. I couldn't bear to tell anyone in Mossy Creek about my widowhood, my grief, or the nourishing secret I had brought with me to my new town; it was easier to live silently among strangers, pretending I was brand new.

I knew only this much: My future

depended on beans.

Coffee beans. And *human beans*.

"God brought us here as naked human bein's," my grandmother lectured when I was a child growing up with her in a small town south of Atlanta. "And low or high, naked human bein's we all remain." Grandma's country dialect was abetted by tobacco chaws and a thick drawl, so I thought she was saying naked human *beans*. I studied the intricate, twining pole beans that climbed her garden stakes every summer. Finally, I understood. Like beans, people were all the same under their tough green hides.

"Promise me," my husband Matthew said, "that you'll do something crazy and full of joy after I'm gone. Remember what you've told me. We're all just naked human beans."

This was that crazy promise—moving to a new town, giving up my safe job as an insurance adjuster down in Atlanta, opening a coffee shop. The joy, however, had not yet come. I cried quietly and often behind the doors of my lonely new business and in the tiny apartment above it, where I lived with my cat Emma.

Next door, the town's bakery seemed just as gloomy. The owner, Ingrid Beechum, had gone on vacation after Thanksgiving. I heard she was a widow, too. BEECHUM'S, her large, white sign said, as if the whole world knew that name meant fine baked goods. Her sprawling turn-of-the-century brick building made my little two-story clapboard shop feel like a doll's teacup sitting next to a latte mug.

I wandered over during dry spells and peered through the dark windows. Her bakery was beautiful, with handsome white counters, scrubbed yellow linoleum floors, old-fashioned display cases, and a large menu board listing mouth-watering selections. It radiated a homey success I envied. Inspired, I pasted a handwritten Grand Opening sign to my shop's wavy glass doors.

Gourmet Coffees And Teas. Pirollines. Biscotti. And A Friendly Cat.

Mayor Walker came by several times to see if I was doing enough business to pay the rent, I suspect, since she was my landlord. "You'll be fine when the weather clears," she told me. "Plus the Christmas shoppers will begin to come through town. And you'll have more traffic after Ingrid reopens her bakery. It's always crowded."

"I'm really looking forward to meeting Mrs. Beechum. I'm sure we're going to be good neighbors. Maybe we can do some advertising together. That'd be perfect. A bakery and a coffee shop."

Mayor Walker pulled a cashmere scarf higher above the collar of her trim wool jacket, as if protecting her throat. Her mouth flexed. She seemed to be considering some frank answer to my naïve hopes, but then she simply smiled. "Sometimes we Mossy Creekites are a little standoffish at first. Let me know how you get along with her. And don't worry." She left without offering another word.

I should have realized that was a warning.

❦❦❦

The rain ended, and the skies over the mountains turned a bright, cold blue. My spirits rose a little. As I cleaned the cappuccino machine in the shop's small kitchen one afternoon, I looked out the front windows and saw a rusty van pull up. Mossy Creek Woodworks. My sign had arrived.

I slung one of my hand-knitted shawls around my tie-dyed sweatshirt—I had learned to knit, quilt, and tie-dye to keep my mind occupied each time my husband, Matthew, was in the hospital—and rushed outside. The handsome hardwood trees of the town square cast sharp, leafless shadows across the van. A shaggy old man wrestled a large, canvas-wrapped rectangle from the van's open back doors. "Howdy do, good-lookin'," he drawled at me.

I smiled at his grizzled flirtation. Foxer Atlas was a harmless lady's man. He looked like Popeye. "I can't wait to see my sign, Mr. Atlas!"

"It's almost as pretty as you are." Foxer tugged at the canvas, and it fell to the ground with dusty drama.

Goosebumps ran down my spine. I gazed lovingly at the walnut wood outlined in white trim around large, scrolled letters in a café-au-lait color. Coffee colors.

The Naked Bean.

"You did a good job, Mr. Atlas," I said softly. He toed his grimy work shoes together as if Olive Oyl had kissed him. I wiped my eyes. "Would you like a cup of coffee to help me celebrate?"

"Well, sure. I never turn down a treat from one of my girlfriends."

I hurried inside and fixed him a French blend in a heavy ceramic mug, then poured some for myself in a delicate china cup Matthew had given me one Christmas. When I returned I set a tea saucer full of cream on the sidewalk for my cat. Cats should never be left out of celebrations. They have known since the ancient Egyptians worshiped them that their feline approval equals a blessing from the gods. Fat, irascible Emma did not seem very divine as she slurped from the saucer.

Foxer and I raised our cups to the new sign. "Here's to The Naked Bean," I said hoarsely. *Oh, Matthew, I miss you.*

"Here's to The Nekkid Bean." Foxer chortled.

"The *what*?" a high-pitched Southern female voice demanded. "You named this place what?"

I blinked and looked around. Emma hissed. A wiry woman stood in the open doorway of Beechum's. Her flour-dusted pink apron swathed her blue jeans and checkered blouse. She planted her fists on her hips. Cold blue eyes didn't blink beneath a spidery hair net that flattened her thick, graying, brown hair into a stern hair beanie. She made me think of a tightly braided voodoo doll I'd seen once during a New Orleans vacation.

"I beg your pardon?"

"You can't put up that tacky sign on the town square." She waved her hand toward Main Street. "What next? Maybe Pearl Quinlan should rename her shop 'Bare Butt Books.' And maybe Rosie can change the café's name to 'Mama's Shake Your Booty Lounge.'"

Heat rose in my face. Beside me, Foxer shuffled from one foot to the other. "Afternoon, Miz Beechum," he said lamely.

"Don't you 'Afternoon' me, Foxer."

"It's just a funny little sign. Nothin' wrong with *nekkid*."

"Your judgement doesn't count for much, you dirty old man."

So this was my neighbor, Ingrid. "Mrs. Beechum," I said in a strangled voice. "I think you're overreacting. Let me explain the name. And let me introduce myself—"

"Oh, I know who you are. The famous author." Sarcasm dripped from her voice. "Miss Jane Austen!"

I groaned. My mother was a high school English teacher and a lover of Jane Austen's novels. "It's Jayne with a 'y', and Austin with an 'i'," I explained tightly. "And my married name is Reynolds. So I'm Jayne Austin Reynolds. Jayne Reynolds."

"I don't care if you're Wilma Shakespeare, you're not putting up that pornographic sign next to my bakery."

"If you have a problem, take it up with Mayor Walker. She approved my sign."

"I don't believe you."

"That's too bad." Suddenly, from the corner of my eye, I saw Emma crouch. She crept toward the open door of Ingrid Beechum's bakery. I leapt to catch her before she launched herself at whatever was inside the building. I was too late.

Ingrid yelped as Emma zoomed past her. I heard the shriek of a small animal being walloped inside the bakery. A pale brown Chihuahua shot out the doorway, with Emma behind him. She chased him across our side of Main Street, which circled the town square. A pickup truck braked just in time to miss both animals. Emma rolled the tiny dog like a champion wrestler. She boxed him around the head, then pranced with every hair on her considerable body fluffed out and her tail bowed like a cobra's neck. The Chihuahua, yelping, hid under an azalea shrub.

"Oh, Emma," I groaned as I ran after her,

with Ingrid close behind. I threw my shawl over my maniacal calico cat and hoisted her into my arms.

Ingrid, cursing, pulled her shivering little dog from under the shrub. "Bob, Bob, its all right, Bob, it's not a hawk, you're not going to be carried off again," she crooned. She hugged him to her chest then turned to me furiously. "You're nothing but bad luck. You and your damned sign and your damned cat don't belong here."

"Mrs. Beechum, your dog is, well, he's peeing on your arm."

Her face turned beet red. "He's had a bad year." She walked back to her shop with Bob, the incontinent Chihuahua, held out from her body like a wet rat. She shut her shop doors. Hard.

I wearily lugged Emma back to my own stoop. Foxer Atlas stood on the sidewalk where we'd left him. He gaped at me. "Cutie, how'd you get Ingrid Beechum so mad at you so quick?"

"I honestly don't know."

"This ain't good. She's got a lot of say-so around here. If she don't like you, you're in trouble. You might as well be the town Jezebel, now." He rushed to his van and drove away, leaving me standing there, alone and confused, on the sidewalk of my new home.

My heart sank.

❦❦❦

The next day I dressed in a new skirt and blazer, then set out in my small Honda down South Bigelow Road. As I left town, steep hillsides loomed around me in the shadows of the old mountains. Tiny waterfalls trickled down craggy granite faces rimmed with diamonds of ice. Majestic laurel and rhododendron made dark green islands in the winter forest.

I loved this wild northern end of Bigelow County and the isolated mountain valley that enclosed Mossy Creek. Not long before Matthew died, we drove up from Atlanta to camp in the mountains. After a day or two, I could tell Matthew was more tired than he wanted to admit. I faked a sprain in my back. We got out a map and looked for the nearest town.

Mossy Creek. We loved it from the moment we drove across one of its rumbling wooden bridges. The namesake creek circled all of downtown, making a pretty moat. We spent the weekend at the Hamilton House Inn. We made love and snuggled and felt safe. It was our last, blessed vacation together.

My heart filled with those memories as I reached the driveway at Hamilton Farm. A breathtaking expanse of handsome pastures surrounded me on either side of the road. Milk cattle grazed on the rolling, pale-green vista. I felt very small, and very much a stranger. My resolve began to fail.

I pulled into the farm entrance and stopped my car between two stone pillars half-covered in ivy. What was I going to ask Mayor Walker to do about Ingrid? Ingrid Beechum was a native Mossy Creekite. She'd run the bakery for forty years, and her parents had owned it before that. Who was I? A nobody with a controversial sign and an attack cat.

As I muttered dire warnings to myself my gaze rose to the tall white Hamilton Farm corn silo. It towered nearby, just inside the pasture fence along the road. Painted in fat black letters high on its side, facing traffic headed north into Mossy Creek, was the slogan the town had adopted over a century earlier: Ain't Going Nowhere, And Don't Want To.

Maybe nobody in Mossy Creek wanted the town to change. Maybe Ingrid Beechum was the voice of the people. I drove through a patch of forest, then emerged between the wide lawns of the Hamilton homestead. My breath caught. The grand old Victorian house was framed by rounded mountains and shaded by giant, bare oaks. Barns and other outbuildings nestled among apple orchards and vegetable gardens. A small fountain splashed in an old watering trough, carved from solid rock. Softly outlined flower beds—now empty and mantled in thick wood mulch—showed where a riot of blooms would appear the next spring.

Two geese began to honk. A dozen fat dogs galloped from the house's wide veranda. Several cats stared at me lazily from behind the curtains of tall windows. By the time the housekeeper, a youngish blond woman, opened the front doors and waved at me, I was surrounded by a friendly menagerie. One of the geese pooped on the toe of my loafer.

"Sorry about that," the housekeeper said in a lilting Scottish accent, as I scrubbed my shoe on a grass welcome mat. June McEvers ushered me into a beautiful foyer decorated with antiques and portraits of Hamiltons. I noticed a collection of framed photographs arranged on a hall table. There was Ingrid, posed in a huge group of men and women on the lawn of this very house. "Is this a family picture of Mrs. Walker's?"

"Why, yes. Those are the Hamilton cousins."

Ingrid Beechum and Ida Hamilton Walker were cousins. I almost bolted. "I suppose a lot of people from the oldest Mossy Creek families are related by blood or marriage. And they must be very loyal to each other. It's all very private, isn't it?"

June smiled and nodded. "They're as thick as thieves. That's what Madam Ida says."

Madam Ida. I was being presented to the Queen of Mossy Creek in her own castle. June led me into a wonderful sunroom filled with plants and wicker furniture. A glass-topped table was set with linen and china for lunch. Large, brightly patterned cushions filled the chairs. Ida sat at a thick wooden table to one side. She was dressed in trim jeans and a dark blouse and sweater, with her graying auburn hair swept up in a French braid. Her elegant hands were swathed in greasy cotton gloves. She held a delicate can of oil in one and a large pistol in the other. On the table lay a dismantled shotgun, another pistol, and a number of small tools.

"Forgive me, Jayne," she said kindly, setting the pistol and oil down. "Let me just go wash my hands. I thought I'd finish cleaning my guns before you arrived for lunch."

"I don't mind. Do you like to target practice?"

"Target practice? Why, that's no challenge." She laughed, rolled her eyes as if I were making a joke and breezed from the room. Apparently, Hamilton guns were for shooting at real targets. Such as newcomers who crossed the wrong cousin? June touched my arm. I jumped.

"I'll bring you some tea," she said.

❧❧❧

Ida fixed her hypnotic green eyes on me over chicken salad. I could barely chew. "Troublemaker," she said, and smiled.

I raised my chin. "I won't change my

sign. It has sentimental meaning to me."

"Good for you. Ingrid will adjust."

I stared at her. "You don't mind that I upset her?"

"Ingrid is unhappy because I chose you over a tenant she suggested for your shop space. The tenant wasn't appropriate. I told Ingrid so."

"I see."

"I know you don't like to talk about yourself, but may I ask you one personal question?"

I flinched. I nodded tentatively.

"Why do you want to run a coffee shop?"

"I managed one when I was in college. I loved it. The aromas, the textures of the beans, the rich sound when you slide a scoop into the grounds. I loved the different teas we sold, and how ancient the art of tea drinking is. I love the way people enjoy sitting in a coffee shop. They talk, they listen to music, they think important thoughts. It feels very...civilized. Very warm, as if you can find answers in a place like that. And very full of life."

"What will you do if your shop fails?"

"I'll have to move back to Atlanta. Live with my mother. Go back to work as a claims adjuster for an insurance company. I've put all my savings into this venture." I paused, then met her gaze calmly. I was suddenly suffused with dignity. "But I'm not going to fail."

"Good. Then go ye and do battle with

Ingrid."

I sat back, relieved. The mayor's eyes gleamed. I'd earned her respect, to my astonishment. I was okay for now, but I reminded myself Ingrid was still her cousin.

And blood is always thicker than cappuccino.

❦❦❦

Five stern old ladies glared at me over my counter. "May I help you?" I asked politely, straightening from the oven with a baking sheet filled with shortbread cookies.

A tiny, blue-veined woman, dressed in a brown suit with a large silver cross pinned to her lapel, spoke to me in a trilling little voice. "Jane Austen?" I thought of the noise an irate cicada makes when you poke it with a twig.

"Jayne Austin Reynolds. Yes?"

"My name is Mrs. Adele Clearwater." Behind her, her companions clutched their purses and squinted at me gravely. Like their leader, they wore silver crosses. One impish little woman, her hair dyed fire-red beneath a feathered hat straight out of the 1950's, couldn't help craning her head and giving the aromatic shortbread an eager look.

Mrs. Clearwater cleared her throat. "We're from the Mossy Creek Ethics Society. We're a non-denominational prayer group and political action committee."

"Wonderful. What can I do for you?" I held out the baking sheet. "Please, won't you sample some of these shortbread cookies?"

Mrs. Red Hair said, "Oh, I will!" then snaked out a tiny hand. The others glared at her. She bit her lower lip and tucked the hand by her side.

Adele Clearwater straightened her shoulders. "We don't approve of you or your vulgar sign, and we intend to discuss the matter with our entire membership."

"I assure you, the sign's not meant to be vulgar. I'm going to write up a little story about why I chose the name. I'll post it by the doors."

"We're also here about your lack of personal ethics and compassion in stealing this space from another tenant."

My mouth popped open. "Excuse me?"

"You offered terms that the other prospective renter couldn't match. You outbid her, deliberately."

"Now look, that's not true. You can ask the mayor."

Mrs. Red Hair, God bless her, blurted out, "Maybe Ingrid misunderstood Ida's decision. After all, no one can talk Ida into doing something she doesn't believe in, so it could be that Ida just didn't want to rent the shop to Ingrid's daughter-in-law—"

"Nonsense, Eustene," Adele said, her voice full of warning. "Be quiet."

Eustene—Mrs. Red Hair—blanched.

The others looked at their leader worriedly.

Adele scowled at me. "Look to your conscience and seek redemption. We'll put you on our prayer support list. Good afternoon."

She turned and marched out with her troops behind her. Eustene glanced back at me and offered a wistful little wave. "Pride and Prejudice," she mouthed.

I strode next door. A customer was purchasing a sheet cake with "Happy Birthday Melvin" written on it in blue icing. Ingrid's assistant, a stocky, sour-faced Cherokee Indian named Betty Halfacre, never blinked at me when we passed on the street. She didn't blink now.

"Where's Mrs. Beechum?" I demanded.

"Too busy for you to be botherin' her," Betty Halfacre growled.

"Then she'll have to make time for botherin'."

I darted around a display case, pushed past a swinging door, and strode into a large, commercial kitchen. A pair of aproned women turned from their work areas to stare at me. I saw Ingrid through the open door of a cluttered little office. I saw no sign of Wee-Wee Bob, as I'd started calling him. Ingrid scowled up from her desk. Pink reading glasses teetered on her nose. A blue bandanna jauntily covered her hairnet. A gleaming pendant hung over her Falcons football jersey. *Mother*, the pendant spelled in tiny diamonds. As I entered the office, she touched it with a fingertip, as if to ward off evil.

I crowded up close to her desk and leaned over her. "Stop telling everyone I cheated to get the shop space."

She tossed her glasses aside. "You have a bad reputation. I can't stop rumors."

"You know I didn't bribe your cousin Ida to choose me as a tenant."

She stood, thrusting her face up to mine. "I never said you did. But what people decide about your behavior is *your* problem, not mine."

"Look, I'm sorry you wanted this shop for your daughter-in-law and you didn't get it. But please stop punishing me for a dispute that's really between only you and Mayor Walker."

The blood drained from her face. "Who told you about my daughter-in-law?"

"Could I talk to her for you? Has this shop-rental issue caused some kind of family rift?"

Ingrid slammed a fist on the desk. "You stay out of my family business. Now get out! Get out!"

I was stunned at her sudden distress. I saw pain and humiliation in her face. Wee-Wee Bob darted into the office and began barking. Betty Halfacre showed up with a rolling pin in one stocky brown hand.

I left before I got clobbered or Bob peed

on my tennis shoes.

That night I pondered Ingrid's fervent reaction as I stared at myself in the mirror of my bathroom medicine cabinet. I saw reddened eyes that had once been a clear, bright green, skin that had once been porcelain but was now too pale, and a mop of dull brown hair tied up in a brown scrunchie. There was a coffee stain on my pajama top, and my fingernails looked as if I'd clawed concrete with them. Did I seem pampered and conniving to Ingrid? Did I look like a threat to her private miseries?

"The name's Reynolds. Jayne Reynolds," I deadpanned in a tired James Bond voice. "And I like my vanilla latte shaken, not stirred."

I might as well try to shake things up.

❦❦❦

Magnolia Manor Nursing Home was located across from the library on North Bigelow Street. Even in late autumn, vibrant green magnolias towered over the pleasant two-story building like loyal guardians. I faced two-dozen sweet-looking elderly men and women seated on either side of a long table in the cheerful activities room. Some sat in wheelchairs, others in upholstered folding chairs with their walkers and canes beside them. I had covered the table with white linen and matching napkins, delicate dessert plates, and my personal collection of unmatched teacups and saucers, some of them antiques. I'd laid out sterling silver teaspoons with colorful enamel handles. Small baskets of cut flowers decorated the table's center, along with two silver-and-porcelain teacake stands filled to overflowing with cookies, pastries, and biscotti.

If this went well, I'd hold teas for every civic group in Mossy Creek. I'd dispel all rumors that I was an evil outsider. "My name is Jayne Reynolds," I said. "I want to welcome you to Magnolia Manor Tea Time, courtesy of my new shop, The Naked Bean."

An elderly man cupped a hand to one ear. "*What* did you say was naked?"

"The bean, Arnold, the bean," a woman shouted back.

"What the hell does that mean?"

"Just shut up and listen," another elderly man bellowed.

"Why don't we just enjoy some tea?" I said.

I began pouring samples and telling the group about different tea flavors and rituals. They sipped and nodded and seemed to be enjoying my little speech, until suddenly one wizened man set his cup down so hard it rattled the saucer. "You said this is chamomile tea?" he asked.

"Yes."

"That's the one that makes people sleepy. I don't do drugs."

I smiled. "It has a very mild effect. Hardly noticeable. It's not a drug."

"I don't know about that! I feel awful drowsy." He sat back in his wheelchair, shut his eyes, and dropped his chin to his chest. His breathing quickly softened, and he made little snoring sounds.

I stared at him in dismay. This was ridiculous. The others muttered worriedly to each other

"You never know!"

"My grandma always said she turned blue from drinking a wild root tea!"

"Doctor Champion warned me not to try herbs!"

A woman abruptly yawned, pushed her table setting away, then pillowed her head on her arms. "I can't keep my eyes open. Oh, lord, we've been dosed with a potion."

Another woman nodded off next to her, and then a third. An old fellow leaned against his snoozing friend in the wheelchair and dozed off, too. A man at the end of the table wheeled himself to a corner and cushioned his head against a wall.

Six of my audience members were now in dreamland, insisting I'd drugged them with chamomile tea.

The others looked at me in alarm.

"It's not the tea, I promise you," I said

with all the calm I could muster.

"Nurse!" Everyone who wasn't sleeping began thumping their canes and pounding the table. One elderly lady squealed, "We've been poisoned!"

A young nurse's aide ran in. She halted abruptly at the sight of a half-dozen old people facedown and snoring. "I better get help."

I watched in horror as a bevy of anxious attendants woke up the sleepers, checked their blood pressures, and listened to their hearts. The home's director hurried into the room. "I don't know what caused this, but no one seems harmed," she said, yet stared at me oddly.

"Chamomile wouldn't hurt anyone. I swear to you!"

"Of course it didn't do this. I don't know what happened, but we'll look into it." She gave me another awkward look. I knew I wouldn't be invited back.

"Good riddance to the old farts. Leaves more food for the rest of us," a frail little lady chirped, as she reached for her teacup and a handful of biscotti. She munched happily and sipped the suspicious tea with no narcoleptic effect, then filled her napkin with gingersnaps, pralines, chocolate puffs and shortbread. "My daughter Eustene said to get some of your shortbread cookies for her."

Eustene. Mrs. Red Hair, my secret admirer. If I hadn't been numb with despair, I might have laughed.

I tried to pretend a public relations disaster had not permanently damaged my business, but word traveled fast. I got angry phone calls from several of my victims' relatives.

Katie Bell, the business manager of the *Mossy Creek Gazette*, showed up at my shop right away. I had been planning to run a small weekly ad. Katie Bell looked at me sadly. "You might want to think about running that ad this week. You know—to do some damage control."

My face burned. I pictured what I might say in public defense:

CHAMOMILE NOW—NOT HARD
DRUGS LATER
JUST SAY YES TO EARL GREY
THIS IS NOT YOUR BRAIN ON TEA

I closed the shop and went upstairs. I sat in my apartment with the curtains drawn. Emma curled up in my lap but growled each time I hugged her tightly.

She only had so much sympathy for drug pushers.

For the next few days, I laid low. Adele Clearwater and her friends strode past my windows with their noses up and their lapel-pin crosses gleaming in the sun. Maggie Hart, a fellow shop owner and free spirit, wandered in wanting to buy "that tea that put the old people to sleep," and asked me with a grin if I thought it would work on her own mother. The minister of the Mossy Creek Unitarian Church brought me an invitation to sign up for the church's weekly tai chi class.

I couldn't decide where I stood with the townsfolk. Either I was a joke or a witch.

"Oh, don't worry about it, honey," said Rainey, the town hairdresser. "If the Unitarians are cultivatin' you, it just means they think you're a liberal."

I trudged outside one afternoon pretending to sweep my doorsill but really just wanting everyone to see I was too proud to hide any longer. Ingrid lounged on the bench between our shops, her blue-jeaned legs crossed at the ankles, a cigarette dropping ashes on a hunting jacket she wore over her chef's apron. Wee-Wee Bob huddled next to her, dressed in a fuzzy orange doggie sweater. He looked like a caterpillar with ears.

Ingrid looked up at me with narrowed eyes and a cool smile. "Knocked out any old folks lately?"

"You're evil."

"I hear you offered to host a tea for the

garden club, and they turned you down. Said they'd rather not be poisoned with nightshade and foxglove." She chortled.

"No, they just said their programs were already arranged for the next few months."

Ingrid took a drag off her cigarette. "I always cater their meetings for free. My mother was a founding member."

"You could provide the food, and I could provide coffee and tea. If you were willing to work with me."

She ground the cigarette into the dirt of an empty flower pot beside the bench. "Either you have no pride, or you just never give up."

"I'm not going to let you shut me out of the local circles."

"Oh, I'm just getting started."

Before I could say anything else, the rumble and diesel scent of a large tour bus engulfed us. The driver opened the door with a hydraulic swoosh and waved at us as he bounded to the sidewalk.

"Hello! I'm driving the Senior Adventurers Club of Paw Gap Baptist Church. They're from up near Asheville. We're on our way to the dog tracks in Florida. Mind if I let my group take a break here?"

Both Ingrid and I snapped to attention. Snagging a full tour bus in November was a rare feat. We were hungry Eskimos competing for a beached whale. Ingrid beamed at the driver. "Why, lord, hon, you just unload those hungry folks right here at my door."

This was war. I plastered a sugary smile on my face. "I bet you're *so* tired from driving that bus," I crooned to the driver. "Please come into *my* shop and have some fine imported coffee and pastries—complimentary."

The man swivelled from me to Ingrid. "Why, thanks, both of you ladies!" Behind him, the Paw Gap Senior Adventurers began to crowd into the door well, peering out at us.

Ingrid waved at them. "You folks look hungry for some stick-to-your-ribs Southern baking. I'm having a special today. Fifty percent off on everything in the bakery."

"I'm offering complimentary coffee or tea for everyone," I called loudly, "and a buy-one-get-one-free deal on my stock of gourmet Swiss chocolate bars."

Ingrid's control began to fray. "Just don't drink her chamomile tea," she yelled. "Unless you want to sleep for the next twenty-four hours."

I faced her. "You take that back!"

"Make me." Ingrid scooped a handful of dirt and cigarette ashes from the flower pot. And flung it.

I stood there in absolute, skin-prickling disbelief as the mixture peppered my face and hair. "Arrrr," I think I said. I lurched to the flower pot, grabbed a fistful of soil, and hard-lined a wad of dirt right into the center of Ingrid's white apron.

Bob yelped wildly and peed on everything in sight. "Now you've done it," Ingrid muttered. She threw another volley. *Blat*. She got me on one arm. I fired back. *Whump*. Damp dirt rained from her hair. She yipped and threw again. Then me. Then her. Then me. We both looked like earthworms.

Suddenly, the bus huffed away in a cloud of diesel smoke.

Silence descended.

Ingrid and I stared at each other with our fists drawn back, leaking dirt from our fingers. Shame flooded me. Around us, Pearl Quinlin, Rainey, and Dan McNeil, who owned the town fix-it shop, watched in shock. Our tale would be told around Mossy Creek dinner tables and hearths for years to come. The dirt duel at high noon.

Ingrid's face turned as white as mine felt. We both fumbled for our door handles then rushed inside our shops. I put up a *Closed* sign, turned off the lights, then sat on the floor behind the counter with my head in my dirt-encrusted hands.

That evening, I heard a knock at my apartment door. I dragged myself out of my living room recliner and peered wearily through the small security window. A white-bearded old gentleman stood on my landing. Though dressed in a work coat and overalls, he made me think of Santa Claus. I opened the door.

"Yes, may I help you?"

"Miz Reynolds, my name's Ed Brady. I live outside town. I heard about your troubles with Ingrid Beechum. It's time to speak my mind before things get more out of hand."

I sighed. "Don't worry, Mr. Brady. I won't throw any more dirt at Ingrid. Or anyone else."

He smiled. "Reckon you and her were buildin' up to a showdown. Good you got it out of your systems."

"Thank you, but I'm very ashamed of my behavior."

"Well, Ingrid's got plenty to be ashamed about, too." He cleared his throat. He looked very tired, and I felt sorry for him. "Listen here, my wife is in the nursing home. She ain't well enough to come to any talks or play no games; she just stays in bed. I go over there every day to see her. While I'm there I keep up with the news. I heard about your tea party, and I did some snoopin' for answers."

"I don't know what happened at the home the other day. It was the strangest thing I've ever seen."

"Ma'am, I came to tell you that you got your leg pulled."

"What?"

"Those old coots were playin' a joke on you. Pretendin' to fall asleep."

I raised a hand to my throat. "Why?"

"I expect because Ingrid Beechum and

her gal friends put 'em up to it. Adele Clearwater and the like. Told the old folks to play-act falling asleep after they drank some tea."

"Thank you for letting me know," I said tonelessly.

"Ingrid isn't herself these days. She hasn't even started to get over losin' her boy last year. He was her only child. Her husband Charlie Beechum, Senior, he died of some sort of illness so long ago that Charlie, Junior barely recalled him. Ingrid made it up to the boy as best she could. She just lived for Charlie, Junior. I got a son of my own. I understand."

"Her son died?"

"Oh, yes, ma'am. He was only 'bout thirty years old. Got killed in a car accident."

"And his wife—she and Ingrid are close?"

"Well, no. Ingrid's been tryin' to keep up with her, though. For Charlie, Junior's sake. Tried to get her a nice home here in town. Offered to set her up with a business. But, from what I heard, the gal's just no-good, just a moocher, you know. It's been hard on Ingrid, tryin' to hang on to her son's memory the only way she can—through that no-account wife of his. So please don't think too bad of Ingrid. Like I said, she's not herself lately."

"I see."

He nodded to me. "I got to go, Ma'am. Got my old dog to feed. Possum. He'll be in the garbage if I don't get home soon."

"Thank you for coming. And for being so frank with me. Please stop by my shop. I'll let you sample anything you care to try."

"I'll sure do that. I been hearin' good talk about your place. Eustene Oscar says she's never tasted shortbread so fine. And her old mama likes it, too." He put a finger to his lips and smiled. "Now, *that's* a secret."

After he left, I pulled on a sweater and went downstairs, then along a wide lane that ran behind the shops. The creek flowed between shallow banks on the far side of that lane. I listened to the soft music of its water before I took a deep breath, walked next door, and knocked on the bakery's service doors. I'd noticed lights at night. Ingrid worked late. When there was no response, I pushed lightly. The thick wooden double doors eased open.

I stepped inside and halted. The light was dim except for a single metal light fixture in one corner. Ingrid sat in the shadows, huddled on the floor of the kitchen area with her arms wrapped around her knees and her back against a metal storage bin. Her eyes were shut. The room was so cold I saw my own breath in the air. Ingrid had wrapped herself in a soft pink-and-blue crocheted afghan. A baby blanket. I ached for her loneliness.

"Mrs. Beechum," I said quietly. "It's time we talked."

She opened her eyes, red-rimmed and

swollen, and looked at me as if nothing I did surprised her. I stepped closer, into the light. "I want to apologize," I said. "Not just for today, but for every rude thing I've said or done since we met."

She gave me a sarcastic look. "Why?"

"Because I didn't know that you and I have so much in common. I understand your pain, now."

Her gaze burned into me. "What are you talking about?"

"I heard you lost your son this year."

"I can't talk about—"

"I understand. I have trouble talking about grief. It's a shell. It's a shield. Armor. Not talking. When you talk, it opens up all those places where the pain can still seep through."

She got to her feet, swaying. Tears slid down her face. "What would you know about loss? You're too young."

My throat convulsed. "I know how it feels to lose someone you think you can't live without. To get up every morning hating the sunlight because you just want to stay in the dark. And then there are days when the dark suffocates you, and you know you'll scream if dawn doesn't come soon enough. Because every day takes you further away from the time when that person you loved was with you."

Ingrid staggered toward me then stopped. "How the hell do you know how I feel?" she yelled.

Warm tears slid down my own cheeks. "Because my husband died two months ago, and I still don't know how I can go on without him."

She went very still, watching me. Misery burst inside my chest. I rushed to tell her more before she threw me out. "Matthew, his name was Matthew. And he was such a good man, and we fell in love during college when he walked into the coffee shop I managed and—" I told her all about him, and why I named my shop The Naked Bean. "And we visited here a few months ago, and made love in a room at the Hamilton House Inn, not long before he got sick for the last time. I've come back to see if life without Matthew can hold any happiness. Maybe it can't. I've taken my fear of that out on you. You're so successful. You have friends, and so many loving relatives, and a place—this town—that's part of you, that's part of who you are. I'm afraid I'll never have any home like that. Nothing will ever fill up the emptiness inside me. I'm not young and carefree. I'm ancient. Some days I can barely move."

She studied me as if my whole life showed in my face. Her silent scrutiny dragged on until I couldn't stand it. My shoulders sagged. "I won't fight with you, anymore," I said wearily. I turned and walked toward the doors.

"My daughter-in-law is about your age, and I despise her." Ingrid's fervent, tear-soaked voice stopped me in my tracks. I turned slowly, then halted. Ingrid went on fiercely. "She cheated on Charlie and spent all his money and lied to him, but he loved her so much he couldn't see through her. Everyone else could see what she was. I saw it from the first day I met her. I couldn't keep my mouth shut. I told Charlie she was no good." Ingrid paused. Her throat worked. "He never forgave me." She lifted the afghan, then let it fall. "I made gifts for children he never had. Grandchildren I would never get to know. When he died, we hadn't spoken in three years."

I put a hand to my mouth. She stared into thin air and kept talking. "After he died in the car wreck, I swore I'd make everything up to him, even if all I could do was take care of his wife. She came to me for help. For money. She had no pride. Neither did I, by then. I told her I'd help her start her own business. A lingerie shop, that's what she wanted. I had it all planned. I'd take care of her, if she moved to Mossy Creek. That's why I wanted your shop space. I went to Ida to set up the lease. Ida told me I was a fool. That I couldn't bring Charlie back and I'd break my own heart all over again. She wouldn't give me an answer about the shop. Then you came along. You were a good excuse for her to do what she felt was for my own good."

I felt washed out, defenseless. "Ingrid, I

only have a six-month lease. That's all I could guarantee Ida. My business probably won't last beyond that—not at the rate it's going. If you and I can just keep a truce between us until then, I expect you'll get the lease. Maybe it won't be too late to coax your daughter-in-law to move here."

Once again, Ingrid went silent. Either I'd stunned her or she'd decided I was still too worthless for words.

"I don't know what else to say," I went on. "Except that I do understand how badly you hurt. And I understand how much you loved your only child. Because. . *because I'm pregnant.*"

There. I'd finally told someone. "Three months pregnant. You're the first person I've confessed to. I want my child to grow up here. You see, I'm certain—" I cried quietly—"I'm certain my child was conceived here. In Mossy Creek."

She looked at me speechlessly. I walked out the back doors and stood in the cold evening air. A majestic purple sunset filled the deepening sky, infinite and painfully beautiful.

Matthew and our unborn child were with me.

🍂🍂🍂

It was mid-morning. I dutifully opened my shop, brewed my coffees, arranged my tea bags, and tidied the café tables as if crowds of customers would use them. Nothing looked right. I broke out in a cold sweat as I pondered Ingrid's sorrows and mine, the humiliating scene we'd caused the day before, and life in general. Soon my heart was racing, and I felt sick at my stomach and a little dizzy. I filled a coffee mug with cold water at the sink. My thoughts circled endlessly.

You let yourself down. You let Matthew down. Quit now. Give up for the baby's sake. This shop was never going to work, anyway.

I uttered a soft sound of despair and bent over the sink. I couldn't give up.   Couldn't stop trying. Couldn't. But how, how in the world. . .

"I have something to tell you. Something I couldn't bring myself to admit last night."

Ingrid's voice. Dazed, I straightened up. She had come into the shop without my noticing. She stood at my counter looking stern and tired. She gaged my disheveled appearance with her sharp blue eyes.

"Are you all right?" she asked.

I nodded and quickly wiped my face with a paper towel. "It's just morning sickness. Tell me what?"

Her face began to soften, suffused with sadness and shame, but also determination. "My daughter-in-law took the money I loaned her to buy inventory for her lingerie shop. She used it to move across the country with her new boyfriend. She won't be back."

"Oh, Ingrid, I'm sorry."

"No, I'm sorry. Sorry I looked at you and saw her. And I'm sorry that I blamed you for Ida's decision about this shop. Ida was right. I can't change what happened to my son, or any mistakes I made, or any mistakes he made. I have to live with the past. Find something hopeful to hold onto. And someone to talk to. Someone who understands." She paused. "Like you."

My throat closed with emotion. I clutched the counter and gazed at her happily. She took a step forward and held out a hand.

"No more dirt," she said hoarsely. "Please forgive me."

I grasped her hand. "We weren't throwing dirt," I whispered. "We were digging holes to plant seeds."

"I have some afghans you might be able to use when the baby comes."

"Yes. Oh, yes."

She went to my doors, threw them open, stepped outside, and gestured for someone to come along. I stared as a stream of people came into my shop, all carrying small gifts. Looking sheepish, Adele Clearwater and her gang bore flower arrangements, potted plants, and cookies. Eustene Oscar and her mother, in a wheelchair, smiled at me over a basket filled with napkins, silverware, and teacups. Eustene took a handful of small bronze marbles from a gift box and set them in front of me. On second glance, I realized they were shaped like...beans. "Tag Garner, our local sculptor, made these for you. Now you have naked beans to set on your window sill."

Everyone smiled. I cupped the bronze beans in my palms. "Thank you," I whispered.

Adele and the others began brusquely setting the tables. "We're giving you a tea party," Adele said with unbowed authority. "Where no one will pretend to fall asleep."

I choked out a laugh. Soon half the town merchants were crowded in my shop, eating, drinking, visiting with me—just like old friends. I looked up to find Ida Walker on the edge of the chattering crowd. She glanced from Ingrid to me and nodded with satisfaction. Ingrid clinked a silver teaspoon against her cup.

"Here's to Jayne and her baby," she said. "Welcome to your new home."

"Welcome," Ida seconded.

I bent my head, shut my eyes, and whispered silently to Matthew. *You were right about human beans.*

From the desk of Katie Bell

Dear Vicki:

I've avoided telling you the rest about Isabella and Richard because here's where it turns sad. As I've said, after she spurned Lionel Bigelow he swore to chase off the Salters, the Hamiltons, and every other Mossy Creekite who sided with them.

The feud split Bigelow County down the middle, with Mossy Creekites on one side and Bigelowans on the other. Farms were burned and livestock shot. People were hurt. Some were nearly killed. The Hamiltons climbed up on their corn silo and painted "Ain't Going Nowhere, And Don't Want To." The final straw came when the Bigelows put a price on Isabella and Richard's heads.

The next day, they vanished.

Oh, what a search there was! Creekites hunted the countryside for weeks. Signs were posted in every town from the North Carolina line all the way down to Atlanta. But it was no use. Isabella and Richard were gone.

Lionel Bigelow collapsed and died. Some say he was brokenhearted and filled with regret. Others say his evil heart had turned on him. Whichever it was, the feud ended with grief on both sides. Isabella Salter and Richard Stanhope were never heard from again.

Salters have the worst luck with happily-ever-afters. My editor and publisher, your cousin Sue Ora Salter, is just about the only Salter left in Mossy Creek, now. You're not going to believe it when I drop this bomb on you, after all you've learned about Mossy Creek's history between Hamiltons, Salters, and Bigelows, but here 'tis:

Sue Ora's husband is a Bigelow.

Is it any wonder she doesn't want to admit that? Salter women pick a man and stick with him, one way or another. They either do a good job of picking, or they're just too stubborn to change. They're like our creek: They go with the flow or pretend they don't give a *dam*. I'm telling you, it's something in the water.

You might not want to mention any of this stuff about Salter women to Lord Stanhope, since you're a Salter woman, yourself. And I sure wouldn't show him my next story, if I were you.

Ssssh, Katie

Sue Ora

The Bereavement Report

To Mossy Creekites, I'll always be that *odd* Susan Ora Salter, but at least I'm *their* odd Sue Ora. That's the thing about small towns—the residents may question your choices privately, but to an outsider they'll defend you to the death. Death is a subject Salters really love. We have a morbid fascination with it, and maybe it makes us distrustful of the living.

You see, we were a pioneer founding family in Mossy Creek, but we haven't prospered the way the other old families have. Our men were swallowed up by wars of one kind or another, and our women tend to make bad choices—starting with their men. Isabella Salter was the first recorded woman to leave the town when she married an Englishman and ran away from Lionel Bigelow. Isabella was my idol. She found a way to escape from a Bigelow romance and by all the accounts we're getting from Lady Stanhope, she never regretted it. I'm not sure how I went astray. I left, but I came back. "You're a Salter. Act like one," I was told repeatedly by both my mother and my eighty-year-old Great Aunt Livvy.

"If I acted like a Salter, I'd leave or die," was my standard reply when I was a teenager. I'd never gotten over my father's death. I was just four years old when he was killed in Vietnam, but I already loved him dearly. I grew up knowing I was the last in line to bear the Salter surname in Mossy Creek. And I knew when I married, Daddy's name would be gone forever. I vowed to never marry. I broke that vow, and it haunted me.

Names are important in Mossy Creek. First and last, middle, maiden, even nicknames. People solemnly account for each one. I'm named Susan Ora Salter for my daddy's aunt Susan Elizabeth (Great Aunt Livvy) and my mama's sister Ora Juanita. Ora Juanita ran off to Hollywood before I learned to walk and was never heard from again. There was probably a Bigelow man involved, but nobody's talking.

From the beginning, I was ornery and didn't fit in. I had red hair. I got in fights. I wrote poems about dead Salters, particularly my beloved, dead father. I read indecent books. Because of me, the Mossy Creek Public Library hid its copy of *Lady Chatterley's Lover*. My teachers down at Bigelow County High School (the only high school in the county, after Mossy Creek High went up in flames—a mystery Mossy Creekites have tried to solve for twenty years) told my mother I was incorrigible. Mother agreed. At fourteen, I started signing all my homework with my initials—S O S!—with the exclamation point at the end. I thought it was pretty cool. Unfortunately, the teachers didn't.

Eventually, I found a way to escape. I played my *Get Out of Jail* card when I was a senior in college. John Willingham Bigelow, of the *Bigelow, Bigelow, and Bigelow Attorneys At Law* Bigelows, and I fell in lust and eloped. And thus, I thought I'd escape the Salter curse by swapping the last S in my signature for a B. I already wanted to be a writer, and I figured any author who could autograph her books *S O B!* made a statement. I considered myself an author with an attitude and a good marketing tool.

When my new young husband fondly called me *his* unpublished smart ass, I thought he was proud of his rebel. That should have been my first hint that I'd never be a dignified Bigelow wife. After my first bridal shower at the Bigelow Country Club, I took one long look at gifts that include prim little crocheted doilies, ostentatious china, and a sterling silver tea service with a big 'B' carved on the monogram, and I knew the Bigelows would swallow me alive and spit me out.

With a big B carved on my ass.

The truth was, I had fallen in love with

the last man on earth I should have, a man buried in family tradition as deep as my own, buried so deeply I couldn't dig him out. I thought I'd teach him there was a world away from country clubs, law firms and power-grabbing family schemes. I didn't. He thought he'd tame me, a wild Mossy Creekite. He couldn't.

Within two weeks after our marriage, we were fighting so much we could barely say a civil word to one another. When we weren't fighting, we were in bed. It was crazy. I've never cried so many tears in my life. I cut my losses and ran. John drowned his misery in law school, and I headed for California—hey, it was good enough for Ora Juanita—where I was sure nothing less than fame and fortune awaited my writing skills. It wasn't that I didn't love Mossy Creek; I did. But I was a free-spirited woman eager to tackle the world's real problems and forget that Salters were fading away. Mossy Creek had no real problems to tackle.

At least, not after *I* left.

Then I realized I was pregnant. There was no way I was going back to the one place I didn't want to live—Mossy Creek, near John. He refused to give me a divorce unless I promised to let him have the baby. He knew I'd never do that. So we drew a line in the sand. I'd keep our child with me in California but remain Mrs. John Bigelow.

Salters know how to get even with Bigelows. At least, that's what I told myself.

In a moment of post-childbirth, drug-induced sentimentality, I named our beautiful little boy John Willingham Bigelow, Junior. When John, Senior arrived to see him, I said, "I woke up in a stupor and realized I'd named him after you. Too late to change it. I plan to call him Willie. Hope you're happy."

"I'd be happy if you'll quit pretending you have any talent as a writer, and you and Willie come home with me."

"Where I can pretend you and I love each other?"

I hurt him as badly as he hurt me, that day. From then on, he never asked me to come home again. I never offered, either. But there's a problem with a proud attitude—you can't eat it and you can't spend it. And there comes a time when you put dreams away and accept the truth. I loved my child, and he needed his father. Every time John came to visit or Willie came home from visiting John in Georgia, Willie moped for weeks. I knew what I had to do. What I owed Willie.

When my mother died five years ago and left me her house next door to Great Aunt Livvy in Mossy Creek, I gave up my meager living as a reporter for the *Village Crier* in San Francisco and came home. It wasn't an auspicious return. I was broke, and jobs for unsuccessful writers were in short supply in

Mossy Creek. I had a son to support. John had always been generous with money for Willie, but I never used a penny of it for myself.

Miss Mitty Anglin, the elderly owner and publisher of the *Mossy Creek Gazette* back then, was happy to give me a job as a reporter. But Miss Mitty's idea of a big paycheck was twenty hours a week at minimum wage, with a free Gazette subscription thrown in. So there I was, scratching out a living at the newspaper, wincing every time somebody chortled at my lowly return. When Miss Mitty retired, she offered to sell the paper to me. I couldn't believe it. She wanted such a ridiculously low price that even I could afford to buy it, if I could get a small business loan.

I went over to Mossy Creek Savings and Loan with a knot in my stomach and true humility in my soul. I had no collateral, no cash for a down payment, and a history of late credit card payments. I knew it was hopeless, but I had to try. Not expecting anything but a polite rejection, I laid out a big presentation about how I'd manage the newspaper and make a profit if the savings and loan would just give me a break.

Damned if they didn't give me the loan. I was stunned. And thrilled. I was able to buy new printing equipment and hire Katie Bell, who runs the office, sells advertising, and writes her own column. I write editorials and cover the hard news in town. I added Jess

Crane, part-time, to cover sports and men's features, and I've got several teenage interns who write up the garden clubs and other fluffy community stories. Plus every cranky old timer in town gets to write a column regularly, and those who don't write columns keep the letters' page filled with rants and loony commentary. I don't kid myself that the Gazette offers great journalism, but with Jess and the interns covering every local person in eye-popping detail and Katie dishing up funny gossip in her weekly column, *The Bellringer*, we've managed to triple our subscription numbers and line up a dependable base of advertisers. Every smart editor knows that name-dropping gossip and outrageous editorial pages guarantee a readership. And I'm nothing if not smart.

So I've been happy enough in the five years since we came home, and Willie is thriving, though he lives two lives. John takes him down to Bigelow every other weekend, where he dresses in crisp khakis and golf shirts and is known as—drum roll, please—John Willingham, Junior. Back up in Mossy Creek with his Great Aunt Livvy and me, he's still plain Willie, a good kid, grinning and sloppy. I let him wear a fake nose ring once, and I thought John's mother would have me arrested. "He's only thirteen," I told her. "He's a Bigelow," she retorted, as if that nixed his teenage dreams.

But Great Aunt Livvy and I see his baggy

warm-up pants and untied Reeboks simply as innocent signs of Salter creative rebellion. "Just like you, at that age, Susan," Great Aunt Livvy says, her false teeth clucking in appropriate disdain as she tries unsuccessfully to hide her pride.

❦❦❦

There's only one thing I try to keep from Willie: The Salter preoccupation with death. Every morning Great Aunt Livvy prepares her bowl of cornflakes and takes it to her tiny breakfast table, where she listens to our local radio station WMOS air its morning *Bereavement Report*. That means they announce who died, of what, and when the funeral will take place. My aunt measures her life by days of survival. "If I don't hear my name, I start plannin' lunch," Great Aunt Livvy says.

So far, I'd managed to avoid this fascinating family hobby. But then our cousin Hattie Almond, down in Yonder, died peacefully in her sleep at eighty-nine. It was the first week of December, the weather cold and clear. When a neighbor went by Hattie's little farm cottage to take her a pan of biscuits and a bowl of sawmill gravy, he found her Christmas tree lit in the living room and Hattie dead in bed.

Great Aunt Livvy called out her side window to me as I was leaving for work. I'd already waved Willie off to the county school bus. Great Aunt Livvy cupped her hands around her mouth. "Susan, you have to carry me down to Yonder. The radio says Cousin Hattie's dead, and she hadn't even put up her mistletoe yet."

"How did the radio know that?"

"Now, don't you change the subject. Have some respect."

I nodded. We both bowed our heads for a few seconds. Hattie Almond was the sister of Granddaddy Salter's aunt by marriage, meaning no blood kin to us. But that made no difference to Great Aunt Livvy. As far as she was concerned, Hattie was a Salter, period. I felt bad suddenly for not visiting Cousin Hattie more often. Yonder is just southeast of Mossy Creek, but its only excuse for existence is the store at the crossroads and the best trout fishing spot in the area. It once won itself a spot in a commercial naming RC Colas and Moon Pies as the fishermen's meal of choice.

"Do we have to go to Yonder right away?" I asked. "She's already dead. Unless you think she's joking, I don't know what you can do about it."

"Hattie planned her whole funeral. She liked a good celebration. We just have to see to the details."

"Can't I drop you off and come back by Hattie's house later? I have to lay out the paper, and now I have to write an obituary. If the paper doesn't get out, I don't get paid by the advertisers. You know this is the week of the Christmas manger sale at the Feed and Seed store and Hamilton's is running their annual pre-Christmas blowout. Besides, you don't really need me at Hattie's. I'd just mope around."

"Honey, I know you've hated funerals ever since your daddy died when you were little, but just try to think of 'em as parties for the living. Hurry up. I've got to get back in time to make a chicken pie and a congealed salad." She sounded almost merry, her false teeth tap-dancing in time with her list of funeral foods. "Hattie always said that congealed salad is old fashioned, but I say if the cook down at Mama's All You Can Eat Café would put it on the menu she'd see her profits go up. I'll probably unthaw a pound cake too. You can say you made it, so you won't show up empty handed."

"Everybody knows I can't cook."

"Well, I'll tell 'em it's a Christmas miracle."

"Listen, I'll take you to Cousin Hattie's, but I'm not—"

"Yes, you are. No use a grown woman actin' like a fool over dead folks. Time to grow up and get on with the living, Susan."

I sighed. There was no stopping my daddy's aunt and her long experience with death. Great Aunt Livvy was the only girl in her generation of the Salter family. She'd outlived her brothers, nephews and nieces, and so the fewer kin she had to remember, the more she honored them. I hadn't yet told her about my recent letters to Victoria Salter Stanhope. I knew Great Aunt Livvy would want to get on the first plane to England, and neither of us had that kind of money in our savings accounts. Katie Bell was sworn to secrecy and given the task of helping me hide our British Salter, for now. At least Victoria Stanhope had escaped what I've darkly named *The Salter Women's Call to Bereavement.*

"You promised your mama you'd look after me and be kindly to me in my old age," Great Aunt Livvy prodded. "And do whatever I want."

I squinted at her. "Mama's will said you promised her you'd look after *me.*"

"I'm old. I get my wish first."

I sighed and gave in. An hour later, I found myself meeting with the minister of the Yonder Faith and Forgiveness Baptist Church, whether I wanted to or not. "First," Great Aunt Livvy told him, "we have to arrange for the people who will sit up with the body. Hattie left a list."

"Body sitters?" I spouted.

"It's a matter of respect," the elderly mister explained. "Of course, I still like the way we did it in the old days. When I was a boy, the body was displayed at home. Sitting up then was so much more personal."

I'd heard enough funeral stories to know the only reason Mossy Creekites wanted to sit with the body at home was so they could privately share a little moonshine and be close enough to the kitchen to eat from all the platters of food brought in by the neighbors, but I said nothing. There was no arguing with Great Aunt Livvy.

"She left a list of music, too," Livvy said. "She wanted it loud."

The minister nodded happily. The congregation of Faith and Forgiveness believed in making joyful noises. If you asked their neighbors, the tone-deaf congregation probably sounded more like a joyful attempt to scare crows out of a cornfield. I'd heard rumors they accompanied their gospel music with a piano, horns, guitars and a tambourine—all off-key.

Unfortunately, Cousin Hattie's sitting-up list was twenty-five years old. She'd already outlived all the sitters, including her pallbearers, most of her respectful mourners and her immediate family. No matter, the minister assured us, God would send what Hattie needed. I hoped so. Otherwise, I pictured Great Aunt Livvy, Willie and me rolling the casket into the church with one hand and shaking a tambourine with the other.

With my hope of making the newspaper's weekly deadline rapidly disappearing, I called

Katie Bell and told her to do whatever it took to start laying out the paper without me, then drove Great Aunt Livvy over to Hattie's house. To my surprise, the house—a small square brown cottage that had last seen paint after the Big War—closely resembled an anthill that cold December afternoon. God had provided an army of short, plump women in print dresses, who were cleaning furiously, and tall, white-haired women with big bosoms, who rearranged the furniture to accommodate the folding chairs brought in by the funeral home in anticipation of the visitors and family who would surely come.

I could have told them that Livvy and I were all the family left. I didn't argue, but I knew none of my friends would be trekking to Yonder for the food or the moonshine. And I had no intention of inviting John. I couldn't imagine him in the Faith and Forgiveness Baptist Church. His Rolex watch would stop from shock.

Hattie's services were scheduled for two o'clock on the coming Friday. The three-day delay was to allow plenty of time for friends and family to arrive. My suggestion—that even if there were family and friends they were not coming by horse and buggy—went unnoticed.

"Of course, lots of folks will come," Great Aunt Livvy said, her lips stretched thin with shock at my newest cavalier observation. "People in the mountains understand about respect."

Respect I can take, up to a point. It was the tradition and the next day's Bereavement Report that reared back and kicked me in the heart. "Murial Bigelow died last night," Great Aunt Livvy yelled out her window as I headed for my car that frosty morning. Murial Bigelow was John's grandmother. I stood there feeling bad about Murial for a minute, then began to brighten, I'm ashamed to admit. Why? Because Bigelows don't believe in sitting ups or sitting withs or gospel singings. Too many festivities. Interferes with their golf schedules. Grandmother Murial's services would be quick and easy.

I called John. He told me the funeral was set for two days hence, at eleven a.m. He asked me to come and bring Willie. "Of course we'll be there," I said, a little wounded. "Murial is Willie's great-grandmother. He liked her. And so did I."

"You never admitted it."

"I should have. I'm sorry."

There was a quiet pause over the phone. Then, "You and Willie come to her house early, and we'll drive to the church together. After all, we should look like a family in times of trouble. Present a united front."

"Keep up appearances."

"Suzy, it's not that," he said wearily. "Look, if you need anything for yourself, use my account at Hamilton's. I mean, I know you don't own many nice dresses, and your money's short." He added quickly, as if he realized I might take offense, "A lot of potential advertisers for the Gazette will be at the funeral."

"I'm not going to Grandmother Murial's funeral to scope out business, John."

"I didn't mean it that way. I just know that you buy nice clothes for John, Jr. but not for yourself." He hesitated. "I bet you still have the dress you wore when I proposed to you fourteen years ago."

The one he was referring to was a little black number that hit me about thigh high and swished when I walked. It was a dinner-dancing-and-to-bed dress. I haven't worn it since the night John proposed, but it's still hanging in the back of my closet. I evaded his question. "I'll get a decent dress to wear. I don't need any help, but thank you. Willie and I will see you at Murial's house."

I rushed to the newspaper office in Mossy Creek. Now I had to get the paper out, attend two funeral services a day apart, and write two obituaries—one for cousin Hattie in Yonder, whose friends would send her off with a Hallelujah Band and a sheet cake that said *Say Hello to Jesus*, and another for Grandmother Murial in Bigelow, where the food would be catered by servants wearing tuxedos and bow ties, and the music would be provided by a string quartet.

Late that afternoon, I dragged myself home. Willie had hung a homemade Christmas wreath on our front door. He'd made it out of old light bulbs painted green. I smiled. "I'm up with this, homeboy," I said, doing my best imitation of a hip-hopper.

"*Word*," he answered solemnly, which in hip-hop meant he agreed.

Great Aunt Livvy was waiting in my living room with her coat on. I drove her and Willie down to Hattie's house. As we helped Great Aunt Livvy make her way across the stubbly brown grass of the cottage yard, she began listing chores. "We still have to pick out Hattie's coffin at the Mossy Creek Funeral Home, choose the flowers, and settle on the music. I think she'd like *Shall We Gather At the River*. Oh, and you have to call her insurance agent about her burial policy." Great Aunt Livvy was willing to contribute her management skills to anyone's funeral, but so far as the expenses were concerned, dead people were on their own.

I gaped at her. "I thought Hattie had all these details planned out."

"I lied. She liked planning Christmas better. But on a happy note, Hattie's neighbors will provide the church coffee pot and keep a running account of the food donated so that we can write thank-you notes."

I groaned. As we stepped up on the porch, Willie stared inside. "Mom, why are all these people sitting around Cousin Hattie's house eating and drinking and smoking?"

"They're here to show their respect," Great Aunt Livvy interjected, beaming. "Just wait until you see the viewing. I bet she'll have at least fifty people peering at her."

I groaned, again. Could there possibly be fifty other people as fixated on funerals as Great Aunt Livvy?

❦❦❦

I soon learned that I had underestimated the compassion of Mossy Creekites. I shouldn't have. I was related to a prime example of Mossy Creekite philosophy—Great Aunt Livvy. She had once organized a thousand people from Bigelow County for the funeral of a child whose anonymous body had been found along a back road. "People come together over the dead," she always told me. "That's the gift the dead give to the living."

The next day, between errands, I bought Willie a new suit at Hamilton's and got a dress for myself by bartering advertising credit with Robert Walker, the department store's president. Robert sent flowers to both Hattie and Murial's homes. So did Ida Walker. Amos Royden scheduled Mutt Bottoms to direct traffic outside Faith and Forgiveness's little chapel. Michael Conners hung a Celtic cross in the window of his pub with a black bit of paper ribbon tied around it. And on and on. I got teary.

I took Willie over to see Rainey at Goldilocks' Hair, Nail and Tanning Salon, and she gave us both a nice trim. I paid for Willie's haircut but, as usual, struck a deal with Rainey for credit on her advertising account, too. Rainey had already put a sign in the window that her shop would be closed for Hattie's funeral. Rainey understood proper bereavement, too.

I decided I'd leave Great Aunt Livvy at Hattie's on Thursday to visit the sitting-with crowd, then Willie and I would head down to Bigelow for Grandmother Murial's funeral. But I should have known Great Aunt Livvy would never miss a good passing. This was a double-header.

"I'm not missing Murial Bigelow's funeral," she declared. "We'll go, say our consolations, then come back to Yonder for the viewing of Hattie's body."

Great Aunt Livvy practically trembled with excited tradition. I sighed.

When our doorbell rang, Willie grinned and went to answer it. It was Rosie Montgomery, the cook at Mama's All You Can Eat Café, bearing a platter of crispy fried chicken and a bowl of macaroni and cheese. "I know you won't have time to cook," Rosie said politely, then gave me an unexpected hug. "This food is for you, not for the funeral. I thought you were more in need than the mourners."

Great Aunt Livvy nodded approvingly. Rosie knew proper protocol. Unlike me, she'd paid attention to the Mossy Creek Rules of Bereavement since childhood.

"Wow, Mom," Willie said, tearing into a piece of fried chicken. "I could get into this funeral stuff."

Great Aunt Livvy nodded. "Just wait 'til you taste the Jesus cake."

🐛🐛🐛

The next morning, I drove Willie and Great Aunt Livvy down to Bigelow. We curved through an old neighborhood where huge lawns fronted enormous old homes and finally arrived at Murial Bigelow's big brick mansion. We were directed to pull off the driveway and leave our car behind a stand of ornamental shrubbery bordering the pool. "If I park back here, I'll never get out," I protested to the attendant, solemnly attired in a white dress shirt with a black armband, bow tie, and black trousers. The temperature was about thirty degrees. He shivered, and I felt sorry for him. "Oh, never mind," I said. "I'll figure it out, later."

"Not to worry, your car'll be taken care of, Ms. Salter."

"Mrs. Bigelow," I corrected. I never wanted Willie to think I wasn't proud of his father's name.

"Mrs. Bigelow. Sorry."

"No problem."

We were early, very early. The mansion's huge, enclosed sun porch was awash in tables covered in crisp linen and lace tablecloths and flowers. Silver holders supported baking dishes of breakfast casseroles. A silver chafing dish was filled with cheese grits. Other trays contained assorted sweet breads, croissants, and fresh fruit. There were coffee urns, juices, and plates. I was right about the waiters wearing tuxedos and black ties. In the background came the comforting strains of live music.

For breakfast. At a funeral.

Hattie's funeral plans were intricate but this party was beyond description. I'd spent half the afternoon at Mossy Creek Flowers And Gifts while Great Aunt Livvy decided which flowers she wanted on Hattie's casket. She went for gaudy color and show—a huge blanket of hot-pink and purple carnations. Here at Murial's breakfast wake—or whatever you'd call it—tasteful arrangements of white roses bloomed from crystal vases.

"Have you ever seen anything like this?" Great Aunt Livvy asked in a whisper. "I feel like we're at a fancy dress ball, and somebody forgot to mention the hostess is dead."

"Why, Livvy," John said behind us, his voice deep and tingling on my spine, "I'll take that as a compliment."

We turned and looked at him. "Nice set-up. I'm takin' notes," Great Aunt Livvy retorted, unabashed.

"Hey, Dad," Willie said, and they hugged warmly. I looked up into my husband's guarded eyes. "Hello, John."

Several of our fellow breakfast mourners arrived at that moment. As if aware of the curious looks they gave us, and the potential for Willie's approval, John suddenly slid an arm around me, pulled me close, and kissed me lightly on the forehead. When he stepped back, I was speechless. "Hello, Suzy," he said.

Why'd he do that? What was he up to? And how could I help but feel warm and alive?

I hated funerals.

🐞🐞🐞

Murial Bigelow's funeral procession was an orchestrated parade of big cars and fat cats. Governor Bigelow was there, with his wife and kids and his powerful, viperish mother, Ardaleen Hamilton Bigelow, who is my kin on the Salters' Hamilton side but never acknowledges me. The funeral director said Willie ought to ride with John and John's great aunt—Muriel's sister, Louise—in one of the Bigelows' black Lincolns. Willie wouldn't budge. "Not without Mom and Great Aunt Livvy," he said.

John nodded grimly. "You're right, son." He turned to me and Livvy, holding out an arm to each of us.

Great Aunt Livvy shook her head at me. "You go with John and Willie. I'll stay behind. This is your son's great-grandmother's funeral. And you're still John's legal wife."

"But you're my wife's great aunt," John countered. "And that makes you my family, too."

She looked ruffled but misty-eyed. I felt the same way. John put her in the front seat. Willie and I sat in the back along with him. His Great Aunt Louise turned up her nose at us and took the next in a long line of black and gray vehicles.

I sighed and gazed out our window, dabbing my eyes. I'd already seen Governor Bigelow and a couple of Bigelow-related state senators. To my surprise, Mossy Creek's Mayor Walker was there. Miss Ida knew about respect and tradition—plus she knew about politics. This was no different than a Mid-East Peace Summit—everybody was expected to show up and make the right noises, then go home and check their arsenals. I noticed that the governor avoided Miss Ida and how Miss Ida's older sister, Ardaleen, turned her back. Miss Ida just smiled like a cat.

The funeral procession wound slowly through the streets of Bigelow. A half-dozen City of Bigelow police cars shooed other traffic away from us. Stoplights were set to blink, so the procession didn't have to pause. People stopped on sidewalks and in crosswalks to wait respectfully. When we reached the Bigelow Covenant Presbyterian Church, the entire center section of the sanctuary had been roped off for the family. Great Aunt Livvy, her expression suitably pious, joined me, Willie, and John alongside dozens of Bigelows in the pews.

"Will you look at *that*," she whispered behind her lace folding fan. There was no way anyone could *not* look. On one end of the communion table sat an ornate brass urn. On the other end was a large portrait of Murial painted sixty years ago, when she was kicked out of the debutante ball at the Piedmont Driving Club in Atlanta. She wore a slinky gown cut down to her, well, her piedmont.

Willie, sitting between me and his father, turned and gave me a toothy smile and a thumbs up. *Great-Grandma was a babe*, he mouthed. Murial, wherever she was, had to be grinning outright at the reaction of the mourners. They weren't sure whether to laugh nervously or frown in horror.

"Where's the casket?" whispered Great Aunt Livvy.

"No casket," I answered. "She was cremated."

Aunt Livvy was too shocked to reply.

The services started, formal and

reverent. Prayers were spoken. Hymns were offered up by members of the choir with voices so professionally trained that they could have joined the Mormon Tabernacle Choir. Finally, friends and family members were invited by the minister to come forward and say a few words.

"Are you going to say something, mother?" Willie asked.

"No, I—"

"I told everyone that you would," John said and looked at me with quiet challenge. *Get up and show them you belong here*, his look said.

Willie persisted. "You liked Grandmother Muriel, didn't you, and she liked you?"

That was true. Muriel had schemed with me to defy Bigelow snobbery from the day I married John. I hugged my son and nodded. "That's all that matters, isn't it? You're right."

I stood. Every eye was on me, including John's, as I made my way to the aisle and up to the front of the church. I almost chickened out but looked at Murial's portrait again and saw that devilish glint in her eyes.

All right, Grandmother Murial, I'm up with this. Word. I hope that your urn is big enough for more ashes because after this speech, I may be toast.

I faced the audience. I looked at John, and at Willie, sitting beside him like a miniature shadow of his father. They were so much alike. I nodded to Great Aunt Livvy and suddenly understood what she'd been trying to teach me. Sometimes, respect for the dead means respect for the living. I stared at all the cool-faced Bigelows staring back at me. *Even when they don't deserve it.*

"Grandmother Muriel was a special woman who gave little pieces of herself to everyone. She's gone now, but she lived a good life—on her terms. I salute her, and I thank her for accepting me." I grinned at the racy portrait. "Miss Murial, wherever you are, I hope the music's loud, the food is good, and the men are buying you margaritas."

Almost every Bigelow in the audience scowled at me, but John and Willie smiled, and that was all that mattered. Afterwards, I left Willie with John in Bigelow while I drove Great Aunt Livvy up to Hattie's house in Yonder. But we had just stepped onto Hattie's front porch when Miss Ida dropped Willie off. Willie looked subdued. "If I hang around with Dad too long, I miss him more when I leave," he explained. "So I got Miss Ida to bring me home. I told Dad I had to find out if you were gonna say something weird at Cousin Hattie's funeral, tomorrow."

"I don't think so," I said, my throat tight. "I've been weird enough, already."

"Of course you are," Great Aunt Livvy snapped in double denture time. "What was appropriate for Murial Bigelow is certainly appropriate for Hattie."

I didn't argue. I'd learned enough about

respect for a lifetime.

The hard dirt of Hattie's yard had been swept clean. It had become a parking lot filled with pick-up trucks and sedans around whose open doors gathered clusters of strangers.

"Now, what we do, Willie," Great Aunt Livvy explained, "is welcome the family members."

"Great Aunt Livvy," I remind her, "we *are* the family members."

"Then we let everybody console us." Her dentures clicked in somber step. "Then we go to the coffin and pay our last respects."

"And then we eat?" Willie asked, an old hand at funerals now.

I took Willie's arm, and we followed Great Aunt Livvy indoors, listening for tambourines. According to Great Aunt Livvy, viewing a body in the deceased's own living room isn't morbid. It's an excuse for a mini-reunion of old friends and family to share stories, a *remember-when* kaleidoscope of the past. So we politely allowed ourselves to be consoled, then we ate and listened to stories about Hattie's life as a young woman.

Hours passed. People began to drift away until late in the afternoon it was just me, Great Aunt Livvy, and a few ancient neighbors. "She was the prettiest girl in Yonder," one elderly man confided. "I was sweet on her myself." His voice dropped. He looked around furtively, then whispered, "But she never had eyes for nobody but Ronnie Bigelow."

My ears perked up. I was glad Willie had fallen asleep in Hattie's bedroom listening to the latest rap CD on his headphones.

"Shush that loose talk, Bart Smith!" Great Aunt Livvy snapped, slapping her hand to her mouth to restrain her escaping upper plate. "Don't speak ill of the dead."

"Ain't nothing ill about my speaking. The only ill was that the Salter family kept them two apart. Just think what might have happened if they'd run off and got married before Ronnie went off to fight in the Big War."

I looked at Great Aunt Livvy with questions in my eyes.

"Nothing would have happened," she insisted. "And the Salter family had nothing to do with it. Hattie was a lot like Muriel Bigelow. She always went her own way. Doesn't matter, anyway. Ronnie died in Europe—Christmas 1942."

"Yeah," Bart said, "and Hattie spent the rest of her life alone—grieving for him."

That news sent me to the back porch, where I sat on the steps in the cold, staring up a small pinecone wreath Hattie had hung from the rafters not long before she died. It occurred to me that maybe she hadn't been celebrating Christmas, she'd been celebrating the man she secretly loved and lost.

I married a Bigelow and lived to regret it.

Hattie didn't marry one and spent the rest of her life grieving. All because the Salter women were doomed to make bad choices, especially when it came to Bigelows.

But had I made a bad choice? I was a Salter who'd felt out of place at Muriel's services, but I suddenly felt even *more* out of place at Hattie's. I missed John's arm supporting me, and the feel of his hand on my back. I'd watched Willie with his dad today and felt his pain when he had to leave him. For years, I'd told myself Willie wasn't being damaged by our strange marriage. Now, I wasn't so sure.

The back screen door opened. I knew who it was even before he spoke.

"You know," John said, "Hattie was just as tough as you are, Suzy. And, so, I'm beginning to think, was my Grandmother Muriel."

"What are you doing here?" I said that softly, not accusing.

"I came to show my respect for your family. The Salters don't have a corner on the respect market. May I sit down beside you?"

No! I wanted to say. We'll only make more mistakes, and hurt each other, again. But I couldn't. Something had changed, and I wasn't sure what. Instead, I whispered, "Yes."

He carried a paper cup and a plate full of Jesus cake, balancing it on one hand as he lowered himself next to me. He licked some icing off his fingertips. Neither of us said anything for a moment, as if he were waiting for me to set the terms of his encampment. "Tell me what you know about Hattie," I finally said. "I just found out she was in love with a Bigelow."

He nodded. "Here's another secret-- something Great Aunt Livvy says I can tell you, now." He hesitated. Then, "Ronnie and Hattie got married the night before he shipped out."

I gaped at him. "Married?"

"Yes. She inherited his share of the Bigelow Banking Company, despite every effort his family made to take it away from her. She used part of the money to build the Faith and Forgiveness Baptist Church. She gave the rest to other charities. The Bigelows could have killed her." He smiled. "Wasting money like that."

"How long have you known this story?"

"Grandmother Murial told me not long after you and I separated. She said Salter women are stubborn and proud—but they don't stop loving a man, once they've chosen him."

My throat worked. "Did you believe her?"

"Not right away. Too much Bigelow in me." He smiled wearily. "Too much pride."

"What do you think would have happened if Ronnie had come back from the war? Would he and Hattie have been caught up in the old feuds and differences? Would the Bigelows have disowned her for being from Mossy Creek?"

He jutted his chin forward as he always did when confronted with a problem. "I don't know. I'd like to think he and Hattie would have made a go of it, but I don't know. What do you think?"

"I think they would have. She married the man she loved, and he loved her, and that would have been enough."

"Why do you think that?"

"Simple. The name of the church she founded with his money. *Faith and Forgiveness.*"

"I never thought about that, before. But it occurs to me that my grandmother was right about Salter women. You don't need the Bigelow name and money. You've been determined to make it on your own. And you have." He paused. "But does that mean you can't be my wife? And that I can't take care of you?"

I cleared my throat, and then, trembling, I asked him the hardest question I'd ever considered, one that dogged the back of my mind for five years. "John, did you have something to do with my business loan to buy the *Mossy Creek Gazette*?"

Slowly, he nodded. "Don't be angry. I wanted you to have a chance to prove yourself. And I knew it was the only way you'd stay in Mossy Creek."

"And you wanted me to stay?"

"I did. John, Junior—sorry, I mean Willie—is my son. Our son. I wanted him close by. And, I wanted you close by. You don't know how much I missed you, Suzy. How much I still miss you." That statement shocked me into silence. He straightened, and stared out into the night. His throat worked. "But I won't give you a hard time any more. If you still want a divorce, I'll give it to you."

After all this time, his offer came as a surprise. Finally, I managed to ask, "Why are you saying all this, now?"

"Great Aunt Livvy convinced me."

"I don't understand."

"She says maybe the star-crossed love affairs between Salter women and Bigelow men should end with us. Maybe she's right."

From somewhere in the forest came the cry of a fox, followed by the joyous call of its mate. Star-crossed love affairs? I answered him the only way I could. "You know I can't let you off this easy."

There was a long moment before he said, "Do you mean about getting the divorce or being mad about the business loan?"

"Either one. I'm a Bigelow because that's my son's name. But I'm a Salter, too. I'll always pay my own way, but unless *you* want a divorce, I think I'll leave things the way they are."

We both knew what I was trying to say. His eyes warmed, and relief washed over me.

"Well, Suzy," he said softly.

Laughter broke out in the house behind us. It was obvious that Great Aunt Livvy had been right; this wasn't a time to mourn but a time to share good memories. Stories about families, their joys, their sorrows, the very pain and laughter that held them in this place. Stories that didn't change, even as life moved forward.

"Want some Jesus cake? It's pretty good."

He held out the plate. He'd managed to carve out the *Jesus*, in purple icing. From inside the house came the sound of a tambourine and a banjo. I knew I was teetering between my old ways and the new. Arguing with my husband to stay married when I wasn't sure where we were headed wasn't fair to him. Still, Salter women don't give up.

"Sure. I'll have some cake, but only if we warm up with moonshine while we eat it," I said, my teeth chattering in the cold. I sounded like Great Aunt Livvy.

"Brought that too," he said and held out the paper cup.

As I reached for the cup, I looked up at Hattie's little wreath. *You kept loving him, and you survived.* John took a bite of the cake then held it to my lips, and I took a nibble, too. We looked at what was left. The *Jes* was missing from Jesus. All that was left was *us*.

I raised the cup of moonshine. "Here's to the Salter women and the men who are crazy enough to marry them."

John nodded. "And here's to you and me, Suzy. I only hope our Willie will learn from us and get it right."

"He can't miss," I said. "It's in the genes."

John and I spent the most wonderful night together, and went to Hattie's funeral together, the next day. We realized we shouldn't try to live together—at least not anytime soon—but we're happy enough, just visiting. I decided to start a new hobby.

"Hey, Great Aunt Livvy," I called this morning, across the cold December yard between our houses.

She opened her kitchen window. "Eh?" she called back, as she ate her breakfast cereal next to the radio at her table.

"Are we still alive?"

She gave me a thumbs up.

"Then let's start planning lunch."

From the desk of Katie Bell

Ho, ho, ho, Vick!

Do you want to know what I believe about Isabella and Richard? I believe they ran away to save Mossy Creek. If they'd stayed, the feud would have gone on for years and hurt a lot more people. Isabella knew there was no other way around Bigelow revenge and Mossy Creek pride, so she gave up her home and her family forever. How noble she must have been! How homesick she must have felt for the rest of her life!

I like to think she knows we never forgot her, especially at Christmas, when Mossy Creek celebrates its memories. Christmas is when all of our traditions seem to gang up, draw a line in the dirt—or snow, depending on the weather that year—and dare us to change a one of them.

Mossy Creek Elementary has a Christmas program that nobody misses. Every kid in the school is in it. Forget the three wise men, the three kings, and the three shepherds. The Mossy Creekite kids decided if three was good, a dozen would be better. If our herd of paper mache stage camels ever gets loose, they'll clean out every fruit stand from the mountains to Atlanta.
Christmas in Mossy Creek is a little over-the-top, but we like it that way.

That's why it was so sad this year, when we

almost lost one of our *best* traditions. Ever since I can remember, a local farmer named Ed Brady has played Santa and Ho! Hoed! all the way around the square. Mr. Brady has always been the perfect Santa, right down to the white hair and beard. He works magic on the kids. They're convinced their wishes come true because of him.

But even Santa can't make every wish happen. And what do you do when Santa himself needs a miracle?

Under the mistletoe,

Katie

Ed

The Ugly Tree

The room is cold. The house is always cold now. And there's no reason to get out of bed anymore.

Except for Ellie.

And she doesn't know.

Possum, my hound dog, is getting restless. I can hear his toenails clicking on the bare floor as he moves around. For most of my seventy-eight years, I've opened these tired old eyes in this same room in the same farmhouse in Mossy Creek. Never left but once and wouldn't have left then, except for the Big War. Figured the folks in Washington knew what they were doing when they sent us to France. But I won't be surprised if one day some smart fella says otherwise. Back then though, I believed.

And I spent enough time fighting on foreign soil to learn that there was no dirt like the dirt my daddy plowed. After the war, I came home, married Ellie and plowed that same dirt. Grew tobacco then, just like my daddy. Never thought to apologize for what we grew. By the time the world decided that tobacco was bad, I'd already quit farming. Now the soil is worn out, and so am I.

Still wearing my socks and winter underwear from the day before, I slid out from under the bedcovers and into my overalls puddled on the floor where I dropped them last night. They were stiff like me, and unforgiving. There were no dying coals of heat in the fireplace. Haven't been since Ellie left.

Poking my feet into my work boots, I stood, pulled the overalls up to my hips, then reached my arms into the corduroy shirt hanging on the bedpost. As I latched the suspenders on the overalls' denim bib, it surprised me to see how much the pants gaped, even after I fastened the waist buttons. When had I had lost all that weight? Ellie would fuss, but cooking takes more effort than I'm willing to expend. The only real meal I ate anymore was breakfast with Ellie, and if I was going to get into town in time to feed her, I'd better hurry.

I let Possum out the kitchen door, then filled his bowl with those little chunks of what the commercials say is real meat. If the picture on the box was right, that meat's been somewhere for longer than I'd want it to be before I chewed it.

I saw myself in an old mirror hanging on a back porch post. Nothing I could do about my ragged beard and mustache. Ought to just shave them off. Never would have let them grow anyhow if it hadn't been for Ellie coaxing me to play Santa Claus every year. "Nobody else looks like Santa except you," she'd say every December, and send me to the barbershop to get prettied up for the children in town.

I didn't look like Santa Claus anymore. To me, the old man in the mirror looked more like Scrooge.

Didn't much matter. Ellie wouldn't know. Setting a stained, green John Deere tractor cap on my head, I headed for my truck. My, "Bah Humbug!" sounded like I meant it, and I did.

A blast of December wind almost knocked me down. I went back for a jacket. Ought to get me some glasses, too. I hated the wind now. It made my eyes water. I left the back door unlocked. Nobody's gonna steal anything. They'd be welcome to whatever they need; none of it matters.

The faded green truck under the shed had once belonged to the National Forest Service. They replaced a fine-running truck with a sports utility vehicle. I bought it back in ninety-one. It was already ten years old then. You can still read the Forestry Service letters on the doors. Ellie fussed some because I bought something already worn out.

This morning the engine grumbled

about starting, sputtering before it caught. I patted the dash. "Me and you are a lot alike these days, old buddy. We're slow to get up and cantankerous about moving."

Sleep crusted my eyes, leaving a patchy film that made it hard to see. Course, it didn't matter about the road to town. I could drive it blindfolded. Squinting helped me focus, but the painted centerline seemed even more blurred than usual this morning. The wind, I told myself. But the truth was, it was cataracts. The only good thing about cataracts is they keep me from seeing the run-down condition of the farm, the peeling paint and the way the barn droops at the front corner. I must have a dozen pairs of glasses. They don't help me see better, just like medicine don't help my arthritis. Just like the once-a-month call from Ellie's and my only son, who lives out of town, don't stop the loneliness.

There was only Ellie, and I was late.

By the time I got to South Bigelow Road, the old Ford was warmed up and purring. Satisfied that nobody was coming from the direction of Bigelow and nobody was headed out of Mossy Creek, I pulled onto the highway. As I drew near the big Hamilton Farm, I glanced up at the corn silo and grinned. One of the few things I could still read were the words at the top: Ain't going nowhere, and don't want to.

Mayor Ida was upholding the town real

well, I thought. Her and the younger crowd were just flat determined to keep everything the same. I could tell them that wouldn't work, but they wouldn't listen. Change came, no matter what. People got sick, and old, and died. New people forgot them. I pulled out my handkerchief and blew my nose. In that second, a horn honked. I didn't take my eyes off the road, but I realized I'd crossed the centerline.

"Doggoned eighteen-wheelers!" I swore and jerked the wheel of the truck to the right, then when it run off the road, back to the left, hard. Too hard. The old truck shot all the way across the road, bounced into and right back out of a ditch, then plowed through Miss Ida's white wooden pasture fence. When it was over, the truck's bumper was resting against the corn silo.

I just sat and waited, cursing the eighteen-wheeler. He didn't even stop. I heard noises after a while, and a Mossy Creek police car pulled up. Mutt Bottoms jumped out and ran to my open window.

"You hurt, Mr. Brady?"

"No." Hurt, I thought, hurt was a bullet that cut through your shoulder so quick that you didn't know you'd been shot until the hole it left turned into fire that burned like the blaze from a fat lighter. But even that kind of hurt ain't nowhere as bad as the kind that sucks up a man's life force and makes him wait to die.

I focused on the skinny deputy wearing a police cap bigger than his head. "I'm not hurt, Mutt, but I reckon Miss Ida's fence might need some fixing. I'll take care of it. Just stand back and let me get outta here."

I tried to goose the old truck into moving. The wheels spun in the soft dirt. "Come on, buddy. You got me in here, now you get me out before Miss Ida comes with her shotgun."

"Mr. Brady," the deputy said, "I don't think you'd better back the truck out. You know you're not supposed to be driving. Chief Royden told you the last time you ran somebody off the road that you weren't goin' to be allowed to drive anymore. He's gonna take your license for sure."

It's hard to take a person seriously when his name is Mutt. I had business in town, and his job was to help the citizens of Mossy Creek. "Son, the only person I run off the road is me, and I'm drivin' in a pasture. Ain't nobody gonna keep me from havin' breakfast with Ellie like I do every morning. So you just get in front of this truck and help me shove it away from this silo."

We both pushed, but the truck refused to move. Half an hour later, a tow truck was hauling the old truck to the barn, and I was being hauled into the police station like a prisoner. Chief Royden took my license and gave me what my daddy would have called a dressing down.

"No more driving, Mr. Brady. I don't want you to hurt yourself or anybody else."

I didn't argue; it wouldn't have done me any good. Amos Royden wasn't much like his daddy, Battle, who woulda let me off and come over to take me fishin', later. "Your daddy is spinnin' in his grave, boy," I said. Amos just looked at me, and I felt kinda sorry for my words. But I didn't take them back.

From the police station, I walked up Main Street and then onto North Bigelow, to the nursing home. Thank God, it was only a little ways. Nobody saw me, but the whole town would know my problem soon enough. When I got to Magnolia Manor, I found Ellie lying in her bed staring at nothing. Like she did most of the time.

"Morning, pretty girl." I picked up her limp hand and leaned forward to kiss her forehead. Her face was turned away from me so that I couldn't see the contorted expression that drew the corner of her mouth into a permanent frown, from her last stroke. But then I never saw what was, only what used to be—a smile that had warmed my heart for fifty years.

"Sorry I'm late, hon. Got held up at Miss Ida's for a while. I'm glad you waited breakfast for me. Let's see what we got."

She didn't respond. I didn't expect her to. It had been almost a year since she'd recognized me. But that didn't matter. I knew who she was. She was my wife.

I turned away from her and uncovered the dishes on the breakfast tray. Everything was cold, thanks to my little side trip through Ida's pasture.

The nurses' aides didn't pay any attention to me as I carried Ellie's tray back to their break room. Squinting at the numbers on a microwave, I punched the pad and waited while the food warmed. Operating a microwave was something I'd learned for Ellie's sake, so she wouldn't have to eat cold food. I didn't have to see the numbers to do that. The numbers didn't matter anyway. I just had to pay attention to how long it ran before I opened the door.

"Mr. Brady," one of the nurses' aides said, "you know you're not supposed to be in here."

"Neither is Ellie," I said. "But she is."

Back in her room, I raised the bed so I could spoon food into her mouth. Some days, she swallowed obediently. Today, she didn't. Only once did she move, and that was to look past me and into the hall. I thought at first she was looking for someone, but then I saw the blinking lights in the recreation room.

A Christmas tree. Ellie had always loved Christmas. She used to start cooking fruitcakes right after Thanksgiving. People at Mossy Creek Mt. Gilead Methodist said nobody could make divinity candy like Ellie. And nobody loved decorating more than she did. She'd get on the phone with Hattie Almond over in Yonder, and they'd plan their bows and wreaths and garlands. Then every year she'd send me out to cut down a tree. "The ugliest one you can find," she'd say. "We'll make it beautiful for Christmas." And she would. At least me and Ellie thought the crooked, scrawny trees were special. Once, our boy came home for Christmas when he was in college, took one look at our tree and bought us an artificial one. Ellie smiled and let him put it up. She didn't want to spoil his pleasure, for he'd meant well. But the minute he left, heading back to the big city and his fancy friends, she took it down.

"Don't fret, Ed. He just doesn't understand that love doesn't need perfection. It makes its own." She rescued our pitiful little tree from the trash heap and put it back up. "Every living thing becomes beautiful when it's loved."

A lump filled my throat. Remembering always made me feel as if I was watching me and Ellie like we used to be. I can still remember the way I felt then. I never was much with words, but I loved my Ellie, and she knew it. The blinking lights on the tree in the recreation room blurred, and I went light-headed with memories.

Love doesn't need perfection. It makes

its own. Ellie believed that. If she hadn't, she wouldn't've of married me. The bullet that brought me home from the war left me as damaged on the inside as she was now.

"You like the tree, Ellie? Wait, I'll move it, so you can see it better."

Over the nurses' objections, I went into the other room, unplugged the artificial tree and moved it closer to the open door.

When I went back to Ellie's room, I said, "Doesn't look much like one of ours, Ellie. Too perfect." I leaned down and whispered in her ear, "Say, I'm thinking, I could bring you a little tree for your room. Your decorations are still in the hall closet. You just say the word, and I'll go get the ugliest one I can find."

Ellie didn't answer. She clamped her mouth shut when I tried to slip one more spoonful of grits between her lips. She didn't want anymore of her breakfast, so I finished off her food like I usually do, then put the tray in the hall.

When I came back in the room, Ellie's eyes were closed. There was no point in hanging around. Our day was finished.

I waved at the nurses and went out the door, then remembered that I had no way to get home. Even if I had my truck, I had no license. And Chief Royden would make good on his threat to lock me up if I got in my old truck, again.

I stood on the sidewalk, then headed

back toward the square. I walked into the police station with my head high. It came to me that Amos Royden had caused this problem, not me. By George, he could fix it.

"I got to have my truck, Chief," I said. "Ain't no other way. I can't desert Ellie."

"Mr. Brady, you don't know how sorry I am about this," the chief said. "I'm going to try to work out some transportation for you. But for now the only truck I want to see you in is the Mossy Creek volunteer fire truck bringing Santa Claus to the tree lighting in the square."

"Not this year. Don't feel much like playing Santa anymore. Find somebody else."

"You know we can't do that. You've been Santa for thirty years. By appointment of every mayor. It's official. If you want to resign, you'll have to take it up with Miss Ida."

I swore under my breath.

Chief Royden looked at me with a thought in his eyes. "I'll tell you what, Mr. Brady. You play Santa, and I'll guarantee that you get to the nursing home every day. But you're not to drive that truck again. Do you understand?"

I nodded. But what he didn't understand was that it wasn't me that didn't understand. It was him. I'd be at Ellie's side in the morning for breakfast—one way or another, whether he guaranteed it, or not. I'd think of something.

The chief put a hand on my shoulder as if I was an old man who needed support.

"Come on, Mr. Brady. I'll give you a ride home."

❦❦❦

Once I got home, I let Possum in. I usually just sit at the little table in the kitchen by the cook stove, but the kitchen was for remembering. This time, I sat down in the old leather chair in front of the fireplace. Didn't take long for me to decide a body can't think when it's too cold. So I built a fire that night. I can always look into a fire and think up a solution to any problem. Fire talks to people that way. But for the first time in my life, an answer didn't come.

Turns out I didn't need one. Old Bart Smith came along the next morning, headed for Mossy Creek.

"Heard you were on foot, Ed."

"Yep. Back where I started as a boy—on foot. Well, that's not exactly true. Back then, I had a mule."

"Get in," Bart said with a grin that showed the vacant space where his front tooth used to be before he knocked it out chopping firewood.

"I remember that mule," he said as I climbed into the cab of his truck. "Remember the day you rode it up the front steps of the old high school, down the hall, and out the back door? Said you were through with school, joining the army to save the world."

"That's what I thought."

"Your Pa thought different though, didn't he? Sent you back to school the next day without the mule. As I remember, you spent the rest of the year on foot."

"I did. But you've given me an idea. Maybe I'll just buy myself a mule. No law says you have to have a driver's license to ride a mule."

"True," Bart agreed. "But the mules you get nowadays are a stubborn bunch. Nobody rides them. You might start out for the nursing home and end up in North Carolina—or you might end up with your head broke before you even get outta the yard."

"Then I'll just walk to town."

The next morning, I was reconsidering the mule when Adele Clearwater's big blue Caddy came rumbling up the drive.

"You're up early, Adele," I studied her suspiciously. "If you've come to talk me into going to some meeting over at the Baptist Church, I'll tell you again. I'm a Presbyterian. Always been a Presbyterian, and I reckon I'll go to my Maker that way."

Adele was scrawny but righteous. She pretty much meddled in everybody's business, her and her Mossy Creek Ethics Society. She'd nearly sunk young Jayne Reynolds's business last month, and I was still aggravated with her over that foolishness. She frowned at me. "Mr. Brady, I've got a back seat full of pies for the

Christmas Festival, and I thought if you could help me deliver them to the church, I could drop you off at the nursing home while I'm setting up the booths. Then we could ride back together. I could really use the help. And I have an extra pie for you."

For Ellie, I'd ride with Adele. The possibility of being given a pie didn't sway me, even if my mouth did water at the smell of apples and cinnamon.

On Tuesday, it was Jamie Green—my rural route postman—in my driveway at the crack of dawn. Jamie's not called the postman anymore; now he's a rural letter carrier. When I saw him, I put on my coat and went out on the front porch.

"Get in, Mr. Brady. I got a special delivery for Magnolia Manor. You can sit with Ellie, and I'll pick you up when you're done." He took a look at me, frowned and added, "Thought you might want to get your beard and your whiskers trimmed before the tree lighting ceremony."

"Don't think so. Not sure I'm playing Santa Claus this year. Still thinkin' on it. But I'll take you up on the ride."

My Wednesday driver was a surprise. Casey Blackshear was sitting in her specially outfitted van, honking her horn. "Mr. Brady, I'm on my way to the library with some kittens for story time. I wonder if you'd help me out."

I frowned. "Help you out, how? Unless

you're reading the Farmer's Bulletin to those kids, I'm not likely to do you any good."

She laughed. The sound was musical, catching in the wind like bells, and for a minute, I thought I heard Ellie again, laughing like a girl. When Ellie laughed, even the birds listened.

"No, Mr. Brady. I can handle the reading. What I need help with is the basket of kittens in the back. I plan a theme every week, and today it's stories about cats. The children love it when I bring animals—though I'm not sure the library staff is as enthusiastic."

The girl had a happy smile, and she never asked for an ounce of pity about her circumstances. When I saw an orange and white kitten climb across her shoulder, I decided she could use my help.

"Oh, all right," I said, and went 'round to the other side. The kittens had escaped from their box and were having a town meeting in the middle of the van. Corralling them was about as easy as it had been convincing Ellie to marry me after the war. But I was determined, still am. And finally, they were boxed up, and we were ready for travel.

It wasn't until we got to the library that I learned Casey had a real cat carrier in the back, hidden behind her wheelchair. Casey Blackshear was a smart one, all right. She'd come prepared to deal with an ornery old man.

"Next week, we're reading *Rudolph the*

Red Nosed Reindeer," she said.

"A basket of kittens is one thing," I said, "but I'm not rounding up reindeer back here."

She said she was just joking about the reindeer, but she'd pick me up bright and early.

I liked her.

Thursday brought Robert Walker, Miss Ida's son, who didn't even offer an excuse for his presence. "Ready to go, Mr. Brady? Mother said to take you to see Miss Ellie and bring you over to Hamilton's when you're done. We've just gotten in a new Santa suit. She had it custom-made for you."

"I like my old one fine," I grumbled. "Now look, a ride is one thing, but what makes your mama think she can just run my life?"

"Mr. Brady, that's between you and my mother. By the way, she wants to know if you'll look at one of the muscadine vines you sold her. She hasn't taken it out of the pot yet. She left it at the store for you to see. She says it looks spindly, and her new farmhand pruned it by mistake. She's not sure it'll make it through the winter."

"Well, I guess I could take a look at it," I said.

By lunchtime, I left Hamilton's Department Store with a new jacket, a pair of trousers and a shirt. Payment, Miss Ida said, for pruning services on her grape vines. But I refused to look twice at the new Santa outfit Robert pulled out of a clothing bag. When Ida

Hamilton Walker sets her mind to something, she gets it done, and I wasn't about to get caught up in her scheme or anybody else's. I know how things are in Mossy Creek.

Neighbors helped neighbors. People meddled. Young folks set their sights on a certain intended, for example, and pretty soon half the town would be playing matchmaker. Not that me and Ellie had needed any help, way back then. Course, I wasn't planning on marrying nobody. Farming was too hard a life. I wanted to see the world.

That was before Ellie's folks came to live in Mossy Creek that summer. Before we met at the old swimming hole behind the Hamilton House Inn. Before Ellie took my hand and told me she'd wait for me to get back from the war.

When I got home a few years later, I took a long look at myself in the mirror and grimaced. I was rail-thin and looked like I'd aged more than my time. And I'd seen things I still couldn't get out of my dreams at night. Ellie said she loved me no matter what, and I was not getting out of marrying her even if my hair did have an extra part in it, courtesy of a German sniper. In the end she won out. We married. I started to farm, and we were happier than I ever hoped to be. But that was then, and this was now.

And now she was in a nursing home, and I was reduced to depending on others to get me to town. I gave myself a strong talking to. I'd stop being so disagreeable. If folks were going to help me, I'd try to help myself, too.

I lit a big fire in the fireplace of the main room. Possum woofed like he couldn't remember what heat felt like. While the flames were licking at the logs, I gathered up the dirty clothes—everything I owned—and put a load in Ellie's Kenmore machine. Once I decided to do something to make myself easier on the eyes, it made me think I ought to do something about the mess around me. I wondered where all the boxes along the wall had come from and knew Ellie would have a fit if she could see how I'd let things stack up. She'd always prided herself on a clean house. Dragging the boxes into the spare room got them out of sight 'til I could do better.

By the time the heat got to circulating, I'd put some order to the place. At least it looked as if somebody lived there. Then came a real shower in a bathroom warm enough so's I could wash my hair and my beard without worrying about giving myself pneumonia.

Over the next week, people continued to show up in my yard every morning. Folks who "just happened" to be going to town and stopped by to give me a ride. I didn't much like it, but I didn't argue. Human nature being what it is, I knew sooner or later Miss Ida and the chief's taxi service would end. In the meantime, I fed Ellie and talked to her about Christmas. She never responded. But from time to time, she'd look at the tree in the recreation room across the hall.

The morning finally came when I was ready to leave, and there was no one outside my door. With only four days before the great tree lighting, everyone was too busy to remember me. I'd known this would happen, but I'd hoped it wouldn't happen until I figured out how I was going to get back and forth to the nursing home on my own. I'd have to drive.

Except, as if it had taken Chief Royden's orders personally, the old truck refused to crank. Sitting there in the cab, I rubbed my chapped, aching hands together and studied the sky. Snow was coming. I could feel it in my swollen knuckles. The weatherman wasn't forecasting it. But I knew. Snow always fell on Bigelow County, even if no other town in North Georgia got weather. Mossy Creekites loved it. Everybody pitched in and turned the square into a palace of snowmen where younguns had snowball fights and made snow angels. The merchants down in Bigelow would complain that the snow interfered with business and the tourists they tried so hard to attract. But a white Christmas would be welcome in Mossy Creek.

Ellie always liked the snow, and though I grumbled, she knew I liked it, too. Except today. I was worried. Frustration had set in. The thing that had kept me going for the last year had been my breakfast with Ellie. Now it seemed that was about to stop, too.

Crawling out of the truck, I reached back for my work gloves. Neither police officers, trucks, nor the elements were going to stop me. When the chief first took my license, I'd toyed with walking up to the highway and hitching a ride. Today, by George, I would.

I put on my gloves, pulled the earflaps down from inside my winter cap and started around the end of the truck.

There was my answer, staring me in the face. The green John Deere tractor I had used to plow my fields. I hadn't used it much in the last few years, but it was worth a try.

Minutes later, I'd fired up the old girl. We made it down the driveway and, finally, onto South Bigelow Road. I might not be able to drive my truck, but a farmer has always been able drive his tractor on the public road.

Some things ought not to ever change.

❧❧❧

At the South Bigelow Bridge, I hit a patch of ice and went straight down the bank. Me and the tractor slid right into Mossy Creek. I woke up in a bed at the Mossy Creek Emergency Clinic wearing a skimpy hospital gown that left my hind-end bare. I said a few bad words about Dr. Champion. When I tried to move, I discovered how bad my right leg hurt. Gingerly, I twisted it and decided that being still was better.

On the other side of a curtain, I could hear Mutt Bottoms. "Chief, everybody in Mossy Creek knows that Mr. Brady is as blind as a bat. But this time it wasn't his fault."

"Just like it wasn't his fault that he took down Miss Ida's fence and put a dent in her silo?"

"Ah, Chief, you have to understand. He wouldn't've run into Miss Ida's pasture if it hadn't a-been for that eighteen-wheeler. Ought not to have been on South Bigelow going fast in the first place. Them big trucks just cause trouble."

"You got that right, Mutt," I growled, but somehow my voice wasn't loud enough to attract anybody's attention. If I hadn't known I was talking, I wouldn't have heard myself either.

"Mutt," the chief said patiently. Just the tone of his voice said he wasn't going to listen to any excuses. "I've got a John Deere tractor in the creek and Ed Brady on the other side of that partition waiting to get a broken leg set." The chief hesitated. "And I've got the governor in Dwight Truman's office at the chamber, threatening to raise hell if I don't drop charges against his driver."

"I feel like it was my fault, Chief. I was supposed to pick Mr. Brady up and bring him into town, but I got hung up by a wreck out on

Trailhead. Then, on the way out to Ed's place, I met him driving that tractor up the road as big as you please. He was almost to town, not going more than ten miles an hour. I turned my patrol car around and fell in behind him, figured I'd follow him the rest of the way. Then the governor's big black Lincoln came up behind us, with the driver honking his horn like he was an ambulance on an emergency. He didn't have to do that! Mr. Brady was just crossing the South Bigelow Bridge, and that Lincoln could have waited another minute. The governor's driver zoomed around me and crowded up beside Mr. Brady's tractor just as Mr. Brady was heading onto the bridge. You know how old and narrow the South Bigelow Bridge is. Mr. Brady got rattled, I think, and swung out too far—just trying not to get sideswiped. The next thing I knew, him and his tractor were down in the creek." Mutt snorted. "If you ask me, Chief, ought to have been the *governor* and his driver in the creek, not Mr. Brady."

"Hello, boys." I heard Miss Ida's voice. She sounded mad.

"You've been over to the chamber office to see the governor?" the chief asked.

"Oh, yes. I dropped in unannounced. I took Sue Ora Salter and her camera along with me." I could almost hear the sly smile in Miss Ida's voice. "Sue Ora snapped a few shots of Ham shaking his fist at everybody. That quieted him down. She told him she's picturing a headline that says, *Governor's Speeding Limousine Injures Elderly Farmer*. Along with a lovely article describing how he was rushing to a meeting with Dwight. And why? Because our own Dwight Truman has agreed to serve as one of Ham's key political organizers in this part of the mountains. The traitor.'"

"If Ham gets elected, Dwight will be his 'Director of Brown-Nosing,'" the chief said dryly.

Miss Ida laughed. "Maybe, but look at the bright side. I had a little talk with the governor. Ham will be paying all of Mr. Brady's medical expenses, plus repairs on the tractor."

"Good work, Mayor."

"So for now, let's just go have a little talk with Dwight. I want him to know that if I catch him helping Ham plot against Mossy Creek he'll need protection."

"No guns," the chief ordered.

"Oh, Amos, you have no sense of fun."

I muttered to myself as I heard Miss Ida, the chief, and Mutt walk away.

"Hey," I called out, "what about me? You're not going to leave me in this bed half-nekkid. Bring me my clothes. Do you hear me?"

Nobody did. Or if they heard, they ignored me. A nurse scrawnier than Adele Clearwater came in, stuck something in my ear, grabbed my wrist, and shushed me so that she could take my blood pressure. "Dr. Champion'll be in in a minute to put a cast on that leg," she growled. "Now you calm down. Your heart's just racing." I could have told her it was racing, but she didn't give me a chance. Instead, she fed me a pill and left the room.

When Dr. Champion came in, he told me I'd bruised my shoulder and busted my leg. "I don't think you can use a crutch yet," he said, "and with a broken leg, you can't go home alone."

"'Course I can. I've been alone for over a year."

"Not with a broken leg. I've tried to get in touch with your son, but his office said he's skiing in Colorado."

"Champion, I'm going home. You can put that in your pipe and smoke it."

"Not until you can get around, Mr. Brady. You stay in this bed. If you don't, I'll have the nurse give you a shot that'll make you sleep for two days straight."

I grumbled at him but knew I was trapped. He set my leg, and that hurt like a sinner. Nurse Scrawny gave me another pill, and I dozed. When Miss Ida came to visit, I kept my eyes shut and listened to her talk to the Doc. "I don't know what to do with him," Dr. Champion told her. "He's acting like an old cuss, a regular Crankshaft."

After he walked out, Miss Ida leaned over me and said, "Stop pretending to sleep,

Mr. Brady."

I opened my eyes. "Who's Crankshaft?"

"He's a character in a comic strip. A cranky old man."

"Suits me, then."

"Mr. Brady, I've been thinking. Miss Ellie already has a room at the nursing home. Dr. Champion says he can get you admitted temporarily, while your leg heals. They'll put a bed in her room for you. I know you don't want to move into the nursing home permanently, but would you mind staying there, with Miss Ellie, through Christmas?"

I fought the suggestion just long enough to make sure she meant it. Dealing with the U.S. Army taught me that trick. People always make sure you get the very thing they think you don't want. "Okay, okay, I give up," I said. Inside, I was so full of joy that my leg stopped hurting.

So, me and Ellie were back together again. The answer to my problem had come, and I didn't even have to think about it. Mutt agreed to check on the farm. Casey took old Possum home with her. I worried about Possum, him being a country dog and all, but Casey said he thought he was a cat and was mothering the kittens like it was his job. Reckon he needed one now that we were both too old to hunt.

For the first few days at Magnolia Manor, I deliberately lived up to my reputation as a cantankerous old man. At least that's what I told myself. But in the wee hours of the night, when the nursing home was quiet, I could hear a swallowed sob in the silence, and I admitted to myself that I was covering up my own hurt. Somewhere in that last secret part of my heart, I'd thought that Ellie would start recognizing me now that I was spending all day and night with her. But she didn't. The only thing she ever seemed to see was the Christmas tree across the hall. Once I even thought I heard her say, *"Not ugly enough."*

Outside the nursing home windows, all of Mossy Creek was making ready for Christmas. The square was covered in little white lights, and all the shops had jingle bells on their doors. I watched the Kiwanis and the VFW fellows string lights and hang ornaments all over the big fir tree in the park. Everybody would be coming into town for the tree lighting. Somebody had sure better decide to play Santa Claus, soon. I kept reminding everybody. There'd been a steady stream of visitors in and out of our room all morning. The visitors hadn't bothered Ellie, but they were sure pestering me.

"Mr. Brady," Mutt said, "we don't have another man in town who looks like Santa the way you do."

"Besides," his sister Sandy argued, "the kids are used to seeing you. Golly, Mr. Brady, it wasn't Christmas to me and my brothers until we saw you each year. Look, now, the volunteer fire department has got the old truck out, and I've been helping 'em clean it. It's polished and shined up like you wouldn't believe. But it won't be the same without you on top."

"Nothing's ever the same," I said, wishing they'd go away. "Ain't no use trying to make it so."

On the day of the tree lighting, Miss Ida walked into the room. She looked like a racy angel in a soft white pantsuit with a long white wool coat and a white furry hat to match. She liked to dazzle people, and she'd turned all her charm on me. "All right, Mr. Brady, it's time to talk straight, here." She dragged a hard-back chair to the side of my bed and sat down. "Ed Brady, you're a pain in the butt, and you've got a problem. And I've got a problem. It's two hours until the tree lighting, and I still don't have a Santa."

"Yes, ma'am, well that's *your* problem. *I've* got problems of my own! I'm too blind to drive anymore! I'm old and useless!" *And Ellie won't ever recognize me again*, I added silently.

"This town needs you, Mr. Brady."

"For what? Somebody to practice bossing around?"

"Mossy Creek has always depended on

you to bring a certain kind of magic to Christmas. And you've always come through."

"That was before Ellie got sick, and I lost my sight."

"I can't do anything for Miss Ellie, but I am going to take care of your eye problem." She smiled slyly and leaned closer. "The governor is paying for you to have cataract surgery by the finest eye specialist in the state."

I lay there a minute. I needed a mouth specialist to get any words out. Finally, I managed. "Thank you. But if Ellie can't see me, it don't matter much *what* I see. I'm thinking I just might let Casey Blackshear keep Possum and move in here with Ellie for good."

Miss Ida looked at me sadly, finally understanding. She stood and walked over to Ellie's bed, and stroked the soft gray hair back from Ellie's brow. "Everybody loves Miss Ellie. She had a special way about her, a look that could convince people into doing anything she wanted, and they didn't even realize she was doing it. She was so pretty, too."

"She's still pretty to me," I said. Ellie looked past Miss Ida at the tree in the recreation room. Her face changed, slightly, not much, just enough that I could almost see that special look of hers that always got to me, no matter how cantankerous or bull-headed I got. "Ellie?" I whispered. Then the look was gone. But I had seen it for just a second, and that was enough. "You know I never could resist that look, Ellie. If you want me to play Santa, just let me know."

I couldn't touch her with my hands, but I could touch her with my heart, and I reached out to her with all the love I felt. And as I watched, through the cataracts that were stealing my sight, I saw my Ellie blink. In the mid-afternoon light, her faded blue eyes looked moist, and I thought for a moment that she was about to cry.

"Ellie?" At that moment I understood. She might not have known yesterday, and she might not know tomorrow, but for right now, Ellie knew. She knew that it was time for me to play Santa, just like she knew that the recreation room tree wasn't ugly enough to be beautiful.

Sliding out of my bed, I hobbled over to her and took her hand. "It's Christmas, pretty girl. I know you're in there somewhere. Come back and tell me. Do you want Santa to get you an ugly tree?"

Finally, Ellie Brady nodded her head.

I turned toward Miss Ida. "Get me some helpers, Miss Ida," I said. I stumbled to a little clothes cabinet and pulled on my coat, buttoning it over my bathrobe. "I've got to go find my girl a Christmas tree. If I can do that, I'll feel like Santa, again."

"All right, Mr. Brady. That's a deal." She waved for somebody to come in. Mutt leapt to the door and caught me by the arm. "Just hold on a minute, Mr. Brady. I'll get a wheelchair. Then I'll take you wherever you want to go. We'll use the firetruck. Then we'll come back to the square. If we hurry, we'll be just in time for the tree lighting. After that, we'll bring Miss Ellie her tree."

Getting up on the firetruck bench wasn't easy, but I did it, with a little help from Jamie Green and Mutt. Letting Mutt drive the old fire engine along a logging road north of town was hard; that had always been my job.

"Are you sure this is legal?" Mutt asked. "I think we've just crossed over into national forest land. The chief won't be too happy if one of his officers gets arrested for stealing government property."

"The kind of tree I'm lookin' for ain't worth nothing to the government, boys. Stop! Over there." I pointed to a lop-sided scrawny pine with a large bare spot in the middle. "Just cut out the top, the part that's leaning."

"Are you sure? Mr. Brady, that's the worst-looking tree I've ever seen."

"Yep." I smiled. "That's the one I want."

My mind flew back to the first ugly tree I'd cut down. That was the year Ellie was carrying our son. She was due within a week, and the doctor had forbade her to go into the woods. Afraid to leave her for too long, I chopped down the first tree I came to and carried it home. Proudly, I nailed it to a wooden plant base and carried it into the living room, where Ellie started to laugh.

"I'm sorry, Ellie. I know it's the sorriest tree you've ever seen. Birds probably wouldn't nest in it. I'll get another one."

"You'll do no such thing," she'd said. "It's Christmas. When we get through with it, it will be beautiful. You'll see."

And it was. Ellie went into labor that night. She delivered our son at home, in the bed where I was born and where we'd conceived him. Afterwards, I unwrapped my gift for her, a cradle—sanded and stained, though a little uneven.

"Just like our tree," Ellie had said. We laid Eddie in the cradle beneath the pitiful little tree, and suddenly it became beautiful.

Every year after that, the most beautiful woman in the world had helped me pick out the ugliest tree in the woods. This time I did it alone, but all for her.

❧❧❧

The children didn't notice that the small tree Santa carried atop the firetruck beside him was crooked, with missing branches on one side. Before I knew it, a half-dozen people had climbed up real quick and decorated the tree with lights and bows. I held it up on the seat beside me, with Mutt's help. The kids of Mossy Creek couldn't see the cast on my leg; it was covered with Santa's brand-new, custom-made, fake-fur-trimmed robe. They couldn't see my uncombed hair. It was covered by a handsome new Santa hat. They only saw a happy old Santa who waved at the crowd and led the countdown until the switch was pulled and the big fir tree in the park burst into light.

I was Mossy Creek's Santa once again, and I'd brought the magic back. Miss Ida read an announcement that said Santa's friend Governor Bigelow wished everybody in Mossy Creek a very merry holiday and how he would help make sure the town always kept the spirit of the season in its own special way. Nobody believed a word Ham Bigelow said, but we were glad we forced him to say it.

The Mossy Creek church choirs began singing *Deck The Halls* and massing a parade. The whole town fell in behind the firetruck. The truck rounded the square and started up North Bigelow to the nursing home, coming to a stop outside Miss Ellie's window. The firemen lifted me to the ground and into a wheelchair. As I looked up at the window, it started to snow.

"Take the tree to her, Mr. Brady," Miss Ida said softly.

Mutt rolled me, still dressed like Santa Claus and carrying the little tree, inside Magnolia Manor, down the corridor, past the grinning patients and into Ellie's room.

"Open the window, Mutt, so Ellie can hear the carols," I said. He did that, and the songs poured in. He propped the tree against the wall near the foot of Ellie's bed. "Anything else, Mr. Brady?"

"No, thanks. Just close the door as you leave."

For a moment I sat, looking at Ellie's blank face, and listening to the whole town sing to her. Then I rolled the chair close to her. "Here it is, pretty girl. One ugly Christmas tree. Do you see it?"

With the notes of "O Holy Night" floating through the window, I pulled myself to my feet and plugged in a cord. The lights on the little tree came on, turning the room into a myriad of reflected color.

I hobbled to Ellie's side and leaned down to kiss her. As I pulled back, she smiled and looked up at me with love. Ellie never spoke, but for one moment she came back to me. Her ugly tree was never more beautiful, nor was my pretty girl.

We had Christmas together in Mossy Creek.

From the desk of Katie Bell

Dear Vick,

Now you tell me! Isabella and Richard disappeared a *second* time after leaving their baby boy with Richard's family in England? You mean there's more to the world travels of Isabella Salter Stanhope than either you or me can figure out? All right, I agree then, we'll just have to keep writing to each other until we solve this mystery.

Besides, you're a Creekite now.

Look at us—we met way back at the start of the year as strangers, and now the year is almost over, and we're good friends. That's the magic of Mossy Creek. You've become an invisible member of the community. Kind of like Elvis. We believe in you and expect to see you someday. And we're glad to have you on our side.

This was a watershed year in Mossy Creek, and the trouble's just getting started. Is Ham Bigelow really going to run for President a couple of years from now? Could we Mossy Creekites and our stubborn ways be such a worry to him that he'll try to tame us? Could Mossy Creek end up preening in the national spotlight—or be defeated and forgotten? On top of all that intrigue, there'll be the usual dramas around here—love affairs, feuds, and what-have-you.

Here's to Isabella's mysterious past and our interesting future, dear friend!

Your fellow Creekite,

Katie

Mossy Creek

And A Prosperous New Year

Del and I stood in the dark on the front veranda of the Hamilton Inn, him looking handsome in a black tuxedo, me as sleek as a cat's meow in a snug and glittery ball gown just one shade darker than the pale gold of fine champagne. Above our heads, the veranda rafters twinkled with tiny white lights. Every pillar of the big, rambling Victorian hotel's wrap-around porch was decorated with aromatic cedar boughs streaming silver and gold ribbon. The windows glowed. Cool winter moonlight shimmered on the Inn's front lawn and gardens. The Inn stood at the southeastern corner of the town square, with all of downtown Mossy Creek spread out peacefully before us. It was a perfect night. The muted sounds of music and conversation from within heralded Mossy Creek's annual New Year's Eve party.

"What a year it's been," I said. "All's well that ends well, at least."

"It's not over yet, Ida." Del flattened one hand in the small of my back, pivoted me on my toes and looked down at me with a provocative gleam in his blue eyes. I felt a little guilty for escaping Mossy Creek's biggest annual dress-up party to make out. Fifty-six years old and playing the ol' smooch-and-tickle in dark corners. How undignified. I wrapped my arms around Del's neck. "You're a bad influence on a mayor."

He kissed me. I kissed him back.

Smiling, we strolled back into the inn's ballroom, which ordinarily served as its restaurant. Several hundred guests munched hors d'oeuvres, chatted, sipped their drinks or danced on a central dance floor. The room vibrated with the raucous country music of our all-female band, The Screaming Meemies. Rainey was their temperamental lead singer, which said a lot. Thanks to her, the band members all had big, bleached hair.

Six Good Women With Bad Attitudes, the Meemies billed themselves.

While Del fetched me a Scotch, I surveyed the crowd. Ham commanded a large group of family, friends, and toadies in one corner of the ballroom. Another fifteen minutes and he'd be on his way to another party in another part of the state, shaking hands, making promises, forging a political base—and plotting ways to dam up Mossy Creek before we gave him any more black eyes in the news.

We had our work cut out for us.

Dwight Truman stood in Ham's circle, furtively making nice while avoiding the glares of his townsfolk. Sue Ora was watching him like a hawk with her husband John Bigelow beside her. Sandy and Jess Crane stood nearby, with Sandy giving Dwight and Ham an evil eye that said she'd like to do a thorough cleaning on both of them. On a gentler note, I was pleased to see Ed Brady sitting in a circle of old friends, willing to celebrate a new year. As I watched, Ham went over and shook his hand. Then Ingrid Beechum and Jayne Reynolds stopped by to sign Ed's leg cast. Jayne's pregnancy was very obvious, now. Ingrid pampered her like a future grandmother.

Clamped under Ingrid's left arm, Bob the Chihuahua—dressed in a furry white collar, a Santa hat, and tiny white diapers—growled at Ham.

A bevy of waving guests caught my eye. Nail, Geena, and Wolfman grinned at me. I waved back. The Foo Club was on patrol. At a table nearby, Hank and Casey Blackshear cuddled like newlyweds. I watched old Millicent Hart slip up behind their table and reach out to filch Casey's sequined purse. Tag Garner, who had proven himself a fine gentleman, caught Millicent artfully. He tucked her sneaky hand inside the crook of his tuxedoed elbow and led her back to Maggie, who smiled at him.

"Miss Ida?" I turned at the sound of a familiar, bird-like voice. Eulene Watkins, Mossy Creek Elementary's oldest living teacher-emeritus, was draped in a black crocheted sweater with fake-diamond buttons, a silver blouse, and a long silver skirt. With her white hair and pooched little face she resembled a graying sparrow caught in a black crochet net. She peered at me through small, round, steel-rimmed bi-focals. I took her outstretched hand. She had been old when I was a first grader in her class.

"My announcement," she said. "It's time for my announcement. It's nine o'clock and past my bedtime. I've had two glasses of champagne, and I'm giddy. I might take a nap, or I might dance a jig."

I gently led her to the center of the dance floor as the Meemies finished a loud, up-tempo rendition of "Crazy." Rainey could really wreck a nice old ballad. When she saw Miss Eulene, she squealed, pushed electric guitar cables aside on the band's raised dais, and adjusted a microphone. "Lor' Miss Eulene, don't you look pretty!"

"I give your music an 'F' on behalf of Patsy Cline."

Rainey laughed as she and I helped the elderly teacher step up on the band's platform. Everyone in the ballroom stopped talking and waited with affectionate respect.

Miss Eulene tapped the microphone expertly. Not for nothing had she presided over hundreds of rowdy elementary school assemblies. "Next year," she said in a somber voice, "we'll celebrate the fiftieth reunion anniversary of Mossy Creek Elementary." Everyone applauded. "We'll have a whole weekend of get-togethers and events at the Mossy Creek church campground and elsewhere in town. We're sending out invitations to all the alumni, and we're expecting the reunion to bring back dear, sweet former residents of Mossy Creek whom we haven't seen in many, many years."

More applause. Miss Eulene pushed her glasses up her nose and peered into the audience. Tears glittered in her eyes. Everyone who knew what was coming ducked their heads in sorrowful expectation. I found myself doing that, too. Miss Eulene cleared her throat. "And we'll also be commemorating—" her lips trembled, and she struggled for a moment— "we'll also be commemorating the twentieth year since Mossy Creek High School burned to the ground."

The facts surrounding the loss of our beloved town high school were few and vague. The truth was submerged in a wild night no one had ever been able to sort out. The state had refused to rebuild Mossy Creek High, and ever since, Mossy Creekites had been forced to send their children down to the big county high school in Bigelow. The loss of our own high school was a blow Mossy Creek would never forget.

I darted suspicious looks around the ballroom, watching people's faces, hoping for a guilty twitch, a nervous smile, anything that might begin to solve the old mystery. But I saw nothing.

Miss Eulene took a deep breath. "Now children, that's enough moping. Life goes on. Before you leave tonight, stop by the door and buy your tickets to help fund the reunion expenses. I'll be sitting there collecting money. And I don't want to hear any excuses. Thank you."

The applause rose loudly. I went to help her down from the bandstand, when suddenly the ballroom's double doors swung open with a clatter. I turned, startled, along with everyone else. We stared at a pair of burly men dressed in the uniforms of a well-known shipping company. But we stared more at the enormous box they guided between them on a dolly. It was the size of a phone booth, looked sturdy, and was wrapped in gaudy Christmas paper with a giant red bow on top.

Amos, Mutt, and Sandy immediately strode over to investigate. "Stop right there," Amos said. "Let me see some I.D."

"Look, we're legit, and we're just here to deliver the box," one of the men answered. He and his coworker opened their jackets, displaying the delivery company's employee badges on their shirts. "We were paid to wait until the old lady got up to tell everybody about the reunion. That's all we know. You can call our supervisor if you want confirmation. Okay?"

"Okay, but leave the box right here. And wait while we open it."

"Sure, whatever." The man pulled a small clipboard from his back pants' pocket. "But somebody's got to sign for it." He shook his head in amazement. "Whoever sent the thing didn't put a recipient's name on the address. It just says 'Hamilton House Inn, Mossy Creek, Georgia,' and this." He held up an invoice and read loudly. *"To Anybody Who Has The Courage To Find Out The Truth."*

"I'll sign," I said. "I'm the mayor."

Del blocked me. "We don't know what's in that thing."

"Well, I'm going to find out."

"I'll sign," Dwight Truman squeaked. He rushed past me. "I'm the chamber president. It must be a gift to the town from one of our wonderful alumni."

He scrawled his name on the form. The deliverymen backed away from the box. Everyone gazed worriedly at the strange, anonymous gift. "Lucky us," Michael Conners called from behind the bar, "but would it not be best to hunt for a greeting card before we open the monster?"

"Good point," Amos muttered. He,

Mutt, and Sandy did a thorough search of the exterior. "No card stuck anywhere," Amos announced.

"Tear off the paper," I told him.

He nodded. Sandy leapt ahead of him. "Stand back, Chief, I'm good with paper." She clawed the box like a small blonde cat. The huge bow and colorful Christmas wrappings fell away, revealing only a rough wooden crate.

Del stepped forward. "Let's look for a latch." He and Amos felt along all the seams, to no avail. "Go over to the station and get a pry bar," Amos told Mutt.

"Hold on, no need for that." Dan McNeil, our town fix-it man extraordinaire, marched over with an unlit cigar butt clenched between his teeth and his rented tux open to show a World Wrestling Federation belt buckle. "I'll open that baby," he growled.

He plucked an all-in-one screwdriver gadget from his pants pocket then began probing along one edge of the giant box. "Right here. I found it. Come on, Mama. Open up for Daddy."

"Wait a minute," Amos ordered. "I want everyone to back up. Everybody, back. I'm going to call for a bomb dog."

"Too late, Chief." Dan popped the door open. Suddenly we were face-to-face with the box's contents. Around me, people gasped. After a stunned moment, I put a hand to my throat. I couldn't believe what I saw.

The Ten-Cent Gypsy.

Dwight backed away from the box unsteadily, his eyes shifting, looking for escape. All the blood drained from his face. "You can't blame this on me," he said in a high voice. "I didn't know what her card meant."

Ham Bigelow whipped a cell phone from his tuxedo pocket, punched a speed-dial number, and hurried off to a corner for a private conversation. Similar frantic conferences were going on among all the other longtime Mossy Creekites. Hank Blackshear took Casey by the shoulders. "I promise you, I can explain," he said in response to her bewildered scrutiny. "And I want you to remember this, no matter what happens: None of the rabbits were hurt."

Rainey dropped her guitar. "I only mixed the perm, I didn't put it on her," she said, and fled the room.

Jess Crane turned to Sue Ora. "I want to do a story about the elephant."

She nodded. "There's a Pulitzer in this. And maybe a screenplay."

"Ida, what the hell's going on?" Del asked.

I leveled a somber gaze at him. "All I can say right now is that this has something to do with the fire at Mossy Creek High School."

Amos, still staring into the box with the expression of a soldier facing a war, turned to speak to Sandy. He opened his mouth but she cut him off.

"I'm on it, Chief. Come on, Mutt." She and her brother ran into the inn's foyer, grabbed their coats, and left the building.

Amos and I traded a stricken look.

"Look at this way," I said. "Your father couldn't stop what happened then, but now you have a chance to make things right." I paused. "Or at least you may find the elephant's bones and the plastic Easter duck."

Amosmuttered, "ThankyouGladtobehere."

"I hope to shout."

From the corner of my eye, I saw Ham Bigelow slink out a side door.

And so, the old mystery began to trickle into our lives again like the cold, muddy water of Mossy Creek after a storm stirs up the silt. We Creekites are patient, stubborn people, not going anywhere and not wanting to, so we know this much about our creek and our lives: After the mud settles, someone gets dirty, but someone else comes clean.

It was going to be another interesting new year in the old town.

From the desk of Katie Bell

Vick,

We're all speechless over the New Year's Eve incident. I can't even bring myself to describe what was in that gift box. It's at the center of a long story. An elephant was involved. And fireworks. And the last, fateful, high school football game between Mossy Creek and Bigelow.

Judging by what happened at the party after everyone saw the box's contents, we're in for one wild time! I can say this much: Somebody knows who burned down Mossy Creek High School twenty years ago. With the town's big reunion plans in the works, I think more than the usual suspects may be on hand. I'll write again as soon as I figure out how to protect the innocent and point fingers at the guilty.

Or when I know some really good gossip.

Take care, Vick. Now, I'm off to find out about the Ten-Cent Gypsy...

Up the creek and looking forward to it,

Katie

The Voices of Mossy Creek

Ida Hamilton Walker	Deborah Smith
Sandy Bottoms Crane	Donna Ball
Chief Amos Royden	Debra Dixon
Casey Blackshear	Sandra Chastain
Jayne Austin Reynolds	Deborah Smith
Sue Ora Salter	Sandra Chastain
"Father" Mike O'Conners	Virginia Ellis
Ed Brady	Sandra Chastain
Maggie Hart	Nancy Knight

What's In The Box?

What in the world has gotten the residents of Mossy Creek so stirred up? And what is the twenty-year-old mystery of the fire at Mossy Creek High? What is Ham Bigelow up to?

Join us in the spring of 2002 for Reunion at Mossy Creek when all your favorite characters gather again (as well as some you've never met) and all your questions will be answered.

In the meantime, keep up with the goings on in Mossy Creek by visiting our web site at **www.BelleBooks.com**.

Also Available From *BelleBooks:*

Sweet Tea And Jesus Shoes

Wise and funny stories about growing up Southern
"Joyful and endearing"—**Phyllis George, former Miss America**

Stories include:

THE JESUS SHOES
By Sandra Chastain

The rituals of the summer of 1945 were observed even in the midst of a war about which I knew little. Shoes were rationed and I, in my sublime ignorance, had no idea of the sacrifices my grandparents made to provide me with patent-leather sandals. No matter that my body was adorned with sun dresses made from chicken feed sacks, my patent-leather clad feet were on the Glory Road.

UP JUMPS THE DEVIL
By Donna Ball

There are two things that all native Georgians worth their peanuts have in common, if you look deeply enough into the weeds that obscure the family tree: the once-upon-a-time ownership of great sprawling expanses of land, and a Cherokee princess ancestor.

COOKIE THE ONE-EYED HORSE
By Virginia Ellis

When you live out in the farm country of Florida, you don't have a wide choice of kids to play with. When I was seven, I had three best friends: Mary Jo Taylor, a boy named Jesse, and Cookie, a one-eyed horse.

GRANDPAPA'S GARDEN
By Deborah Smith

Grandpapa's roses bloomed their prettiest the spring he died. The roses, like our family, had been established in rich earth. Grandpapa, after all, was a gardening man.

UNCLE CLETE'S BELL
By Nancy Knight

Death is serious business. Everybody knows that. And when somebody dies, people do the dangdest things. They may start to squabble over who gets what or who the deceased loved best--or even worse. Sometimes it takes an extraordinary event to make folks come to their senses.

SWEET TEA
By Debra Dixon

In the South you grow up steeped in tradition. It's not that you find the South particularly quaint or interesting. You simply have no choice. You know four very important things that will shape your life. You know who your people are, where the homeplace is, and that you will never, ever like playing the piano. You also know precisely how much sugar to put in a gallon of tea.

BIGDADDY'S OUTHOUSE
By Sandra Chastain

Indoor plumbing didn't come to our house until I was in junior high. That never bothered my granddaddy. He'd used an outhouse all his life and continued to do so, even after the facility took a dangerous tilt to the left.

FINGERPRINTS
By Donna Ball

Scratch any Southern family and you'll find a story of a young boy who fought a wild cat with a pocket knife, a mother who hid her children in a well to protect them from marauders, a husband who crossed a mountain barefoot to bring nourishment to his starving family. These are not heroes, they are not legends. They are simply men and women who did what had to be done.

ALICE AT HEART
Deborah Smith

Among the sultry society of coastal Georgia the Bonavendier family of Sainte's Point Island is considered mysterious, notorious, and extremely odd. For more than two centuries, rumors have swirled about the Bonavendiers' seductive charm and strange physical talents. Now, simple, plain Alice Riley, an outcast young woman who is far more extraordinary than she ever imagined, is about to find love, kinship, and adventure in the family's amazing world.

Deborah Smith, New York Times bestselling author of Southern family fiction including A PLACE TO CALL HOME and **ON BEAR MOUNTAIN**, welcomes readers to an enchanted South where anything is possible. **ALICE AT HEART** is the first novel in her Water Lilies series, exclusively for *BelleBooks*.

ALICE AT HEART

I hovered like a ghost, shadowed in the ultraviolet glow of the fish tanks at the Riley Pet Shop, waiting for the three webbed-footed women to find me. I heard the whisper of their fabulous feet on the concrete lane, there; I imagined just the slightest, alluring tang of sea salt in the air around them.

Watching me was a menagerie of hamsters, mice, parakeets, snakes, iguanas, and hundreds of small fish. Every creature, whether fin, fowl, fur, or reptile, moved to the fronts of their cages and tanks. I sang to them every day. They listened.

The sound of my breathing made a low roar in my ears.

Click. The shop's back door opened, followed by the softest padding of footsteps beyond the doorway to a storeroom. "Alice," the silver-haired one called quietly from the storeroom. "Shall we enter?"

"I'm here," I said in a voice that shook. "With the fish."

The three women entered the shop's main room with the gossamer grace of leaves floating on a stream. Silver Hair stepped in front of the other two like the queen of a small delegation. My name," she said, "is Lilith Bonavendier." She nodded toward the dark-haired woman. "This is my younger sister, Mara." And in the other direction, toward the redhead. "And this is my second younger sister, Pearl." She paused. I suddenly noticed that the fish, the mice, the hamsters, the snakes, the lizards, and the birds now faced *her* way. None of them moved or made so much as a peep. "And you," Lilith Bonavendier went on, looking straight at me, "are our *youngest* sister."

"Only our half-sister," Mara corrected, then blanched when Lilith gave her a hard look.

I took a step back, pressing myself against a wall of aquariums. Like all the other small creatures, I gazed at the three women in hypnotized wonder. "What kind of game is this?" I whispered. "You're too old to be my sisters."

"I am seventy and quite pleased to be so," Lilith countered, nodding to indicate her own lithe form. She lifted a hand toward Mara, who yipped in dismay. "Sixty-five." And Pearl, who laughed. "Sixty-two."

I stared at them. Mara and Pearl couldn't possibly be much older than me, and Lilith had the skin of a beautiful forty-year-old, despite the silver hair. Southern socialites are notorious for lying about their ages—gilding the magnolia—so to speak. But none ever claim they are thirty years *older* than common sense says is possible.

"I see."

Lilith watched me closely. "No, you don't. We don't live by the rules of ordinary people. You know that, in your heart. You know anything I tell you may be possible. Look at me, Alice. Please. Have faith."

In the deepening silence between words, the pauses of reflection and emotion, the acidic wash of stark scrutiny and shock, in those spaces where the truth lives, I knew, I felt, I saw. But I shook my head.

"Faith is a blind word, used to excuse every mistake."

Lilith took a step toward me. "No. Alice, say what you will, but you do *want* to believe me."

"This is all an elaborate defense for a tragedy that shamed you."

"Yes, I'm ashamed we never knew your mother—and you. And yes, this is an elaborate effort to redeem that terrible crime. But then, we Bonavendiers are an *elaborate* kind of being."

"Oh, more than elaborate," Pearl interjected brightly. Mara scowled at her.

"If I am going to believe any of this," I managed, "then please tell me why we're so different from everyone else."

"You aren't ready to hear that, yet. You're consumed with anger and pain and distrust. Come with us to our home, Alice, and learn about us, and learn about *yourself*. And then you'll understand. And you'll believe."

"I prefer clear answers instead of vague promises. *Simple* answers."

"That's not possible. The truth, my dear, is far more complex than you've ever imagined—and far more wonderful." She went on in her lovely voice, telling me that she and her sisters—*my* half-sisters, if I believed her—come from one of the barrier islands off Georgia's coast, a small isle named Sainte's Point. She said it has been owned by Bonavendiers since the late 1700's. "Our ancestor was a French privateer," Lilith said.

"A pirate," redheaded Pearl interjected eagerly.

Lilith silenced her with a stern glance. "A *privateer* in service to the American revolutionary government. He fought off a British warship that threatened an American village on the mainland. After the war—in return for his service—President Washington deeded him the small island across the cove from that grateful village. Our ancestor named the island Sainte's Point. He settled there quite happily, bringing with him a quite *remarkable* wife."

"And *she* is responsible for the very special circumstances that have existed in all her Bonavendier descendants ever since," Pearl put in, shaking an elegant, webbed foot for mysterious emphasis. "Because she was a. . ."

"*Ssssh.*" Dark-haired Mara hissed at her. Pearl's eyes widened. She huffed. Lilith gave both women a rebuking stare. They lowered their eyes. Lilith looked at me again. "Our family has so much lovely history to tell—so many traditions, so many proud memories. But you, of course, simply need to know your own history, at the moment."

I took a deep breath. "If I do believe you, then tell me this much. *What kind of monsters are we?*"

Pearl sputtered. "Monsters? *Monsters?*"

Lilith inhaled sharply. "Say no more."

"But we're *not* monsters," Pearl cried, her expression wounded.

"Pearl, say no—"

"We're *mermaids*!"

Silence.

"Oh," I said. "Mermaids."

And, moving as casually as I could, I left them there, with the fish.

THE STONE FLOWER GARDEN
Deborah Smith

Deborah Smith, the New York Times bestselling author of **A PLACE TO CALL HOME** and **ON BEAR MOUNTAIN**, sets her next novel inside the glamorous lives of a wealthy North Carolina family beset by tragedy and secrets. **THE STONE FLOWER GARDEN** will be available in hardcover from **Little, Brown, & Company** in February, 2002.

❦❦❦

On a dark spring night twenty-five years after I helped bury my Great Aunt Clara Hardigree, I found myself digging her up. I felt as if I was playing the lead in a scene from some grotesque southern soap opera. Scarlett O'Hara does the gravesite scene in Hamlet.

Alas, poor Clara, I knew her well.

A propane camp lantern hissed and flickered among the ferns by my feet. I dug for my great aunt's bones as quickly as I could in the moonlit woods. A huge marble urn loomed over me, its cascading marble flowers and marble vines poking my shoulders and head like hard fingers. The Stone Flower Garden was as much a part of the forest, as much a Hardigree symbol, as Clara's hidden grave. I shivered. Appalachian mountains as old as the earth looked down on my shame, and beyond the deep glen with the bones and the marble urn, the lights of Burnt Stand, North Carolina, my sleeping hometown, winked knowingly at me.

We always suspected you weren't cut from the strongest Hardigree stone. The Hardigree name stood for unbreakable women and unbreakable marble. But I, Darl Union, granddaughter of Swan Hardigree Samples, great-granddaughter of Esta Hardigree, had cracked.

And it was all because of a man. I looked up at Eli Wade, the man whose trust I'd betrayed, just as my silence had betrayed his wrongfully accused father, twenty-five years earlier. Eli watched me with no understanding of what I was about to show him.

I finally found Clara's skeleton no more than an arm's length down in the loamy forest sod. When I was a child, watching my Grandmother Swan dig the grave, it had seemed like a mile. Now Clara was just dirty bones waiting to be pulled up one at a time. Perhaps I should have brought one of Swan's finest linen tablecloths to wrap her in. A monogrammed one. We Hardigrees set a nice table.

The only thing that startled me was a necklace I plucked from the grave soil. When I wiped its small pendant and held it to the lantern light, I saw the twinkle of a diamond set in a tiny, polished chip of milk-white Hardigree marble. Grandmother had one just like it. So did I. It was a tradition in our family. Not a family crest, but the next best thing: Hard stone on hard stone, tinged with the soil of our ambitions.

I shivered again. *Done, then.* Every piece of infamous misery lay exposed. Nausea rose in my throat and I sat back on my heels with Clara's pendant clasped in my fist, my head bowed, my eyes shut. As a child I never meant to help Grandmother murder her and blame it on someone else. Like all the unforeseen fates -- hate and true love and success and failure -- it just happened.

"Your father didn't kill Clara," I told Eli. "Swan and I did."

Eli looked at the grave in shock, and then, slowly, back at me. Ineffable sadness and anger began to crowd the night air between us. I believed at that moment that he could never forgive me, and I could never forgive myself. "How could you do this to me?" he asked.

"Family," I whispered.

Children lose their innocence piece by piece. The layers are carved away until our hearts have been exposed and polished into an unnatural gloss. We spend the rest of our lives trying to remember why we ever loved so passionately and how we dreamed so simply, before life chiseled us down to the core.

THE WEDDING DRESS
Virginia Renfro Ellis

"We began the dress on the last evening in October." For three sisters, it will become a banner of hope, spun from delicate memories of genteel tradition and woven with threads of possibility.

Award winning author, Virginia Renfro Ellis' extraordinary work of historical fiction evokes the tattered essence of the post-Civil War South where widows and scarred veterans were left to reconstruct a country. Available from **Ballantine** in June 2002.

THE WEDDING DRESS

October, 1865

The war has been over for six months, yet the dream came again last night. I'd thought it had left me, after plaguing me for two years without mercy, then inexplicably stopping. But as I lay motionless in the darkness, alone, eyes wide open, held prisoner by the familiar overwhelming sadness, I remember.

It is my wedding day. And in the dream William stands tall and handsome at my side proudly wearing his lieutenant's uniform of the 24th Virginia. In this welcome glimpse of the past, my William, my husband to be, looks fearsome and beautiful, so alive and in a fever to claim me as wife before going to war. The beloved vision of him breaks my heart. Because I know what comes next. I remember the weary path of this dream well. What comes next is that as I stand there, in front of family and friends—half of Patrick County—on the happiest day of my life, I look down at my beautiful, heirloom wedding dress, the same gown my mother wore to pledge her life to my father, and see that it is covered in blood.

The blood of war and mortal men. Of broken dreams and severed vows.

You see, I am the middle child of three, all of us girls. Our duty, and the best we could do for ourselves and our family was to marry well, have fine, healthy children, be obedient wives and good Christians. So far, my sisters and I had failed on every count beyond marriage. My elder sister Victoria should have married first, but when I met William and fell heels over head in love, my father thought it circumspect to marry us before our passion got out of hand. William's family agreed. So, I was the first to take the vows, to become Lieutenant Mrs. William Lovejoy, wearing my mother's dress.

So much has happened since then.

The authors of Mossy Creek would love to hear from readers and welcome fans to their individual websites.

debbsmith@aol.com
www.authordeborahsmith.com

sansmy@bellsouth.net
www.sandrachastain.com

Ellislyn@aol.com
www.superauthors.com/Ellis.htm

Martha@marthashields.com
www.marthashields.com

debradixon@aol.com

novelkid@aol.com   (Nancy Knight)
Bellebooks@Bellebooks.com